Rebecca Entel

Fingerprints of Previous Owners

A Novel

The Unnamed Press
Los Angeles, CA

The Unnamed Press
P.O. Box 411272
Los Angeles, CA 90041

Published in North America by The Unnamed Press.

1 3 5 7 9 10 8 6 4 2

Copyright © 2017 by Rebecca Entel

ISBN: 9781944700232

Library of Congress Control Number: 2017940133

This book is distributed by Publishers Group West

Cover design & typeset by Jaya Nicely

For my parents,
Esther and Leonard Entel

too slow the stones crawling toward language...

Derek Walcott

Pain—has an Element of Blank—

Emily Dickinson

*There is no place you or I can go, to think about or not think about,
to summon the presences of, or recollect the absences of slaves...
There's no small bench by the road.*

Toni Morrison

Fingerprints of Previous Owners

Chapter One

When the planes landed out on the key, we would gather on the beach. We draped ourselves in sheets, the wind turning us into shifting shapes of brown and white, like sea creatures wrestling our own bleached shells.

I'd never arrived here from somewhere northern, frosty. But I imagined that when they filed out of the plane, it was hard not to go rigid, expecting the January cold. The sun would come down to massage their shoulders. They would relax against its warmth and squint through their sunglasses against its glare. From there, they headed to the resort on Furnace Island, though their boarding passes had said the destination was *Cruffey.* They didn't know what it meant for this place to have two names.

I'd never even been on the key where the resort landed its planes to see the island as a dot out in the ocean. I'd never arrived here from anywhere.

When they moved toward a gravelly area labeled *Baggage Claim,* a flurry. A team of people with the name of the resort scripted across their chests would appear, arrange its bodies as prosthetics for whatever they needed to do: move luggage, climb into the small boat that awaited them. Scaffolded in wooden masts and adornments, bearing a flag with the resort's sunset logo imprinted over a red-and-yellow castle. Across its side in regal script: *The*

Pinta. The boat would jostle against the dock, clacking and swishing, as they waited to be unmoored.

After heaving all of their luggage in a human assembly line
onto a twin boat labeled *The Nina: Luggage,* some team members
would don felt hats with feathers and put on the bug-eyed faces
of actors. Those staff members without costumes—the ones who'd
done the lifting, the ones *from* the island, the ones like me—would
sit down on the floor of the boat and wait.

Some of the newly arrived faced toward the island, some faced
backward toward the airport key or the open water. Their backs
would touch. The stepping-stone trail of clouds in the sky would
lure some of their eyes out to sea while others would lean away,
waving their phones around for a signal, frowning. The boat
would begin bobbing along.

A throat clearing, followed by a sandy boot planting itself on the
bench next to them, bringing all the eyes back.

"Then the *Pinta!*" the befeathered man would bellow. "Being
faster and in the lead! Sighted land!"

Some of the other men would jump up around him, pointing
excitedly at the beach that had been in view even from the key.

"In the presence of all of my crew!" the bellower would continue, *Columbus* embroidered across the front of his hat. "I ask you
to bear solemn witness that I am taking possession of this island
for their lord and lady, the King and the Queen! And I will call this
island, in all her glory, after our sovereigns Ferdinand and *Ees*-a-
bella: *Ferdin-Ees* Island. And oh, the glorious heat of the sun that
circles our God-given Earth: Furnace Island, then!"

Kids would clap. I imagined the adults, too, cheering.

"Lo and behold, sir!" One of the hatted crew members would
put his arm around Columbus's shoulders. "Natives!"

Finally every head would turn to the beach. The beach where we
waited. They'd see a cluster of women gather slowly to face them.
Just the local women, no flown-in-from-the-States staff with skin
lighter than our driest sand.

"Why, they go about as naked as the day they were born!"

Laughing, they would all feel lighter. Drifting farther from home and its tethers as their boat rocked ever more slowly toward the shore.

They must have seen that the women on the beach were distinctly not naked. The draped gowns shaped out of white bedsheets would whip around in the unpredictably looping wind, both revealing and distorting the shapes of our bodies. Some of us would seem to be looking right at them, our faces hardened into expressions they couldn't read. They would look away, to the smiling faces with the slightly downcast eyes instead. A hatted team member would begin handing out pennies.

"We will give them coins of small values," Columbus would shout. "They will be so delighted, as they are so eager to please and will give us anything we should ask for!" His hands would take wing as he spoke, flashing rings with the sunset insignia carved into them.

We women on the beach would begin unlooping necklaces over our heads and pulling bouquets of suckers from bags sunken in the sand. The colored wrappers shimmered in the heat. Our stiff arms would reach toward them like branches. Murmurs of approval would flutter through the crowd.

"And now all of *you!*" Columbus would flourish his hand around the boat. Even the people who'd been grumpily waving their phones around on the key would relax, docile hands at their sides and their chins pointed ever so slightly toward Columbus. "Our natives take anything and give willingly whatever they have! Our staff shall be so eager to please you during your stay on Furnace Island. They shall be called *eeeeyes.* A-Y-S: At Your Service. You need *eeeeyes*? They will provide!"

The staff would motion for them to climb from the boat and would press pennies into the squishy pockets of their hands. Kids would cry for suckers, jump happily at receiving them, cry again when they ducked into the sand, sticks up.

Our group in white would begin to disband, pulling sheets from our shoulders, revealing the maid uniforms that would make them think of fifties sitcom reruns on late-night TV. We, the women, would disappear through a break in the fence they would never see behind.

They would tell one another and themselves to forget any dropped pennies as they were directed away from the fence, up a graveled path to where the pool sat on the beach, hugged by either wing of the hotel. Speakers hung like bats under the roof's edge, vibrating with the pock of steel drums. They'd hear the faint sound of someone sawing very dry wood.

At night the speakers and the sawing would fall away, but the sounds of Furnace Island would keep them alert. The *whoosh* of the waves, a sound that was supposed to put them to sleep but was called a roar. After a night or two, they'd dream through everything.

Archipelago, the maps in their rooms would tell them: scattered seeds floating away from the finger of Florida, that imperative pillar to our point of exclamation. A tiny island way out from any mainland, quivering like an unattached period in the water, seemed like an invitation to decide how to complete the sentence that had brought them here. Sentences started elsewhere; we were just a dot. A dot named twice, neither time by us. They would hone their geographical grammar, tracing the explosion of islands across the map's flat sea. Or they would turn away, be no place. The rooms would be full of no one's history, never belonging to anyone.

They would end up sitting by the pool most of their days at the resort, reaching out for drinks on trays. Flipping through magazines, maybe forgetting the books weighing down their oversized pastel bags they'd bought to bring here. Most of them would never swim. Those who did would dip in the pool, never the ocean. Their loungers would face in toward the pool, the hotel. Never out to sea. Some would do laps, strapped with full snorkeling equipment. Back and forth, slow-motion lawnmowers, finally emerging like primordial creatures with the baggy seats of their bathing suits leaking water down their legs. Plastic masks and the snakes of their snorkels like plumbing for their heads. The soupy words they called out to the staff would sound like complaints or warnings.

They would eventually discover that the sawing was the sound of the maids sweeping crabs from the deck with wire brooms. Back onto the sand to scuttle in loops down to the beach or into the truck parking lot.

I was one of the maids they heard but didn't see, sweeping away. By day.

By night I swooped with gravity like a ghost was crocheted around my arm, the machete its extension. Not hacking away like a crazy bitch. My brother, Troy, did that. He couldn't be taught, Mother used to say, and she had been a teacher. He was the bad one, the one who'd left her for work in the capital on Wells Island and wouldn't ever be coming back. I was the good one, the one who came home every night, bringing money. I was the one who would never leave.

She had no idea I went where I wasn't supposed to go. Wandered along the stones that peeked from the earth like calluses hardened from time. Slicing a path big enough only for me, not caring if the nettles picked at my work uniform, which would cost us money when it had to be replaced. Sliced and climbed and grubbed and tiptoed around anthills to walk inland among the dead.

Those are not our bones, she would have said to me. She would not have meant people. She would have meant the ruins: the stone walls creeping up within the brush, which led nowhere, which told you nothing, which were built only to keep in. I knew; I had followed them.

I didn't know what I was looking for. Mother loved the knowing. Knowing Bayard a third of a mile down the road in the lime-green house could fix your car. (We didn't have a car, but Mother knew Bayard could fix it if we got one. And she liked knowing exactly how far it was to walk if someone else broke down in front of our house.) Knowing a whistle in the air meant Hebbie was coming around the bend. Knowing her hair'd be some shade of red you'd never find growing in your garden. Knowing Miss Patrice's store would always reopen after lunch and would always have ibuprofen when you couldn't find it anywhere else. Garrett would always stop by when he'd been catching crabs, and we'd always eat well each night that he did. Miss Minnie would ask every time I saw her if Mother would join her in selling at the Straw Market that coming Wednesday or singing at church that coming Sunday. And the answers would always be *yes* and *no*. Knowing her brother, my uncle Q, lived as far from us on this oval as you could get, but he wouldn't go three days without seeing on her. And Mother knew I'd wash all the plates if she'd grab a needle to fix up the edges of my work apron until her hand was too stiff and came to rest in her lap, a knobby cavern. She didn't wonder how it got torn up, because she hadn't been inside the resort to see they'd cleared away the brush so you'd walk through the entire stretch of the place without anything touching you. For all she knew my uniform got snagged all day at work.

Haulback, we called those nettled plants. They dug into your skin and your clothes when you tried to get by, hauled you back.

Before the resort, most of the men went to the capital for work. Many still did. My dad had. And my brother, Troy; Troy's best friend, Andre; so many. Some women, too. And way before that, there was only the land you were in a relationship with for anything you could plant or pluck. Everything else had you waiting for a boat to come in. Those boats came slowly, infrequently. Still did.

And before that, long before our time, life—if you could call it that—was only on the inland. Working the land for someone else who'd claimed you, corpse that you were, from the ship that docked in the capital and put you on another boat to this bitty outermost island. Once you were here, you were *theirs*. Even if you could slip the inland to reach the shore, there was nowhere to go, nothing to take you away. The horizon surrounded you. The sun and the water promising escape only in surrender, only in giving yourself up to the waves instead of to your master. The platform of sale in the capital was now where the cruise ships docked, and with every arrival Americans in visors filed down to the beach. That's what Troy had described.

Even Ole Mr. Vit was too young to remember the move down from the inland, but he once told me about it when I was young enough not to know I shouldn't ask. He was just a boy when the oldest people around would remember *their* parents reminiscing about it. Each family turning its back on the high inland, a while after the masters had deserted this place and its miserly soil.

New houses were put up just back from the beach trim, and a road ringing our oval island was built in one swoop. Still our main road. After a storm its potholes became mini-oceans, and rocks rose like icebergs. They ruined cars that went too fast.

Water and electricity came more slowly, each family saving up week by week to pay for the connections. Those of us who still weren't on the water grid came to the spigot at the gate of the resort with jugs the size of calves. Six dollars came out of my pay each month.

I had a water bottle from the resort's gift shop that I took with me when I went inland. (I found it, still shrink-wrapped, behind a bush by the resort's main gate.) *See you,* Mother would have said if she saw me using it, *you don't belong up there. See you, like a tourist. You're making yourself a tourist up there.*

But she would never say that, because she stopped speaking once Troy was gone, and because I would never tell her where I'd been. Except in my imaginings: when I sat on a wall and collected her next to me, a ghost girl with old eyes, sucking the thiflae flower for sweetness. I never liked it, this red bud that felt like fabric in your mouth, until I saw all the kids at the resort—couldn't keep their mouths from taking on the colors of their suckers. All sticky. *Thwuck, thwuck* sucking. Made me see that we had to work our mouths a little for *our* sweetness, and it was a sweetness that grew on your tongue, didn't just spike your mouth. Made me see who I was a little bit.

Mother would be right, though, that only tourists went inland. The resort had cleared a path to a ruin that looked like a house— the only one that looked like *anything*—and took packs of guests up to see its walls. They didn't tell the tourists what the walls had been a part of, what they sat on. Just an old house, just a formation of stone to pose yourself against. Stone spangling in the sun until it was cooked into something else. I didn't know exactly what they told the tourists, their path off-limits to me. I could see only the ruins still shrouded in the brush that shrouded me, too.

The resort owned most all the inland. No one was allowed to go among the ruins beyond this little tourist patch. The ruins of the estate that all of us on the island, way, way back, came from—now a trap of trespass. I waded through the brush like a ghost, a nocturnal animal, a thief.

Except for the house they'd claimed for the tourists, all I could find remaining from the plantation: these stones and stones and stones piping the hills, holding themselves against the overwhelming brush.

I pictured what it must have been like moving down from the inland to the edges of the island. I pictured everyone moving all at once, like an exodus, though I knew it wasn't really like that. I pictured every single family creeping down the same ways I went up, carrying sacks of all they owned—not much—the ones in front swinging their machetes. Reverse invasion, I thought, a dispersal. Moving from the center out, out, finding space between all of them, to set up where they could actually see the sky and the sea. The brush filling in behind them almost as soon as they passed through. Almost like water, how you couldn't keep it from taking any little space you might try to carve out for yourself around here. This tiny oval, quiet and loud at once.

Most of those very first houses had been abandoned. People just left whole houses behind, took what they could carry. There was a piano in one of them. We used to have parties there when I was a little younger. Somewhere to sit and get out of the sun, hear someone plucking at the keys. Even if my friend Hebbie was the only one who really knew how to play, it was something to hear besides the dogs bickering on the road, the scribbling sound of the waves reclaiming sand. Mother hated when people would go in those deserted houses to take stuff, practical though she was about us collecting trash on the beach to use at our house. Just didn't like the idea of transplanting some piece of that loneliness into your own space. Me: couldn't get enough of the memories of things. Everything I touched dripped with the syrup of the past, even at the resort where the brand new strapped over everything like duct tape.

Last year, just a few months after Troy had joined him in the capital, our dad was dead, and Troy briefly back among us for the funeral. (Not a real funeral, since Dad's body had been buried in the capital—who could pay for otherwise?—but what Mother wanted anyway. Mr. Ken came on behalf of the funeral committee. I walked the perimeter of the house while they sat across from each other at our wobbly table. Took walking only nine of those small squares for them to settle the details of the grave marker without a grave. The empty that would be inside of it heavier than his body had ever been.) Two days, that visit, and then Troy was off again, and the night before he left he didn't even come home. Out with friends all night. Miss Philene had given me a ride to work that morning, and I saw him standing, waiting for the boat to the airstrip. Saw his back and one knee leaning toward the other, unsure. Turtled with his overstuffed red backpack; one frayed strap hung limp. Someone else also waiting stepped into my view, blocked him out entirely.

Right before Troy left he managed to run our cousin's car through the fence and let the cows out. Used to be his best friend Andre'd keep him reined in those nights out, but they'd gone to the capital together, and only Troy had come back that trip.

Guessed Lionel felt bad it had been his truck that did the wrecking, since he offered to take me inland to search the path of broken
brush the cows had stomped out. We gathered the machetes our
fathers had used for gardening and headed up. Or in. The middle
of our island was a big hump you couldn't really see unless you
got way out to sea in a boat or way up in the air in a plane. From
the road and the sandy strip around the island we lived on, it was
just a hill of snarly brush we sometimes dipped a hand into to
pluck leaves for teas.

The cows were so big, how could they hide? So big, how could
we not hear them? So big, roaming the inland like they themselves
were the ghosts that lived up there.

First time I fell over a stone wall was when we were searching
for those cows. Thicket so dense I didn't see a two-foot-tall wall
in front of my legs. Fell over and got a ridge of red scrapes on my
knees.

Lionel was only four years older than I was, but he kicked the
wall as if he'd known something, lived in a different time when
people told you what the walls were for, when you could walk inland for something other than chasing your food. A different time
when you could walk inland to add background to the whispering of the elders who'd been around long enough to have their
grandparents' memories of moving down and letting the inland
seal itself behind them. *There was a time,* Ole Mr. Vit had told me,
that time I was young enough to ask, *before my time, when folks
knew who was or wasn't Africa born and when folks recalled moving
down from the estate and calling themselves "stateless." Then people
didn't want to talk about that anymore. Didn't want their little ones
strapped with sandbags while trying to wade across this life.* Then
he'd stopped talking, too, and nothing you could do to open those
lips again. Sent me on my way.

"Why'd you do that: kick?"

Lionel looked at me like I was a stupid kid, putting him on
with my ignorance. "These *used* to keep cattle in anyway," he
said.

The walls were intact in some spots but mostly crumbling and intermittent. There were so many breaks where the cows could have gotten through. He rolled his eyes at me. I didn't think he'd say more, but he did.

"We're on the estate, Myrna, don't you know that much? These walls were built by slaves."

Word like a bogeyman. Something in the past or in the darkness or in nightmares. Bogeyman Slavery. Worse than a *yeho*, a monster. Monster of death who knew what he was doing. Bogeyman whose name wasn't said. Sandbags we all wore but didn't see.

Only talk of the inland my whole life was when I was a kid too young to really understand much of what I heard, and when I was a little older, the residual trickle of gossip. About the night Miss Philene's youngest son, Jimmy, never came home. His body was found somewhere inland. Came out later that Minister Callaghan had found some teenagers drinking up among the stones. And when Jimmy refused to get going, the minister spun himself into a rage. Beat him, left him bleeding, took his flashlight. Jimmy never found his way out and never went anywhere again, inland or otherwise. No one talked about it that much after it was all settled. Only remembered Jimmy's death same as a person who died in hospital or from old, old age. Seemed like it had always just been the way it was: Jimmy and the minister both gone from the island in different ways, the minister's wife, Miss Wayida, barely coming out of her church, and neither Miss Philene nor Mr. Ken speaking much about their youngest, long gone now. Then as now, that rage about the inland that grabbed the minister? Was a mystery to me the size of the ocean. Felt its depth each step I took through this brush.

And I was also coming to understand something about confusing swirls of anger that could gather in my own gut. Like what I felt when news of Dad's heart attack came to us.

We kept walking, inching along behind our machetes. Thorny branches scraped the tops of my arms, leaving thin lines of white. It was the dry season, and the haulback had lost its leaves. Just gray branches now like a skeleton of itself instead of the cloud of emeralds it looked like in full bloom. (In full bloom leaves wouldn't make a tea any less bitter than the branches would. Coughed a little, thinking of the prickles ricocheting down our throats.) In some of the particularly thick places where Lionel told me to stay back while he swung wide for a good slice, I found angles to stick my arms through the brush to feel the stones of those walls.

Felt some need to run as far as I could and be like Mother, never talking about any of it. Felt some other need just as strong to clear all this brush away to expose it all, clear the brush to explore the nooks and crannies the way Dad had done as the island dentist. He'd once described to me, when I asked why anyone would want to go digging around in other people's nasty mouths, how it made him feel to find where the pain was coming from, to know exactly what to do, and to dig out the source of it. How it made him feel, when people brought their X-rays from the dentist in the capital, to match them up to the mouth in front of him, as different as they seemed just to his eyes. And then using his fingers to carefully feel out, trusting.

I felt dust on my tongue and held it as I watched Lionel's back, T-shirt stuck with what we called island glue, turn this way and that to avoid the haulback. All around me, even with the island glue sticking my shirt up under my breasts and around my belly button, I felt the chill of the past like a ghost pushing its way right through me. Here I was, days after Dad's funeral, feeling out the secret source of pain.

After we'd been at it for a long while, Lionel said, "No way we're finding those cows. Let's get out of here. And don't be coming up here. And don't tell your ma where we were looking."

"Don't, don't, don't, don't," I said, now rolling my eyes at him.

"Look, no one wants to hear about this shit anymore. Leave it gone," he said, interpreting my body language.

I didn't need him telling me that, older cousin or not. Never once heard the word *slavery* spoken above an accidental whisper, not even in school. In history class used to run my finger along the edges of the textbook's sliced-out pages, half hoping for a paper cut that'd remind me later something was missing, something almost invisible that bled easily. Hebbie, my best friend when we were kids and Andre's sister, used to call me Hyphen Hands for all the straight bitty slits on my fingers.

Say the word *estate* at work and look down at your palm for your firing papers.

"Aren't you the Landfill Manager? Dealing with everything that's thrown away?" I didn't know what I meant exactly, but he seemed angry, and I felt like pushing back.

"Yeah, exactly, Miss Smarty. I know how to get rid of everything no one wants and keep it from ruining the whole island. Besides," he said, his tone changing, "the resort owns all this land now anyways. You get caught up here, you trespass. Lose your job. Then how you gonna feed your ma?"

"We're here now," I said, but I mumbled it to myself.

The thing about my cousin Lionel was he was smart, and he did lots of stuff for Mother, especially in the weeks since my dad died. Stuff like that made me swallow what he told me, even if I told him to his face that he should mind his own business.

I kept following behind him, letting him do the machete work while my hands felt through the brush for more traces of walls, places where I could feel the absence of where a wall had been. By the time we emerged from the brush, my arms and hands were maps of where I'd been cut up.

We stood on the road looking at each other. No cows. Lionel pointed up around the bend.

"Thiflae Bar?" he asked.

We kicked dust in front of us as we walked along the road. Lionel pulled his shirt up to wipe sweat off his forehead. The wind had died, leaving the ocean flat with stillness and bugs hanging in the air. The only sound that reached us was of distant cars, but no one drove by as we were walking. Walls of brush on either side of the road looked so thick, almost like it was impossible we could've ever been where we'd been. A skinny blondish dog we both recognized from the landfill, Freddy, zigzagged the road about a quarter mile ahead, probably waiting for someone to come out the bar and drop something. The sky was going pink just as slowly as we were shuffling along. I was thirsty, and I kept my eye on Freddy to see how close we were getting.

When we got to the entrance, the door hung crooked like always so you could see a slice of the room before you went in. I didn't bother looking, knew there wasn't anyone I particularly wanted to see. We could hear voices of all the men hanging out on what had been the bar's back porch. All the slats gone, now just a piece of floor jutting toward the brush like a pier without water. I didn't know how long it'd been since I'd seen my dad on that porch, talking it up with his friends. My memory of coming to find him there—so long ago—was only of legs at my eye level.

"Wanna go on the porch or inside?" Lionel asked.

Usually older folks on the porch, away from the music. How would we explain our machetes this time of night? The coating of the inland all over us?

"Inside," I said, where I knew everyone would be tipsy. I pushed ahead of him through the door.

"Lionel!" Christine's voice squawked above the din of voices in the room and on the TV as soon as we entered. Her hair glowed orangish in the fluorescent light where she had streaked it blond. It hadn't been like that at work earlier in the week. We worked side by side at the resort, and she worked some nights at Miss Patrice's store.

She was calling us over, though I saw only one extra chair by her. She'd always been sweet on Lionel, but I couldn't tell whether he couldn't stand her or was willing. Lately he'd been talking an awful lot about that vet who came from the capital to tend to the island dogs. But she came out to us only once a year, a few weeks at a time, and Lionel wouldn't go to the capital.

Lionel and I sat at the bar instead, on stools he'd once rescued from the landfill when the resort threw them away. Christine walked over where we were anyway and slid closer than I wanted her. I reminded myself of all the times she helped me out, like when she spread early word to a few of us that a new shipment of the good tampons had come in at the store.

"Lem's here," Lionel whispered into my ear. I didn't bother looking around. "Ah. Done with that already?"

I figured he'd known how long it'd been since I'd been done, everyone around here knowing everyone else's business. I didn't think Lem would come over to me at this point, since we hadn't even talked much lately—though we both worked at the resort, him on garbage duty. But then there he was, by my shoulder. The heaviness I used to feel around my hips when he came near, and the furiousness following—gone.

"Hey, Myr."

"Hey," I said.

"Another beer, Mr. Ken," he said. I heard the exhaling sound of the cap being released, and Lem put the bottle in front of me. I put my hand on it for the cold feeling, then rubbed the glass against some scratches on my arm. I didn't feel like having a drink.

Lem's head was shaved perfectly as always along a sharp line above his ear. Breath of beer that used to smell crisp and fun to me, now just stale.

"I could use a water, Mr. Ken," I said, feeling the kind of parched even my hair was soaking up the smell of fritters sizzling in their baskets behind the kitchen door. Lionel and I'd been up inland since before it was even thinking about getting dark.

"Saw Troy before he left again," Lem said. "Told me take care of his sister right."

"What'd you tell him?" I was looking at him now.

"What? Can't tell my old buddy I been hanging out with his sister?"

Christine started *doo-doo*-ing a little tune she thought sounded like something sexy. Lionel laughed, and I glared at him.

"We're not—I— Seriously, what did you tell him that's gonna get all back around to me now?"

"I see how it is," Lem said, stepping back and looking less smi-ley. "Always too good for everyone else around here, right? That's how it's always been with you: biggity. Even before, when we were, you know."

A sourness started collecting in my gut and wanted to come out of my mouth as something nasty, like telling Lem I had more fun by myself than I ever did with him. Wanted to shoot the sourness at Lionel, too, embarrass him about the way he was always run-ning to get messed up with any girl at all set foot on this island from somewhere else. Couldn't even be bothered with Christine and her tune. I took a sip of water and tried to shut off the trickle of meanness.

"Man, Lem," I said. "We haven't even been out together in a month."

He looked at me for a long time. "Sorry 'bout your pa, anyway," he said, and he walked away. Lionel was sucking down his beer, his eyebrows raised, whole forehead in a smirk.

"What?" I demanded, and Lionel shrugged.

"Nothing. Lem's a nice guy, that's all." The two of them hadn't ever been close when we were younger, but with Lem on the re-sort's garbage crew and Lionel at the dump, they'd worked them-selves up some kind of friendship.

"I'm just so *tired* of all this. Of everyone."

I stared at the glass of water Mr. Ken had put in my hand. A bottle broke behind me, and Christine seemed to laugh and shriek at the same time. Then her voice and Lionel's started braiding to-gether until I couldn't make out anything they were saying, but the sounds were there, just nudging against my ears but not go-ing in. Lots of shuffling behind me, too, like everyone had started dancing or moving in some game, but I just kept staring at my own hands.

When I looked up the room seemed shadowy, like a smudgy black-and-white photocopy of itself. Everyone was mulling about more slo-wly, transparent, as if I could see them but through them, only the bottoms of their feet looking heavy and solid. Everyone looking like glass but their feet lined with iron. I stopped hearing the sounds of the conversations in the room and just heard a white-noise sound like the wind or the waves coming in. Like none of this was real, but there was something just beyond. Just under us. Not like a bogeyman either, but something calling me to come see. Like I would come to feel about my dad's gravestone: calling me even if the ground it marked was full of dirt, empty of him.

"I'm going home."

Whatever Lionel said in response sounded too far away.

But I didn't go home. I'd left both machetes at the bar with Lionel, and it was dark out, but I found myself pushing through the bushes, arms raised up, the way I'd seen tourists wade deeper into the pool, shuddering at the chill.

I was trying to follow the stone walls again through the tangled brush that clawed and scraped and twined and wrapped and pricked and caught. The stone walls were meant to keep the cattle in, not the slaves. That was done in other ways. The oval shoreline looped around us all.

It kept me in, too. A year ago I'd been planning to finally get off the island, looking into art history at the university, but then Troy went off, and now Dad was gone, and with all of it there was no way I could leave Mother. I'd never be going. Just walking the oval my whole life. (Always ovals, never perfect circles. Circles smooth and calm; ovals warped by some force. Those months with Lem he was shaving his head smooth, and my hands would absentmindedly run over and over the oval of it. While his fingers scrambled, and when he found the right spot, slowed and stayed, until my mind burst in shards of light. Now my brain was already different, held a thickness.)

No going off the island for me. Going inland, back in time, instead. These stones my ancestors—and almost everyone's ancestors on this island—had quarried and carried and packed in place, like planting gravestones. (Each of them known as Cruffey's so-and-so: the same seven letters painted on Mr. Harper's old rickety

boat, the same surname so many on this island—this Cruffey Island—had, including my own mother's family.)

That first night inland—more than a year ago—I thought the
wall ruins would keep me on a path. I ended up lost in the dark,
cowering, sweeping fire ants from my ankles and then from my
hands and cursing myself for being dumb enough to try to go in
without the right supplies, without even a flashlight. Imagined
them telling Mother they found me, and where, both stupid and
dead, so soon after Dad's heart attack. I'd have to wait until the
sun came up to move or risk getting in deeper. Crouched until
the feeling in my ankles disappeared. Thought about Mr. Harper's
half-leg. Anyone ever ask what happened to it, folks would nod
up at the hump of the inland and say nothing but *Stones*.

I didn't know how long it'd been when all of a sudden I heard
a car going by and realized, like a fool, I wasn't all that far off the
road after all. I ended up crawling toward the sound until I felt the
pavement beneath my hands and pulled myself up to walk along
the road. A bloody, bitten mess.

When I finally got home, deep in the night, I went through the
motions my body had always known. Skipped the broken step;
pulled the doorknob up just so to make the key catch; rattled it
four times before turning all the way; turned back just a tick and
heard the tiny *click*. Did it all without waking Mother. But my
body felt different, heavier.

After that night I went up only if I could make it back out before
the sun went down. But I went up as often as I could, most days
for a year. Always had Dad's machete by my side; after that night
at Thiflae, Lionel had returned it to its place with the other tools
in our shed. I started in the same place every time—by the low,
stooped tree—so I could keep working on the trail I was making,
and I hid the machete far enough in no one else would find it.
Took it back to Dad's old shed when it needed sharpening. Mother
must've thought how much I was missing him, with how often I
was in that shed, his old mill file in my hand going up and down
the blade.

Chapter Two

F *urnace Island*: I sneered every time I walked under the resort sign, tying my apron strings at the last possible second
before the managers considered me "at work" on *their* island: this
landscaped bite of our oval that existed one hour ahead of the rest
of us so that some tourists wouldn't have to adjust quite as much
to the different time zone. Only advantage was I got off work one
hour before Mother expected me: one hour to trek inland. Lionel
laughed each time he saw me in the evening: "Out of the furnace,
into the—what's worse than a furnace?" Guessed most folks I
knew would think the inland was worse, but no one knew I went
up there.

My ID tag said nothing but *Maid*. But it was also my job to be
silent and visible only when the tourists wanted to see me. "At
work" meant not just a place or time. A being, a not being.

Mother would scoff: "Life *is* work, Myrna." Mother in the yard
tending the garden. Mother struggling up from tending the garden. Mother in the kitchen fixing meals with her rewards from
the garden. Doing the wash for Miss Patrice in exchange for some
credit at the store. Packing up what we didn't use from the garden
and carrying a box on her hip around to Bayard's house, where
he'd trade for meat and milk. Mother drying the sisal rope in
the dirt alongside the house. Braiding it once it was dry. Selling

lengths of that rope at the Straw Market, to tourists only, since everyone else around here knew the rope wasn't so strong now that her hands were older. Mother trawling the beach from the sun's first streak in the sky until her stomach was too empty to keep on, eyes cast down for unbroken shells the tourists might buy. Walking home with her skirt pulled into a bowl full of shells, hands raw. After eating a little, Mother flagging friends' cars on the road to drop her at a different stretch of beach where another harvest of shells awaited. Mother on her knees washing out shells in a metal tub. *D-thonk, d-thonk, d-thonk, d-thonk* as they hit the sides. This, for hours, before any shells we'd clean out for dinner. Her knees stiff as bark by nightfall. Mother walking the road, back and forth, back and forth, seeking out the most vibrant buds that would open the next morning. Standing outside the resort's snack bar area, colorful island weeds clutched in her hands and propped in jars at her feet. A cardboard sign resting against her legs: *Tourists: Buy Native Island Wildflowers for 50 cents a bunch. U.S. coins and other OK.* Mother at work.

But never setting foot inside the resort to work, I reminded myself—reassured myself—each time I arrived at the gate.

The key where the planes landed was close enough that not only could I hear them landing from the gate, but from the pool deck I could see how they rattled to the ground. The propellers seemingly no bigger than a truck's steering wheel slowed to show their arms, and then the whining of the engines ebbed to silence. I could even see passengers filing out the hatch, jostled by their own bags. And I would ready myself for another arrival.

"Aye, it's hot today. Sweating in this thing," said Christine, who I'd heard complain almost every day of our lives. Almost rolled my eyes at her but remembered that when I came into Miss Patrice's store for Band-Aids, Christine never asked why I had so many scratches. Though she might have recognized the way the pin-sized bits of skin flipped sideways from my ankles and wrists:

the work of the innermost nettles of the island. I always stuck to this side of the group these days anyway, Hebbie sticking to the other side.

For all her complaining, Christine got into her role. Came alive when the boats approached. She let the wind whip her sheet out in front of the rest of us and waved her arms at the tourists. The look on her face: astonished wonderment, grateful welcome. She could flatten parts of her face into a plane both ancient and without its own story: a trick of the nerves I could never master. She'd once told me she *liked* putting on that sheet to pretend she was somewhere else in history. Jumping from Cruffey Island to make-believe Furnace Island. I hung toward the back near Miss Philene, who hated this as much as I did.

"Your sheet's got a stain, Myrna." Miss Philene's cracked voice was older than she was and stubborn in its boredom. She stood strategically behind me to hide her cigarette from the boat staff. I yanked the tail of my sheet around and saw the stain: a bloom of yellowish brown.

"Blotched paradise, my dear." She chuckled low, a sound that conjured the knobbiness of her face, the bluishness of her lips. She'd said much worse about stains and smells when it was just us soft-padding down the hallway with two rooms' worth of used guest sheets bundled in our arms. Her face always pinched as if she could solder her nostrils. We weren't allowed to push a laundry cart, because it would keep us from ducking into corners when guests appeared in the halls. She always said that walking the halls of this resort, hugging the sheets clean rich folks have made foul in all sorts of ways, didn't mean that foulness touched her. Dropped them at the laundry, did her other chores, went home, and was still herself. She let me steal a drag of her cigarette as Max—Columbus—went through the labored explanation of Furnace Island.

Lionel had been fired from the resort for asking the Arrival Manager if he could edit the boat script. He'd even printed out pages from the Internet showing that furnaces hadn't been invented yet in 1492. Surprise, surprise. She'd pulled out rebuttal pages from a photocopy of Columbus's journal, showing that Max said a lot of what Columbus supposedly actually wrote. When Lionel pointed out first, that the journal was full of nonsense, and second, that none of us was descended from or even remotely looked—in our "sheet-y getups"—like the natives of Columbus's arrival, she banned him from setting foot in the resort. He went back to working at the landfill, where the pay was less but he worked alone most of the day. Getting company when everyone dumped about once a week, when the resort's trucks came about three times a day, when folks came to pick up the good stuff those trucks had dumped. Where he got to reclaim all the decent stuff to help keep all of our houses furnished, comfortable—and to keep the landfill manageable, according to the plan his granddad measured it for years ago when he was still working and walking.

The new batch of tourists started scrambling off the boat; it was impossible to climb off the thing in an elegant way, but the boat staff was there with smiles and hands, twisting and bending their bodies to ease the transition. They were even stepped on where the sand was gummy with strands of seaweed. Some of the tourists looked weary from travel, but most twinkled at us as if we were magical.

So rare a black American came to the resort that we had to notice her climbing off the boat. She was all sharp angles: octagonal bracelets clattering up her arms, the arrows of her elbows facing us. Biggest purse I'd ever seen: a pastel-pink summer-weight bag stamped with an aqua palm tree and a tick of blue paint on the strap. Sharp corners of a book sticking through the fabric against her hip. She'd surely designated it, among all her other purses, "Vacation, Resort." But like that book was pulling her down.

Also had to notice her white-as-Max husband waving his phone around, frowning, and the little boy between them. Far as I could tell, everyone—maids and boat staff and tourists—took note. Then a white girl standing near them in her college T-shirt the color of a cherry sucker, taking the little boy's hand when the woman told her to. Hands free now, the woman shifted her bag to the other shoulder, pressed it close to her hip. (Later I would feel how heavy that book really was, weighed down with time and the smudges of all the other hands that had held it. Weighted with what it was.)

Christine murmuring, speculating: "You think his daughter from a first marriage?"

"Maybe," Della whispered. "But I don't think it's his *wife*. Maybe she works for them, and they let her bring her kid along."

"Naw," Miss Philene tutted. "Seems like wife, way she told that girl to take the boy's hand."

Before anyone answered, the little boy was whining for a grape sucker; he started off a chorus of kids, and pennies started slipping from the sweaty pockets of palms all around us. A few of the maids bent to their knees to save the pennies from the sand.

Max was ambling through the crowd, repeating that there would be a reliable Wi-Fi signal once they were inside the confines of the resort. "Not to worry," he kept saying with a puffed-up chest.

He began barking over the wind again, back on script. "Willing to trade *anything*, ladies and gentlemen!"

Lionel's voice came loudly into my head, swishing in the background. Performing the speech he wrote one night when we were having beers on Junkful Beach, posturing above us on a dune while Christine and I laughed and laughed. That speech was just a joke to her, but I kept imagining it over Max's words:

Willing has nothing to do with it, ladies and gentlemen! Come gaze on these people draped in white because they are darker than the natives who I originally came across in 1492, sent off to the silver mines and otherwise cleared from the island, setting the stage for the other ships that would come later, bringing the ancestors of these people you see before you in uniforms, here to serve because the economy is a rough ocean, my friends. They will smile and greet you. But during your stay they will be a reminder of the sad and punishing history of this island whose beauty you soak in, that you will take with you like the sand that will, I promise you, come back with you no matter how many times you try to shake yourselves free of it!

A giggle rumbled out of my lips, and my cheeks inched up toward my eyes. Max caught my eye and smiled, big and bright, his chest puffing up even more. Like I was finally playing my role with the glee he'd been waiting to see. I had to squint my eyes as his rings caught the sunlight and shot it at me.

Christine and I ducked our heads to remove strands of plastic beads and handed them to the tourists in exchange for pennies. I could see in their eyes: the expectation of gratitude, how the pennies—not worth stooping to the ground for back at their homes—were transformed through some sort of island alchemy. The alchemy of poverty.

And to the Maids' Brigade, I say: our resort will take anything, yes, and shall make you so eager to please!

Behind the fence we stepped around the crabs that'd been missteered by our brooms. But out of the tourists' way still. After I dropped my stained sheet off at the laundry, I took my handful of pennies back to the jar in the kitchen. Their *clink-clink* sounded like a shell cracking under a tire. The Arrival Manager would count to ensure all fifty pennies were returned, then they'd be handed out again on the next boat in expectation of the natives showing up with more trinkets. Which we would, since there was no other work.

The resort's blog mainly told tourists the day's meals (always a buffet with everything) and the day's weather (always warm, sunny) and sometimes where to go (today: the Jamboree). It didn't tell them what not to look at; "at work," we had to keep them from seeing.

> Island Jamboree for kids of all ages. Featuring our local steel drum band and native women selling native crafts. Hair braiding, too! Special guest appearance by our Captain Columbus. Get a taste of the island without venturing too far from the

comfort of your room: the Jamboree will be held
at the snack bars that are conveniently located just
beyond the resort's gate. More details will be avail-
able on *The Beach Blanket Blog.*

We had to memorize the description in case any tourists asked
about the event ahead of time. Only words I'd be allowed to say to
them. Script stuck to my tongue like a piece of a brochure washed
up from someone else's island.

The job of the AYS was to bring water, lemonade, extra-sweet
-smelling punch with too much rum—but not just to serve. They
soothed with drinks, they directed with conversation, they encouraged the purchase of trinkets. The drinks, the braids, the massages
were all free. But the Jamboree was always outside the gate to up
the number of snacks purchased from the snack shacks and the
number of bikes rented from the Captain-on-Wheels bike shack.
(Some of the kids on the island got the old, discarded bikes from
the dump at least. Not even old, just replaced.)

My job was to clear away and not be seen. I was one of the maids
in charge of water bottles. Some others, plates and flatware. Others, trash. The Events Manager thought tables full of near-empty bottles or abandoned plates with sprays of food fork-nudged
to their edges or blooms of crumpled napkins catching the wind
didn't say "Jamboree." Clear it all away and ourselves, too. Keep
moving. Event management didn't want us standing still for more
than eight seconds at a time, and two of us couldn't stand next to
each other at all. If any of us stood still for too long—watching
for a table that needed us, talking to one another, or just leaning
quickly against anything at all—trouble dusted up, like sand you
couldn't get out of your clothes.

Sometimes the sun painted yellow shadows along the sides of
the bottles, making it impossible to see the water level. Half full
or more: give the guests five minutes to return to it, then assume
abandoned. Less: our cue to whisk the bottles away. Then we'd
have to approach carefully, when the guests had left their tables or,

if they were still sitting, when they were engaged by the AYS. Certain times of day, it was impossible to step close enough to reach without throwing your shadow over the guest tables. Luckily today's Jamboree was right after lunch, when the sun pounded our shadows straight under us.

The steel drum players were Floridian. Bought their set off some Jamaican street band in Miami. But the tourists leaned in for every timbred bounce of their mallets. The couple from room B1 was smiling and bopping—wouldn't have guessed from watching them they had so many pill bottles I had to line them up on the floor in order while I wiped their bathroom counter. It wasn't bad music, but repetitive—and, as far as I could tell, all Trinidadian songs on Floridian-Jamaican drums anyway.

Miss Vernie sat behind the table spread with earrings and necklaces, candleholders and straw bags. The resort didn't even buy the bags from Miss Minnie, best weaver on the island. Had them shipped in, big flat boxes of them with plastic bubbles tucked in between. The banner above the table: *Miss Martha's Island Crafts*. Management had told Miss Vernie to keep weaving and unweaving the same four plumes of straw while the maybe-customers browsed.

(Before they started shipping in crafts, and before Lionel was fired, the Events Manager had asked him to bring stuff from the dump. My brother would help him turn junk into stuff tourists would gladly buy. I remembered sitting in the back of Lionel's truck while they worked, watching them cobble before bringing stuff around to the Events Manager for approval.

"Not *authentic* enough," he might say. Or he might put it right on Miss Martha's table. Whoever Miss Martha was that time.

Sometimes it was all just scamming: shards of a broken beer bottle called sea glass. But Troy took great care, sometimes, his artist self not letting his hands rush. His specialty was stitching scraps of brown leather from a thrown-away belt to hooks not good enough for fishing. To the tourists: coconut-shell earrings. He'd soak the leather in salt water, then let it dry around an actual shell for the right curve. With each Jamboree, that old belt hanging from his doorknob inched shorter and shorter.

"Does this look like a coconut shell?" he'd ask me. I'd shrug, which he probably took as ambivalence about the pretense. I just didn't know what coconut shells would look like as jewelry.

But I knew he was an artist, transformation just by turning over in his hands. I was always more interested in how Troy made things, without a tool to his name or an art class his whole life. A brother more distant than the three-plus years that separated us. Led me to try to see into his mind through the steps of his art. Trace back to the thought that propelled his fingers. "Study a work of art to understand the time and place that produced it and the sensibility of its maker." That's what the university art history brochure had said, and that's what I—not a maker myself—had wanted to find out: time, place, sensibility. About Troy, the maker. Before I'd heard back about the application I'd secretly mailed, the major had been shut down. Funds shuttled to the burgeoning Hospitality Studies School. And I went to work instead. With an apron around my waist and the sunset logo stamped on my shoes, like I'd signed up for the hospitality major after all.

When Troy and Hebbie's brother, Andre, first went to the capital, they'd set up a table outside the dock of the big resorts. Andre was the better salesman. Standing there in his always-intriguing T-shirts that tourists came closer to read; aloof with his headphones in, acting like he didn't care if he sold a piece or not. Troy not even at the table. Felt sick to my stomach thinking of them tinkering up their own Jamboree. Hadn't eaten breakfast or lunch, giving the nausea more room to bloom.)

Three women who I also recognized from hall B, my cleaning wing, were trying jewelry on their ankles and wrists. Hands raised to the sun, feet looking soft and rested. The black American woman from B3 was clipping a coconut-shell barrette in her son's curls, the two of them laughing. Not seeing the interested looks shot their way. His head just reaching beneath her squared-out palm tree bag.

Days at the resort now, and we were still talking about that family with the refrain *the woman with the white husband.* Her mix-up kid staying in the room next door with the white girl in her college T-shirts. Some places in the Caribbean were beyond a mix-up from the mixed-up-ness of history—all the ghosts on every dot of an island in this sea—but some places were color coded clearly. Cruffey certainly was. And Furnace Island—*certain.*

Hebbie'd been put to braiding. Joke to me, since growing up I was the one always doing her hair. Not wearing her uniform but not her regular clothes either. I didn't know where they got the getup they'd given her to wear. A dress so long like it was meant for her brother, tall as he was. Her tray of beads rattled with kids and women riffling through for their colors, then sitting and squirming while she worked.

Hebbie's own hair was braided for her to play the role: shooting stars of pink ducking behind black. Wondered who'd done it for her. Her eyes looked sad without her bangs winging above. Looked just like her brother with that high shiny forehead. She caught my eye like she was going to say something, but I stared down at my black sneakers, like I was investigating the sinking spider sunset stitched into my feet, then walked away before eight seconds added up beneath them.

She used to play piano in the abandoned house by the southeastern bay while I talked a streak about everything I could think of. When she was studying in the capital I used to go over to her mother's house for her scheduled calls home. Inseparable as our brothers. Until we got the news about Troy, and Mother stopped speaking, and I couldn't bear to be going around with Hebbie knowing her brother was going around without mine. Knowing her brother knew things about how it all happened. Hebbie was my sister-friend, more than Christine or some of the others my own age, but hearing any of it, even filtered through her voice, would make it all meaner than it already was.

Christine was walking toward me like she had something to say. I turned half sideways and drifted along behind where the braiding was happening, where my eyes wouldn't meet Hebbie's again. The taught white scalps looked so raw they made me cringe. I wanted to muss that hair back over all those riverbeds of skin. Flaming pink burn would spill around each braid soon enough.

Maneuvering around without touching anyone or stopping anywhere felt somewhat like trying to go inland without a machete, dodging haulback nettles and keeping on and on to avoid the insects gnashing on you. Less visible snags here—but nowhere to get to either. Kept walking by the other maids, hearing just snippets of what they wanted to tell me.

Miss Philene, tray primly under her arm like her at-church purse: "Arrival Manager's office. Right after this." Her back to me before I could ask a thing.

Christine right there again: "Trouble brewing." Ripple of her fingers for emphasis. Max walked by in his Columbus hat, reached out and tickled his fingers against Christine's. She half laughed, but I shrugged my free hand into my pocket.

Miss Philene again, trading places with Christine in a figure eight: "Boil and bubble."

One of the AYS stepped in between us. I lofted my tray of near-empty bottles onto my shoulder and kept circulating.

One of the backup Columbuses, also in costume, rode circles on a kid-sized bike, legs sticking out like rifles, throwing his hands up in the air, too, while the kids cheered. Wind almost took his hat into my face before he snatched it back.

The pocking of the steel drums turned into pounding. Not like the rustle chorus of insects inland in the evening, the cicadas crushing the air, like an engine moving me on and on.

I headed back around the brush, circled behind the cluster of padded chairs where Max was now standing next to the AYS who usually did the massages. In one chair was B3's husband, telling the woman next to him about that morning's gecko on his bedpost. (Complaining about my cleaning or just storytelling about exotic wildlife? Hard to tell with his voice that refused to spike with interest.) Max kept pushing up his bulky costume sleeves as he squeezed another man's shoulders.

The man scowled each time the sleeves slid back against his neck. Said to his wife and to whoever could hear: "On our cruise last year we loved the massages from the Jamaicans."

His wife nodded vigorously as an iguana. "Yes, yes, the best hands are the Jamaicans'." More nodding. The chain attached to her sunglasses clinked against her earrings. "Shouldn't you have a local do this sort of thing?" she asked.

Hurried off to the kitchen before I could be recruited. Last time a guest requested a local woman give her a massage, Miss Philene was yanked over. Afterward management had examined her hands for an hour, debating whether it was more or less authentic for the maids' fingernails to be painted when the guests wanted us to touch them. My own nails were ragged and encrusted with the dirt of the inland. Fingertips gouged by the stones. I again stuck my free hand in the emptiness of my pocket. Had a flash of when Mother used to clip my and Troy's nails out on the doorstep, when we were small enough sitting still was an even bigger chore than now.

I placed each empty bottle gently into the recycling barrel that was almost as big as the door. According to management, bottles were placed carefully to avoid clatter; according to Lionel, to avoid the denting that revealed recycled bottles to be not new. There was no recycling facility on the island. But the tourists liked to see the green bins with their happily spinning arrows.

Sometimes Lionel gave kids spare American coins that turned up in the trash for washing the bottles, and we'd sneak them back in. The trick was not to sneak bottles in our bags, betrayed at the gate by the crinkling sound, but to load a pallet of them into Lem's truck when he delivered to the dump. So they came back in via the truck entrance and could be shelved with the new pallets. Lionel our island recycling facility after all.

The trick was to do it only once before the resort's logo on the bottle started to rub off, gave us away with disappearing letters or an asymmetrical sun. If we didn't risk it, though, the piles of plastic at the dump clacked in the wind, rolled against one another as if huddling from the gusts. Could hear them all the way at Garrett and Della's house. Pile of empties so high it could distort the view. Even at the top of the landfill, there was a view.

My next load, one completely empty bottle got picked up by the wind. The plastic crinkled against the gravel as the wind blew it away from me. I stooped, reached out, only to have the wind swoosh the other way. Finally grabbed the bottle by its cap as it tried to sneak around the bend where the resort's landscaping gave way to the bursts of brush we were used to. That grew the way it just grew. I noticed a few other empties rolled up under the brush, and I pulled my apron up and out into a bowl for them.

Looked up to see Lionel's truck parked just out of view of the Jamboree. Lionel himself, dressed like a tourist: bright T-shirt, baggy shorts with pockets bigger than his knees, rubber sandals like spiderwebs. Probably wearing dumped tourists' clothes.

He was talking to B3, the woman with the white husband and the palm tree bag. Showing him something that she'd bought from "Miss Martha." Maybe beer-bottle sea glass, maybe a string of wrinkly tumor-shaped beads called sea pearls. Something shiny and split to pieces.

Speakers from the Jamboree blotted out whatever he was asking her. When they quieted down again, I could hear her describing to Lionel what sounded like his landfill but she called her consignment shop. Explaining how the topography of the shop shifted slowly but remained fully populated: novelty lamps swarming her cash register, a baby buggy filled with lizard skulls, midcentury TVs that were their own furniture, vintage cameras like miniature luggage stacked in a skyline by the window. The objects bearing some marks of their owners. How she liked sorting and recontextualizing the donations into anonymous objects that could belong to someone new, to anyone. People bought this stuff from her, she said. Arranged their purchases on shiny mantels and texted her proud photos.

"We turned a particleboard bookcase on its side," she was saying to him. "Like a holding place for some stacks of smaller items but also a balance beam to travel toward the front of the store. That's how full to the gills the store is sometimes! With a clothesline to hold on to." She mimed it for Lionel: feet shuffling sideways, hands overhead.

Reminded me of the corridors Lionel's father had created along the far wall of the landfill when it was first built, wide enough for one. Few times I was up there with him, each of us tracing a different level, facing each other only every fourth sentence or so. Thinking about Lionel taking an American tourist up there to show her the similarities in their jobs: made me ready to laugh. Once in a while he did get up to forty dollars taking them on what he called the "*real* island tour." But getting paid by an American tourist to take her to the dump? That'd be the same day the resort made me captain.

When I heard Lionel actually offering to show her how he handled the sorting and the navigating at the landfill, I turned my head away to hide my smile, a little bit of a laugh seeping out onto my face.

That's when I saw Mother, facing the road. In the afternoon light her grayish hair shimmered platinum. Lost count of how many times Miss Minnie had asked various managers at the resort not to schedule the Jamboree on Straw Market Day, especially when a new boat of tourists had just come in. She and Mother must've agreed to split up this time. New strategy for selling.

Mother's sign for selling flowers was facing the road. I saw only its blank, dusty back through her ankles. And her own dusty back. Just a slice of face in my view. Resort would let non-employees sell so close to the gate only if they faced out, pretending to sell to their own. Not take a single coin away from the Jamboree vendors if management could help it.

I rebalanced my tray with the partly full bottles and gathered together the empty ones in my apron pouch. Tried to keep them wrapped from the wind so no one would hear me standing there, catch me watching.

Then I heard the word *plantation*, American accent. Stopped dead still. Must've heard wrong, I thought. *Plan, nation, plant, situation, damnation*. Something else said. But still I stood, a stone myself.

Corner of my eye saw B3 clutching to her a book the size and shape of the records Miss Wayida Callaghan could be heard blasting out the open windows of her church no one would set foot in. An old book, corners soft. She turned back to Lionel, lowering the book to show him the cover, and his face folded in. Not his usual eye-and-mouth puppetry, especially when trying to sell a tour. Not his usual shag of braids jumping around with his head. His eyes shifted toward Mother. Hand gently nudging the book back up against B3's torso.

Force between Lionel's eyes, Mother's hunched body, book whose title I couldn't read. Mother shifted her position so I couldn't see her face at all. Shoulder blades a fortress. Her back a curling wave about to sink back under where it came from. Eight seconds, then I had to move my feet so management wouldn't move theirs toward me.

Lionel might have said something, but I could no longer hear their conversation as a bunch of older tourist kids who'd rented bikes zoomed around me, hooting, almost knocking my tray out of my hands.

Before I could round back, an AYS appeared. Skin alive with anger or too much sun. At me standing still? At Lionel being here? At B3 talking to a local? At the possibility she could buy a flower from Mother or something, anything, from somebody else?

Once I got to the kitchen door with my new load, I upturned any bottles that weren't empty. Watched the wet darkness burn off the ground almost instantly.

When I came back, B3 had rejoined her husband. He tapped his hand on his knee to the beat of the music, and the two of them passed a cup of rum punch back and forth. Their kid was sitting in the lap of that white girl while she got her hair braided. Hebbie's hands rushed. She had to join us for the maids' call-up, whatever it was about.

From across a table, Miss Philene's lips reminded me: *Office.*

"What now?" I whispered. Circled a table, counting seconds. Came back around so she could answer me.

"Don't know, dear," she said. "But keep your hands in your pockets, I'd say."

I slid my tray on top of hers by the bar station, and we followed the others out of the sun, waiting for our sweat-soaked uniforms to get soggy and cold in the air-conditioning.

They took us in one at a time. According to the four who'd already gone in, they were each first addressed as "Christine." Christine found this funny, but I saw under the older women's eyes a subtle strain. We stood quietly, each fidgeting with the rim of a pocket or something deep inside.

Only one talking like a rainstorm was the actual Christine. Talking about how antsy she got standing still like we were. How she needed to go out and see things, talk to people.

"No worry," Miss Philene said. "Plenty to see and new people to talk to when they march us back out for the next boat." She rolled her eyes.

"And that's fine," Christine answered, ignoring the shushing of everyone who was sick of her talking. "May sound silly, but I like standing on the sand."

"Standing on sand?" Della snickered. "What are you, taking a break out there?"

Christine shrugged. "Can pretend *and* be myself at different times of day," she said. She stepped out of line and pointed to each of us in turn. "Other girls having so much trouble here? They need to learn how to do that, I think."

"We're all in trouble, that's what we're doing in this line. Over pennies, not pretending." Miss Philene moved to the back of the line. She'd rather wait all day than stand next to Christine.

Christine kept talking by the mile as always, this time about the new tourists and what she'd learned about them at the Jamboree.

"That white college girl is the family's *nanny*!" Her hands star-bursts. It sorta was a revelation, with how interested folks had been.

"Now I've seen everything," Miss Vernie said.

I wondered how Christine learned this, since I'd been cleaning their rooms and didn't know. Talking to them directly? Couldn't be. One time last season when management heard from the AYS that some of the maids had talked all night with tourists who'd been at Thiflae Bar, they'd started asking the guests questions to see if they knew by name who cleaned their rooms or cleared their tables after meals. Even heard they used a poster with all of our pictures, like a mug shot collage, and just asked the guests all sweetly who'd been taking care of them. Nelson'd been fired when three tourists matched his name to his picture. Miss Philene said there was a hidden-away room somewhere with that poster in it, among other things.

Waiting outside management's office like we were was pretty much a lineup anyway, mug shots or not.

I wanted to hear some more about the family, but Christine was going on and on about her own boy being about the same age as their little boy. Miss Philene, still planted at the back, called out to the whole line, "Let's talk about the weather." She was likely to change the subject when it was sons, sons, and more sons. Of her three kids, only one and two—both daughters—still left in the world.

Even I laughed at her idea. So few weather variations around here, not much to say.

"Too bad hurricane season passed us by," Miss Philene grumbled. "Resort's not going to blow away while we're standing here."

I let out a snort.

We marked time by the worst storms, named them, talked about house repairs by how many storms they'd withstood. Last year was the Big Blowout, when the resort had no electricity for a week and a half, though the structures came through all right on the eastern side of the island. When folks referred to *That* Storm, everyone knew which one they meant and which roofs had been made useless by the worst winds anyone could remember. The winds had blown the ocean so far inland, salted up the wells for weeks. Even if you hadn't been born yet, you knew That Storm. We all knew the story of Miss Patrice, pregnant with the youngest of her five kids, and her husband off in the capital. When the roof started blowing off the house, she didn't know whether she was crying or just wet from the rain coming in. A tree crashed into the door, and they had to climb out the window—all four kids and Miss Patrice with her swollen belly. All of them crawled to her brother's house, blinded by wind.

Other thing we all knew was that hurricanes didn't used to slam that part of the island where Miss Patrice's house had always been. But that was before the resort had bought up more land along the western shore and cleared it of trees. You had to go back a *long* time to have seen hardwood all over this island. Most of it had been gone since the early nineteenth century, cut down and shipped off for money by Cruffey, who planted his feet here and claimed to own those trees. And claimed to own the men and women who cut the trees down and loaded them up for shipment. Later a lot of folks built houses on that one slice of the island, where trees pointed toward the storms blowing in. Tall trees with roots that stayed firm in the soil. Used to be those trees soaked up some of a storm, withstood the rage. But the resort came in like a storm of its own and stripped the rest of the hardwood, like leaving a door open to those houses.

Worst part was—and we all knew this story, too—Miss Patrice's late husband had all kinds of engineering know-how. Gave the resort all the right advice about where to clear or not, what to build or not, and was plain ignored. We'd all heard her description of him standing on the beach with all the executives sweating in their suits, their faces red as thiflae in the noon sun, explaining how the small cabin suites they wanted to put in the cleared-out slice couldn't match Mother Nature on that part of shore. Heard Miss Patrice's description of him standing on that same beach when the trees had been chopped and stacked like carrot sticks, watching them loading up with his hands fisted against his hips, fingertips white.

The office door opened, and we all stood more still and quiet than we had been. Hebbie came out with the manager behind her. I avoided her eyes as she walked away. I was next.

"Christine?" the Arrival Manager said to me. We called her this—Arrival Manager—behind her back, because from the first she insisted on being called Claudia. Not Ms. Ricken or Miss Ricken or Mrs. Ricken, not Manager Ricken or even Manager Claudia. Not Madame Claudia, as many of the tourists called her. Claudia.

"Myrna," I said, following her in.

Embarrassed shuffling of papers. "Muuurna..." Stretching out my name while she looked for my last name on her stack of files. Mother used to laugh when she heard Americans say my name. She said they missed the way your lip had to jut out into a tiny half-smile when you said *Meer* or *Mere*; as she called it, "the island *y*." "The island *y*," Troy had said, laughing, "is really a sarcastic sneer."

Claudia said my last name with the same drawn-out *uhhh* sound and with a question mark on the end of it: "Burre?"

"Yes, ma'am."

"Claudia."

"Yes. Claudia."

"You were on the beach last Thursday? For the whole arrival demonstration?"

She knew I was. I had to be at every arrival, according to my contract. And I turned in my time card with all the information from the week: when I was cleaning the rooms, when I was on the beach for the arrivals, when I was assisting with laundry. "Yes, Claudia."

"How many pennies did you receive?"

"That one day?" Sometimes we had more than one arrival per day this time of year.

"The afternoon boat arrival on Thursday. The jar was missing six pennies when the boat staff prepared for Friday's arrival."

"I return the ones that are given to me by the tourists. I don't count them."

"Guests."

"Guests. I don't hand the pennies out."

"You don't hand them—what do you mean?"

She knew what I meant. There were no interviews like this with the boat staff members, who collected the money from the jar and handed them out on the boat. (Or with the guests, who could keep the pennies or throw them in the water for good luck; I was pretty sure I'd seen some thrown.) Waiting outside this beige door was a line of women only like me, "natives," in our maid uniforms.

Claudia closed her files, sighed loudly, and clasped her hands on top of the stack. She kept tucking a straw-colored strand of hair behind her ear, and it kept making its way forward again. Her hair and her skin and the beige shell she was wearing all blended together, her pale blue eyes popping out at me; the contrast was similar, it struck me, as the water to the sand just outside her office. I looked for tides in her eyes. They were ringed by pink. The wide center part in her hair looked like a dried-up riverbed. She looked tired. With the guests she always brightened up, even her faded grayish hair sparkling blonder from the reflection off the pool water.

Her desk faced away from the window, leaving me the ocean view. I knew the setup wasn't for me; this other side of the desk beautified for upper management or guests or both? Through the window, I could see most of the pool deck, the loungers all faced toward the pool. All turned away from the ocean view, which always surprised me, the way the brochures sold our blue seas. From where I sat, I could see the pool and the ocean in sequence, like two versions of one thing: the heated, simulated version and the rough, cold version that was too vast to see all at once.

There was barely movement out there. Just acres of white skin, strung up in spandex, in various stages of sunburn and repose. Except for the one woman from B3. That woman with her sharp bracelets and elbows seemed softer somehow, reclining in her bathing suit, her thighs the shape of upside-down lungs. Pastel bag slumped under her chair. Her husband was on his side, seemingly fast asleep. Even from this distance the back of his neck looked like rare steak. I didn't see the little boy or the girl who apparently was his nanny.

Through Claudia's closed window I could just faintly hear the tinny music still bobbing along. The only movement was a woman snorkeling in the pool, taking in the mural of a coral reef painted on the bottom. The resort used to offer boats to take tourists out to the reefs, but almost none of them wanted to dip into that cold water, real thing or not.

The snorkeler walked slowly out of the shallow end and onto cement in all her gear: steel-colored hair wrapped around her ears and mask, each flipper dropping a short wall of water off its side. She was waving her hand around the same way she had yesterday, when she'd scraped it open on the bottom of the pool and emerged announcing to everyone and no one: "It is so *real* down there! I reached out to touch it!" She sent the AYS in a tizzy to find a bandage. I'd had a Band-Aid tucked into my apron for that night, but I knew I'd be caught out if a manager saw me touching a guest.

But here I was anyway.

"Have a seat," Claudia said wearily, her eyes softening and meeting mine. She fixed me with the I-get-it-because-I'm-really-your-friend look management pulled out of their pockets.

"Look. The international office makes me investigate if we are missing more than ten percent of any supply. *Any* supply. Five? Fine. I would look the other way. There have been many times—*many* times—that we were down one, two, three, four, five pennies, and we made do without reporting a thing. I don't want to go through this any more than you do."

I could tell from the slump of her shoulders that she thought she meant what she was saying. Caught up against her will by the powers that be—and by whoever it was who started this whole thing by stealing or misplacing six pennies.

You could have put six pennies in the jar instead of reporting it, I thought. *You could have assumed the pennies were dropped in the sand and either told the main office that or gotten down on all fours and searched all day for them. You could have told the main office to get the sticks out of their asses.* You *could have stolen the pennies. But we both know you didn't, because we both know that if someone really stole six pennies, that person really needed them.*

One of the AYS came in the office without knocking and didn't even give me a glance. Started fighting with a filing cabinet, and Claudia handed him a tiny key over her shoulder. He unlocked the drawer and took out what looked like a brick of blank name tags. Handed her back the key, left without a word and with the door partly opened. I could feel the ears from the women still lined up in the hallway lean closer to the crack in the door.

I said: "I carefully hold in my palm each penny that is handed to me. I put it safely in my pocket with my hand while I make the walk from the boat arrival location to the counter in the kitchen where the jar is placed. I cup my palm just so as I put the pennies back in the jar so that none can fall onto the floor. I give my bag to the guards every night when I leave so they can search it for anything they think I have stolen, and they hand it back and send me on my way." I almost laughed at the thought of a guard finding a penny at the bottom of one of our bags and assuming it was trespassing there. Spare change wasn't typical on this island.

Claudia shuffled through her files, the desperate fidgeting of her fingers trying to get to the bottom of all of this and set things right. As though she wanted to dismiss me to go back to my work if I could just prove, beyond every shadow of a shadow of a doubt, that there was no possibility I took those coins. If one of us maids could just get her off the hook with the international office.

From where I sat I could see only the black cardboard backs of her picture frames held in place by tiny metal arrows. The faces— of husband, kids, maybe aging parents with crow's-feet smiles— only looked at her. Waiting for her, reminding her to resolve this nuisance and get home to her real life.

She had, after all, dragged the whole family down here for this job. To this dusty place where they didn't have the things they had at home and where they had a hell of a time getting used to the way our people lived. If it weren't for the pool they got to use all the time, and the financial opportunity in this international company that she was scrounging her way through with her tough, clean fingernails, that family would not even be putting up with all of this. I had heard it all, when the staff or their families came into Thiflae Bar. Had one or two too many, told us all how it was, this hard thing of keeping the place going, being here, whole family's life on pause, so a resort could be pushed along. My nose wrinkled itself, as if the sour breath of the night's last beer were in the room with us, right here with Claudia and me and her desk piled high with problems.

She stood up from behind her desk, secured the door, and I found myself taking the seat she'd offered several minutes before. She stood above me, walking from one side of my chair to the other. Through the window I could see the sun starting to bleed out into the sky, its reflection muddling the resort's famed turquoise water with a metallic pinkish edge. Out of place, the moon floated beyond like a memory of a cotton ball.

Claudia's hand was on the pocket of my uniform. I kept looking at the window. She ran her thumb over the knots of my resewn catches that spread like a rash down the front and sides of the skirt and apron. I felt her fingers skimming, connecting the dots that Mother had so carefully stitched for me. Mother stitching without ever questioning what it was that clawed at me, gnawed at the fabric that turned me, each day, into *Maid*. I sat still as one of the stones, speaking as little as they did.

"Hmm." Her voice was calmer, surer. Her fidgeting had receded to allow the tide of power back into her voice and movements. "You put the coins in these pockets?" Her thumbnail scratched at some hooks of thread that hadn't been pulled back through all the way. Hadn't been reinforced.

"Yes."

I could hear the music outside break off abruptly for the announcement that the dining room was open for dinner. The speaker's vowels were flat, the words spreading out like water. That's when I spotted the nanny and the little boy, coming back up from the shore. Sandy feet and ankles. The only two who hadn't stayed up on the pool deck. From where they were standing, I knew she could see the break in the fence, where the dumpsters and trucks were, and I wondered if she noticed the division between the workers back there—no maids, since we were all in here, but the other workers, like Lem, in jumpsuits—and the AYS on the deck in their crisp white shorts and pastel shirts. Not just clothing different colors either. As they approached that nanny's boss, the little boy's mother, I saw the woman dig through her bag as if she'd misplaced something and then stand up and walk toward the doors to the lobby. (Was it that book that'd drawn Lionel's eyes toward Mother, made him nudge the cover away from her?) Some of the AYS who circled endlessly between the bar and the pool deck fetching cocktails turned and watched her go through one of the doors.

Claudia's breath was close to my ear. My eyes left the window.

"And it's not possible," she began, "that with all these tears all over this uniform—*all* over it—that some coins could have slipped through?"

I felt her fingers on all the nubs of thread and fabric, scars of all the trips I'd made inland and back out. The claws of the haulback trying to keep me out, then trying to keep me in.

"Catches in the material like this," Claudia murmured. "Looks like..." Her eyes met mine, one eyebrow in a knowing arc. Some of the resort people around here, a few of them, knew the land. The plants. I felt goose pimples rise up all over my arms.

She stepped away from me, and I looked back up at her. Behind her on the bulletin board were the season's disciplinary write-ups, with a thumbtack staked through the stack. Lateness. Stealing (suspected). Stealing (confirmed). Guest Complaints / Service Negligence. Uniform Divergence. Trespassing.

If she wrote me up for negligence (dropping the pennies) or divergence (tearing my uniform), I'd be better off than for trespassing, for which I'd have to meet with the security team and would almost certainly be fired anyway. And either way, fired or kept on, would be watched. An invisible but thick wall between me and the inland. If I forced her to keep going down the line of women, one of them would have to be written up for suspected stealing, since Claudia wouldn't know how else to resolve this. And whoever it was would never be able to work at the resort again or at any of the resorts in the capital. Why we all lined up so nice and polite even when management got our names—or anything else—wrong. A list, a database, whatever it was that had its way of knowing spread across the ocean. Bad words swam fast.

As they had with Miss Patrice's husband. The resort didn't like that he'd kept talking to people about the whole mess with the trees and the cabins and the storms. Especially when there was no need to be put in harm's way, when he knew better and had said so. Probably couldn't help himself, all that mix of sad and mad and crumpled men got. They also didn't like that he'd kept insisting to be paid the consulting fees they'd promised, even if they'd ignored his advice. He had to go back to the capital for work, but that didn't last long. He kept talking about what happened, and the resort badmouthed him in a way that, after a while, he couldn't even get work on the capital. All the hotels that used to hire him for projects stopped. Some wouldn't even see him when he came to ask for work, even people he'd worked with for years as their go-to man. And then That Storm came and tore his own roof off with his family inside.

Thought of myself wandering the capital alone, no work to be had, while Mother rotted alone in our house. If we even still had a house.

"Well, Murna? Possible?"

I reached into my bag and spidered my hand for change. One dime. I put it on her desk. She shook her head slowly, still standing above me.

"The missing coins are already reported. I can't replace them." Her fingers went back into my lap, pointing to each spike. I didn't squirm; I would not squirm. "Well? Is it *possible*?"

"Are you asking me if it is *possible* a uniform divergence could have caused the pennies to be accidentally lost?"

"Yes."

Above my shoulder, Claudia's blazer was drooping, too big. Like a kid playing at teacher. She looked tired, her cheeks creased like bundles of straw. I went through all the options again and again in my mind. She needed to settle this money thing before she could go home or else she'd spend the night on the phone with management, accused of not doing her job, of letting us natives take the dust from her pockets, as my dad used to say. If not me, she'd convince Miss Philene or Christine or Miss Vernie or someone else. Well, probably couldn't convince Christine. But Miss Philene was now last in line, no one else to move on to after her. I tried to picture who else was waiting in line before I came in. Ticked off all the names of who would go home employed, not written up, with their water for the week. Claudia waited until I had conjured the others who were waiting. Aprons pristine compared with mine.

"Aye," I said.

The rest of the line in the hall dispersed when they saw the yellow paper in my hand. Two weeks of overtime garbage duty without pay.

Bench Story No. 10: Hebbie Whylly

I have worked at this resort for four years. Full-time, four whole years, with almost no time off, even in those August heat weeks when we're all soaking in island glue. Until today I've worked so many days in a row I couldn't tell you the last chance I had time to climb in bed slowly before I was already asleep like the dead.

My mother sent me to the capital for university—this before my brother went off to work there. I lived with my aunt and uncle: my father's older sister who looks just like him, so folks say, since I don't remember my father's face. He went to the States when I was about three. Sent money back for a time and then didn't.

I came back from the capital even though a lot of my friends were staying there, finding jobs, liking the bustle of things. Like a museum with all those different faces to see every day. Especially to kids like us who came from the outer islands to the capital. I remember calling home, both my mother and Myrna—my then best friend, none of you could forget—sharing the phone, and explaining what walking down the street was like in a place where you couldn't count the steps to the next house or face or dog that you knew. Streets you had to wait and see whether it was all right to walk along singing to yourself. A little like the resort that way, since sometimes you had to be a little less yourself in the capital.

Not all my friends there were from Cruffey, but they were all from
outer islands. Capital kids didn't really mix with us. Saw us as be-
hind the times, ignorant. Called us "small islanders." Didn't think
we could get our brains to soak in worldly things if we weren't in the
middle of them. One way to see things forgets the second way to
see things. *My friends from the outer islands seemed to know what I*
meant whenever I said that.

I came home to my mother because even though her sister was here,
her sister was getting sickly, too, and I thought they both needed me.
So I came back here with my degree in music and business—double
major, honors list—and I took the job I could find that would give me
a paycheck each and every week. My boyfriend was in the capital, and
he said we'd still visit each other a lot and figure it out in the long run,
but pretty soon I didn't hear from him so much. You didn't know what
could happen in the capital, all that could change in one sleeping's
time. But Myrna knows that. Miss Daphanie knows.

My brother, Andre, pops in and out to visit, but not everyone comes
back. Changes all of us, all our ties to one another. Right, Myr?

Nothing I could do 'bout anything but do my best at my job. I did
everything they told me to do. No one's guest rooms were cleaner
than mine. No one's walks between the guest rooms and the laundry
were quicker than mine. No one's toilets shone like mine did. No one
cleared away the buffet leftovers as quickly as I did. No one com-
plained less about throwing all those piles of food in the garbage than
I did. I kept my mouth shut while others asked the managers and the
waiters if they could just take some of that unused food home—saying
how many people it would feed if they could just pack up some of the
food in their own paper and their own bags and transport it them-
selves, not asking the resort people to do anything except not insist
it all get thrown away. No one's mouth stayed quieter than mine, no
one's lips pressed together for as long as possible like some kind of test.
No one's tongue so at rest.

Sometimes at night I'd realize I hadn't spoken all day, and the first
few words I'd try to say on the road or at home to my mother would
come out hoarse. That whispery-ness reminded me of trying to draw

words in the sand and having a letter erased by the wind before you even finished making it.

At the end of each day I stood in line patiently and let the guards put their hands in my purse, and then I went home and made dinner with my mother out of whatever we could get from the nothing-nothing soil behind our house combined with whatever we could afford and was in stock at Miss Patrice's store. And then I'd wash my uniform in the basin and put it out where I knew the sun would hit it first thing in the morning to at least make it not so damp when I put it on to go to work again the next day.

Never got in trouble once. No green or yellow paper slips for me. In fact, used to keep others out of trouble, reminding Miss Philene to hide the cigarette smell and Myrna to hush out the obvious annoyance brimming in her eyes. But it'd been a length of time since Myr and I kept each other reminded at work.

(Seeing her at work since was like when that gone boyfriend's chewed pens surfaced in my purse, or like my father's one outfit still on a hanger in Ma's closet: the empty shape of the used-to-be right there inside your home. Long time now. The last time Myr was in our house, at our table, was the night we'd all heard about Troy. Once her ma finally fell asleep, she came straight to me and my ma. One point my ma opened the cabinet to give her water, and before she could even nudge Andre's favorite pint glass aside to get Myr a water glass, Myrna bolted out her seat and off she went and didn't come back to the house again ever. All these months and months and months.)

All of a sudden last month I get written up by my manager, but she wouldn't tell me any of the details of who complained about me. Someone, someone out there, said I was "disagreeable." That's all she told me. Her advice was to keep to myself. I didn't know how to keep more to myself, since I don't even talk to the other maids all that much. Even women I grew up with since we were the height of this bench: at work I just work, I don't hang out with them talking away. I went home that night and studied my employee manual. What was going to happen to my mother if I lost my job and had to go back to the

capital for work? With my brother already there, too? Knew stories
of girls making good money there, doing some things I didn't want
to do. Some guys, too. Anything can sink down or rise up there. You
didn't know what could happen to you in that place. To change you. I
mean, just look at Troy—a guy whose smile you could see all the way
down the road—I never would've dreamed it.

Keep myself to myself: all I can do in this world.

I stayed up half the night studying that manual, all the little de-
tails that might flit out of your head while you're focusing on the
tasks of your job. Mainly I was focusing on the notes I'd taken during
training, because those seemed to be the things they were emphasizing
above the technical stuff printed in the manual. I'd written:

Step aside when guests are in the hallway. Don't just
let them pass—don't make them interact with you by
making eye contact.

Don't knock and say "Room service." If there is any
sign guests are still in their rooms, come back another
time.

If the gate between the garbage area and the pool
deck has come open, close it. Best to stand behind the
gate so no one by the pool can see you as you close it,
especially if you have an armful of garbage.

Reading all these penciled notes in the darkness, two in the morn-
ing, tired like I am after any day, all of this starts to sound like crazy
talk. Like the kind of stuff Myrna and I would laugh at up at Junk-
ful; like the kind of stuff Lionel would scream out into the ocean in
a dreamed-up voice to make us laugh more. And without Myrna to
run it by, I start going in circles in my mind almost trying to invent
a time I broke one of the rules so that I could understand what I did
that didn't agree with someone. Kept imagining some faceless person
out there who could point to me and say there was some disagreement,
something in my manner that suggested I wouldn't do something I
was supposed to. Something they wanted me to agree to.

Then I started thinking of all the men the previous week, down from the international office to check on things but mostly to get red-faced drunk by the pool all day and night.

Then I think of how I'd been following all the rules but some of them kept staring like they wanted *eye contact or stepped out of the direction they were walking like they* wanted *me to be in their way. These weren't regular guests; they were half guests and half people who worked here,* ran *it here, so they sometimes went in the halls that were "staff only" or in the garbage area. There was no way not to be seen or heard because they were coming in all your hiding spots.*

Times I felt eyes on me, like sensing a gecko in your room when you're sleeping. But then I think how I just went on about my business through all of it.

Then I think how Christine told me one of them smacked her on the bum when she was loading drinks on a cart in the back hall.

Then I think how I saw Christine by the pool talking and laughing, but I don't know if it was before or after the smack. (The bum smack, not the ring one. That hadn't happened yet. Lord, I didn't think we'd be counting them up.)

Then I think there would be no way I'd be talking and laughing at work. No way I'd be by the pool unless a manager sent me there, which had never happened. (And after the last few days you won't find me anywhere near that pool.) Tried to remember if any of those men in the hall or the garbage area had said anything, or gestured even, that I should be by the pool talking and laughing, too. Disagree with them just by doing what I always did: my job.

Got about two hours of sleep that night. The sun wasn't too strong that morning so my uniform felt damp under the arms and around the back zipper where the fabric is doubled over. Walked to work with my head cottony from sleepiness. Tight behind my knees from sitting instead of lying all night. When it's cloudy things look dirtier around here. Smell dirtier, too, to me at least. Have to walk around smelling dirty all day long. Wet under the arms feels dirty, too, because how much is the clean wet from washing and how much is the dirty wet from sweating? Can't breathe through your mouth all day long. Have to breathe in through your nose sometime. Hard to tell whether the dirty is me, too, or just all around me.

Chapter Three

F elt a burn to go inland that night, since I'd be working overtime and probably couldn't get up there again for two whole
weeks.

I still didn't know what that first building I'd found even was. It
had taken me months to cut a trail to and around the wall ruins I'd
located. All I knew was that I had cut through the brush to stone,
made out what was left of a corner of a building. Smooth in places,
stones pushing out in others. A horizontal plank of lignum vitae
wood, our hardest wood that never crumbled, showing where a
window used to wait for ghosts—I couldn't imagine them as people—to pass through day after day after day. So grown over with
brush I hadn't yet worked around to see if the other two walls still
stood. Cacti arms burst through the window like warnings. I went
back up to that point over and over, letting myself realize each
time I'd found more than border walls—finally! But there was no
way to figure out where I was on the estate, and it would take a lot
more work to get inside, figure out the building's function. And if
I figured it out, what would I do?

The sun was getting ready to sink, stretching a gray veil over
everything I was trying to see. I should be getting home to Mother,
eat dinner with her before two weeks of not. But... I reached out
to run my hand along the wall I'd found, letting my fingers travel

across where the stone went from rough to smooth and back to rough. My finger caught on a deeper groove, followed it in different directions until I was kneeling, and I was certain it was a diamond shape. Didn't care about the nettles moving in close to my shoulders, my neck, my face, as I leaned in to press with both hands and get my eyes as close as they would go.

Definitely a diamond. Smaller than the platter I was carrying that morning, lines not quite as thick as my pinkie. Pretty exact shape to seem an accident of time or of anything else. Inside the diamond, more lines harder to make sense of. Looked in the dimness like a dropped bundle of twigs. I ran my fingers through and through. Felt like a bundle of tiny sticks, too. But maybe arranged—not time cracking or an animal gnashing or branches scratching. No: etched in by a person's hand.

The veil got thicker, and I knew I had to head down, home. Walked slowly, looking at my fingers, which had now traveled the same lines as fingers of people I'd never know. Felt through the veins in my arms the pressure they put against the stones.

Troy had called home when an art exhibit from the States came through the capital. How much he wanted to run his fingers over the globby ebbs and thinning bays of van Gogh's paint, he'd said. Guards and velvet ropes between him and that paint. Haulback and cacti and overtime between me and the next corner of building.

I used my left hand to protect my face from the brambles, and with my right I kept the machete close to my knees like a shield since bleeding there would stain my uniform. My uniform was filthy. I could even feel the dust on my face, a skin on top of skin. If I kept my face still, it wouldn't break up too much. I eventually reached the road, feeling low. Weeks of no-pay overtime rummaging with the garbage; manager onto my haulback threads. And who knew how much farther I could chop my way through before the rainy season would come around all over again, brush closing in on all I'd cut away. Blocking my view of what I'd just found. Once I got down and let the bend of the road guide me home, I was still reluctant to step too far out of the brush, didn't want anyone to see my scraped-up ankles, ask me where I'd been.

When I got in sight of home, I saw Lionel's truck out front. Guessed he gave Mother a ride home from the Jamboree. Inside he was sitting with her at the table, in my seat. Mother in hers. The two of them were drinking tea, Lionel's braids swinging as he sipped, stopped, sipped. I wondered which leaves Mother'd plucked from behind the house today without thinking the way I'd come to: letting a bit of the inland seep into us. Troy's and Dad's place settings there as usual, chairs empty. When Mother wasn't in the room I sometimes sat in them.

I fell back onto the old loveseat I used to sleep on, wedged in next to the table, and the three of us stared up at the window to avoid looking at the extra place settings. Mother had made a curtain out of dish towels, stamped with the resort's sunset insignia. I would dry the dishes with them, and then I would hang them back on the window. We had stuff all over the house, small as it was, marked with that sunset. All of it fished out of the dump by Lionel. He was thinking, I could bet, about who he could recirculate some of our dishes to since we didn't need those extra two settings. He'd been the one to give them to us way back when our old ones chipped too much.

Lionel glanced at his watch. He knew I'd gotten off work two hours ago. Couldn't imagine the hollering if he knew where I'd been. Though he wouldn't be near as angry as Mother if she knew. I couldn't help but picture her inland, side by side with me as I fought to get deeper and deeper still.

Mother picked up an empty glass and lifted her arms in an annoyed shrug. I could hear her voice asking, *You didn't get the water, Myrna?* She had always pronounced my name *Myr*-na! Like she was always telling me *no*.

"Bayard said he'd bring the water for you, because he has to drive by the resort in the morning anyway," I said.

She nodded. Mood I was in, wondered why Lionel hadn't thought to get it for me when he was nearby that afternoon—he'd been too busy chatting up tourists.

Mother's fingernails were cut too low. I could see red lines between the nails and nail beds, like the leftover imprint of blood. I counted the hours she'd worked that day. And she got dinner ready while I was inland and now ready to lie about it like someone possessed. And now: two weeks without me home to help with dinner, but not a cent more coming home with me. Lionel turned to me, ready to speak up, and I felt relieved to look away from her hands.

"Myr," he said, excited. "Garrett got a cow caught in his barbed wire fence. He found it this morning. Says it's yours. I figured I'd take you over in the truck. Uncle Q said he could store it all for you in his freezer once we get it broken down."

Every once in a while someone still told me they saw a glimpse of one of our cows, threatening a massive car accident by thundering across the night road like a shadowy nightmare you couldn't quite hold in your mind. I always thought that one day, wandering inland as much as I did, I'd come upon one. But no one had ever caught one, and I'd never come across one myself.

Mother urged us to get going by standing up, letting Lionel help wrap her in the cardigan that'd been hanging on the back of her chair.

Back before she retired, my mother was the junior high math teacher. I sat in the row of desks by the window, second chair from the front of the room. She had long talks with me the summer before I started junior high, about what it would be like to be in my own parent's class. I half listened. I'd known every teacher I'd had my whole life in one familiar way or another: my aunt or cousin or so-and-so's mother or father or grandfather. But she kept telling me it would be different. And I wasn't so hooked in by math, finding my eyes tracking toward the windows as if I couldn't control them. So we devised a way to communicate, both so she could find ways to say *I'm your mother!* in the middle of class and to keep me focusing on her, not the windows. Mother almost always wore that cardigan during class, with the drawstring hanging off the bottom corners that she never tied.

One night we measured the strings and notched them with a red marker. In class she would wrap it in two-inch sections around her wrist to send me messages. Two inches, right: *Pay attention!* Two inches, left: *I love you.* Four inches, right: *Start dinner when you get home.* Four inches, left: *This is a very hard lesson; don't get frustrated.* Six inches, right: *This class is getting on my nerves today.* Six inches, left: *Guess what I'm thinking.* It was hard for me to see the teacher in her anymore, but sometimes, like this, she would take up a sleeve edge of a cardigan and wrap it around her finger or her wrist or the pinkish heel of her hand. I stared, measuring, wondering if she was marking out a message for me or if it was just an absentminded motion. The inches of the fabric an alphabet we'd forgotten or the mindless fiddling of an old lady who was tired?

Garrett's was way down on the south side of the island, so I told Mother not to wait up for me. If it got late, to get to bed.

She watched Lionel and me walk toward the truck, along the edge of what used to be a clearing for the cows. Stretch of land so overgrown I couldn't remember the borders where Dad's machete had switched away the brush.

Once we were on the road, Lionel told me about chatting with B3, as if I didn't know. He brought his hands off the steering wheel, stiffened into a *T*, and I knew he'd set up a tour of the island for the American woman, which made me smirk. We'd see if he took her anywhere near his house at the dump after all. I wanted to ask about that book, but I didn't dare with my uniform already a terrain of suspicion.

When I didn't answer except for a shrug, he turned on the questions about where I'd been after work. I thought about making up a story of hanging around with a friend, but who would I have been with, now that I was steering clear of Hebbie? Instead I just pretended the wind was too loud for me to hear. He started yelling, and he knew I could hear over it and over the crunkling of rocks beneath the truck's wheels. I shrugged.

"Ah, OK then."

He looked at my legs, the little tags of skin yanked up by the haulback. Scruffy-looking beneath the uniform I'd been trying so hard to keep neat. *Scruffy Cruffey*: that's what we used to call this island when we were kids. I almost smiled, thinking of that.

"What, you tumbling around with Lem again?"

Then it was my turn to scream, about how a man only thought anyone could be interested in anything if it had to do with a man. Even a man a year in the past.

"Just kidding you. Gee."

We didn't speak the rest of the way, the sounds of the truck coming up out of the darkness. I looked toward the water as we passed Junkful Beach, breathing in its salty luck.

Lionel and I had a tradition since we were teenagers. Troy used to go with us, too, and whoever else we passed on the road who had the time. We went to this beach, the worst on the island, the one that faced east and got hit by the open Atlantic's winds and covered in the ocean's trash. Flotsam like a disease.

The tradition went way back, since when Dad used to tell us about the boats that would try to come in on that side of the island. They'd all get wrecked on the barrier reef, the crew usually panicking and leaving everything behind as they swam for shore. He was just a kid, but he'd swam out with *his* dad and older brothers to the broken boats and loaded up on the supplies: whatever they could carry while swimming. Which he said was quite a bit, since the currents would sweep you back to shore like a twig. And those currents carried lots of stuff to the beach, too, stuff no one even had to hold onto. *Lucky, lucky, lucky,* he used to call this beach— though the tourists avoided its garbage-strewn and branch-filled sands, its weedy braids of seaweed that got stuck between your toes. But we kids knew it was lucky to go collect the junk. Didn't swim out—none of us strong in the water—but didn't need to, just salvaged what washed up. Delivered what we found to someone who could use it. Made room for more luck.

Tourists throwing pennies away in the sea for luck. Us collecting everything we could for luck before the waves swallowed it all.

Even Mother, who wouldn't say whether she'd been one of the kids who'd swam out to wrecks, thought it was good luck. The day Dad first went off to the capital, she waved for Troy and me to follow, and we started toward Junkful Beach, grabbing a ride for part of the trip and walking through the dust and sun for the rest of it. We didn't just fill our arms but our pockets, and then she found a part of a tarp in the brambles and turned it into a sack that we dragged behind us. Projects in Troy's eyes as he spread our findings on the front steps.

There were two men waiting for us at Garrett's. Their faces were smudges in the darkness, except where Bayard's glasses caught the half-moon, a silver apple wedge. Would've guessed it would be him, even if I couldn't see those glasses. Bayard always seemed to be everywhere on this island, helping out. He'd been teaching history at the elementary school since Mother and some of her generation retired, and when any of his students mentioned some task going on at home, there he'd be at their houses, pitching in. Heard him say more than once that *to teach is the same thing as to plant or to build, to feed or to clothe.* Guessed dealing with a cow same as *to feed* for him.

Lionel and I climbed out of the truck. The corpse was enormous, probably the biggest one I'd seen caught. It was already dead, but no one said whether they found it that way or made it that way. If they'd shot it, I was grateful it happened before we arrived.

Bayard was in the middle of telling his brother that some of his students were collecting shells by East Point and could see the resort from there, along the shore. Didn't used to be you could see the resort from anywhere, but they kept clearing out the flora. Those kids saw the boats arriving from the airstrip key, the whole Columbus burlesque. Which meant they saw me and all the others, caught in it.

"It's a distortion of this island," Bayard was saying. "In history, natural and human, and in name. Disfigurement, really."

"Mm-hmm," Lionel piped in.

"No good come from kids seeing that," Garrett said.

"And they're not reacting to folks gathering for a day's work," Bayard went on. "Even working at something that might be termed demeaning or embarrassing or absurd. Work is work is work. They get that."

"And even the kids already know the bullshit about the name," Lionel said to assents.

"That's right, Lionel," Bayard said, like we were students in his class. Didn't bother me much when he spoke that way. Used to drive my brother crazy. Lionel didn't mind, since he would be the next Bayard: telling everyone what he thought but too helpful for anyone to complain about it.

"They came to talk to me, because they heard a very specific word —*native*—that we've discussed over and over and over again in class, even with the very little kids. The complexity, the connotation. Of course I don't use the words *complexity* or *connotation* with the kids. But that's what we talk about, things as long and sophisticated as those words. *Trading whatever you please* or whatever it is they're saying on those boat puppet shows. I'll tell you what I trade: knowledge. I'll tell you what I give willingly: knowledge, food, whatever my neighbors and family might need from me." More assents from Lionel and Garrett.

I covered the roughest patches of my uniform, all the places where Claudia had run her hands over me. Though it was too dark, really, for anyone to see the damage.

Couldn't even tell Bayard where I'd been, catching in haulback. Bogeyman even to a history teacher.

The men started moving more, getting going on this cow. All tangled together, I couldn't see who was doing what. Bayard's voice carried through the darkness, telling us all the definitions of *native* that didn't make any sense on this island, didn't match up to any of us.

"And I'm using *The Oxford English Dictionary*, a book coming from *England!*"

The others laughed.

As my eyes adjusted to the dark I could see it wasn't one of our cows. Lionel stood between me and it, blocking my view. He knew, too.

Bayard's voice didn't stop as they worked. "Definition one: 'under Feudal and similar systems: a person born in bondage; a person born to servants... and inheriting their status.' This one is complicated, I will give you that. But aren't we quite far ahead, now, of the inheritance? Definition two: 'a person born in a specified place... whether subsequently resident there or not.' But that's not what they mean, is it now? Definition three: 'a person resident in a particular place; a citizen.' Resident? Is that what they call themselves when they're at home?"

No one seemed to notice whether I was helping or not, so I wandered a little up the road. Came back for what must have been definition nine or ten.

"'A member of the indigenous ethnic group of a country or region, as distinguished from foreigners, especially European colonists.' Distinguish, distinguish, distinguish: that's what they're best at in that place."

Thought about piping in to tell them about the lineup outside the office today. The natives stealing pennies. My write-up. But instead I just got back in the truck and waited. Like a wave crashing again and again against the dock, wasn't anywhere for anger to go at the resort. Or on an island. A chorus of insects swarmed in a way I could concentrate on instead of on Bayard's voice.

After they'd got it all done, and we took it over to Uncle Q's, Mother'd been long asleep, all four place settings put away. We'd eat meat the next night and the next and the next after that. The air was cool on my skin as I mended my skirt in the dark.

The first couple of nights I thought maybe I'd get used to the schedule and find a way to go inland after the day's double shift. Climb back to that bundle of sticks fenced in by the diamond. But when I finally got off work, I was definitely too tired even to think about finding my hiding spot for had-been-Dad's machete, my tourist water bottle. Took all my leftover energy to trudge home. And Mother'd been home alone all those hours. She ate dinner without me, and then she sat in her chair alongside the window. Each night when I came in, she was looking up at the sky as if she were reading it.

When I came in the house that third night of garbage duty, her back was to me—but she was standing upright, not sitting in her chair. Blocking my view of her plate so I couldn't see right away if she'd eaten. Three place settings around the table for my viewing. The extra two plates used to sit empty, at least then we weren't wasting food. But more and more lately—especially when I wasn't home to take charge of dinnertime—Mother would put food on those plates, too.

As I stepped farther into the room I saw Miss Patrice was sitting in Mother's seat, head unhinged from her neck as if her jaw had split. Mother was standing over her wearing gardening gloves, peeling back the fleshy shades of Miss Patrice's lips and investigating with her fingers each nook and cranny of her mouth.

For as far back as I could remember, Dad had done dentist work for everyone we knew. Sometimes folks came around since he'd died, hoping Mother could help them with what she knew from watching him. She often could; she knew a lot. Miss Minnie said Mother was so good—better than Dad even—that she could get Wayida Callaghan out of her church. It was true: I'd never seen Minister Callaghan's wife at anyone else's table, but she'd twice sat at ours while Mother tended to her toothaches.

My dad used to laugh about *counting all the holes on the island*: his way of remembering all the teeth he'd pulled. Chuckling and palsying his hand like a craps player *like God playing dice*: his description both of the dislocated teeth out there and these scattered islands. "Maybe they'll all come floating back to fill in the gaps when we die," he'd said.

"Zombie teeth!" Troy had exclaimed. "That's morbid, Dad."

As a girl, my dreams were full of maps of the archipelago and clou-dy X-rays of mouths.

If after her examination Mother held up one finger, Miss Patrice would understand she had a minor problem that could be taken care of at the resort clinic. Two fingers held up, she would understand that Mother was telling her to get to the capital to see a real dentist sometime soon. Three fingers, to get there as soon as possible—emergency airlift might even be in order.

Miss Patrice's dog, Catchum, was under the table, sitting on her feet. Still as furniture but breathing loudly. Not disturbing the cracked pedestal of our table, which was held up on two sides by stacks of old books. Two stacks of identical height, collected over a long, long time by Lionel. When Mother held up one finger, Catchum scampered to the door as if he'd timed the whole thing. Miss Patrice waved for me to follow her outside.

Miss Patrice was one person on the island I didn't tire of talking to. Loved to hear how she ran her business. Contacts in the capital helped her negotiate with the mail boat to deliver her inventory quicker so the store's shelves wouldn't be sitting empty. All sorts of smart stuff that she'd figured out over a long, long time. But I could see from her face tonight she was in pain and couldn't be calling me out the house just to chat about day-to-day business.

"How's your ma been doing?" she asked once we were outside.

I shrugged. Wasn't it all the same, since Troy? Same sad puddles of eyes as he had.

"Same," I said.

Catchum worked his head against my calf, and I rubbed behind his ear. His nose kept moving, moving, moving. I smelled like garbage.

"I don't know, girl. I need root canal—your ma confirmed it—and she told me just see the clinic. They don't do that there, you know as well as I do. And she knows better than either of us. Sure used to."

Headlights swung around the corner, dragging engine noise with them, and both of our hands hovered by Catchum's collar until we saw it was a car we knew. We both raised our hands in a brief wave to Bayard even though we couldn't see him through the blackened windshield.

"You heard all about that mess? With Picker?"

Lionel had told me about the passing of one of the dogs that lived by the landfill, Picker. Thought he was one of the dogs fell to a disease that spread across near half the island a couple months ago. But now bits of the real story had been floating to us.

Most dogs on the island belonged to no one and everyone; some of them chose who would be their person. Catchum chose Miss Patrice's store and Miss Patrice. Eppie, oldest one around with her all-white muzzle, usually hung around by the Straw Market, waiting for Miss Minnie to pack up for the day and drop some scraps for her. Picker had liked to be with kids—Bayard's two and Miss Minnie's grandbaby Angelina. Henry sometimes sat forlornly outside Christine's house, crabby at his own paws, then hopped ecstatically when she came around the bend in the road. Queen Isa tended to pick me, at least when I came around the dump. Always came running to sniff me out like we belonged to each other, paying attention to no one and nothing else. She'd get to be in dog heaven with me showing up there now, on and off for two weeks as part of my overtime, while I'd be in hell having to skip my own sniffing around the inland.

"Yes, ma'am. Wasn't a car hit him, from what I heard."

"Tourists, though," she said.

Miss Patrice started lamenting what we'd all been witnessing for a while. More and more tourists on bikes not minding walkers or drivers in the road. More and more tourists in cars rented from the resort swooping around like the road was a highway without a chance of a pedestrian or a dog. Barriers around the resort thinned out enough that Bayard's students caught a glimpse of the arrivals. Heard stories from Christine about tourists and international management alike coming by Thiflae Bar, calling women half-names like "Little Mama," even "Chocolate Milk." It made me tired, thinking about the resort leaking out all over.

I asked Miss Patrice if folks getting out from the resort's gates more often, though, meant any more business at the store.

She scoffed. "Once in an afternoon star." An expression I hadn't heard since Dad used to say it.

The whole time she was talking to me, with one hand ready to clutch Catchum's collar if need be, her other palm never left her cheek. She bent toward him a touch and, even in the dark, I could see the perfect way she always blackened her eyelashes and traced her lips. Face on, even against her palm that held in the pain.

"Come, Catchum," she said. "All right, you just keep keeping an eye on your ma and tell me about anything."

"Yes, ma'am," I said.

She started to turn away, then hesitated and spoke without looking at me. "And Hebbie was in the store the other day, mentioned her brother'd be visiting. Wasn't sure I should tell your ma."

Nawt-nawt. Click of her tongue, and the dog followed her away.

Andre and Troy: inseparable all their lives. Even went to the capital together. I hadn't seen Andre since the two of them had left two years ago. He hardly came back for anything, not even funerals.

When I went back in the house Mother was looking out the window and up at the sky again. Her fingers lay still in her lap, interlaced and dumb, not revealing what she'd told Miss Patrice and why. No numbers for me. Sitting always made her look thicker around the middle than she was. The way her knee sagged to the side, taking with it the whole left side of her body: just slumped, is how she looked.

She kept staring out the window, and I didn't say a word. I hadn't eaten and, before sitting down at my place, plucked a yam off the plate in front of Dad's chair. Quick as could be, Mother slapped it out of my hand, onto the floor. Not even going to Catchum to eat, no flickering movement of a dog cleaning up under the table, just a piece of yam sitting there on the floor until I threw it out later.

I wanted to grab my mother's head like she'd held Miss Patrice's and open her jaw. Diagnose with my fingers. But we sat in our seats and ate dinner as always. Went to bed with that yam still on the floor.

That night the forces of a storm pitched and screeched. I woke several times, grateful for having my dreams interrupted. Dreams of Andre arriving at our house. Couldn't keep him out. He knew just how to skip the broken step, pull the doorknob to catch the key, rattle it four times, turn it all the way, turn it back until the tiny *click*. Couldn't keep his mouth closed, all dream long, no matter how hard I tried.

The morning was full of the season's early sunlight. The brackish puddles stretching along the road the only sign the storm hadn't all been a dream.

Bench Story No. 9: Angelina Eldon

The dogs in the picture books have rounded ears, short scrunchy noses. Light pink tongues, tails the same color as their bodies. Bellies a
perfect oval of white. Dogs around here have more pointy-ish ears
that flap over once about two-thirds the way up. Like this. They have
tongues with black around the edges. Their noses are small at the end
of long snouts. The colors of their tails almost never match the rest of
them. I can't count all the times I've seen tourists pointing at dogs on
the road and laughing. Or sometimes they look really, really scared,
like they don't even realize these are just dogs.

And sometimes tourists tell me all about how their dogs are different from our dogs. Their dogs have stupid names like Sugar and
Snowball. And then me and the other kids laugh when they walk away
because these dogs are not our dogs! Dogs live on the island, same as
people, one or another of them isn't mine. All kinds of things, Daddy
always says, that tourists don't understand. Do differently, Mom
corrects him. She tells me there are things about their home places
that I wouldn't understand. I believe both my mom and my daddy.

All those tourists who are afraid always use their eyes or sometimes
their hands and sometimes their words to nudge me and my friends
toward the dogs, like giving us a sign to restrain the dogs or keep the
dogs' attention until they can walk far away. Like they're scared, but
they don't think we are. Or maybe they think we have some kind of

magic power over the dogs. Funny, looking up at them, all grown up. I mean, we're not scared, since we know these dogs, but still is strange.

Picker was the dog who always came from the landfill around the curve to our house. He liked sitting in the shade of our tree and wagged his tail something fierce when anyone from my family came out to the yard. He was called Picker because you'd see him picking through piles of garbage all the time to find food. Or to find smells, too. I didn't name him this. Everyone called him Picker. Name suited, though. Not like me: people are always telling me that I don't look like an Angelina. I just laugh at them. See the dirt on my knees? I tell them. See the happy way my eyes squint you up and down? That's not just like a little angel to you? *Then I laugh, and they start laughing, but they don't know whether I'm laughing at them or not.*

I played with Picker at the landfill all the time. My big cousin Lionel works there and usually has a thermos of lemonade he'll share with us, or at least some water, and we can run up to the ridges of the dunes around the landfill and see pretty far over the ocean. We like to play a game called Arrival: when we spot something out at sea, whether it's really a boat or not (and it usually isn't), we make up stories about who it is, where they're coming from all the way across the ocean, where they were really trying to reach, what they'd do when they ended up here by mistake. And what they'll say when they step off their boats onto the beach. My friend Manny is always the funniest at that part:

I claim this island in the name of Queen Jellyfish of the Underworld! You will all bow to her and call her Your Majesty and wear stickers with jellyfish on your cheeks. She sent me out to find the lowest point on the seafloor, but the coral got in my way and hurt my little feet, and I figured she won't know the difference if I land here instead because cameras have not been invented yet! I have come all the way from the shark waters of Antarctica where sharks are stuck in blocks of ice, so you can look at them like on a TV without being scared! I have never seen water like this that's not all filled with ice and sharks inside the ice. What is this feeling on my feet in the water? "Warmth," you say? I know nothing about it, coming from the underworld of icy sharks at the bottom of the world!

His little sister, Gussie, likes to chime in once he gets started, and she is pretty serious for being eight. She says things like: So how can jellyfish live there if it's all ice, huh? And Manny says: They swim around with heat packs strapped to their tops. Duh.

Anyway, we play this game all the time, but I just remember some of the stories we make up that are extra funny, like the shark TV one.

But I want to tell more about Picker. Picker died two months ago today, and no matter what anyone tells you, he did not have that virus that lots of dogs up north of town had. I know because when the vet Dr. Amerie was here, she examined him not once, but twice. Two whole times he had an animal doctor, from the capital, who was real smart, checking him all over. Dr. Amerie examined Picker when she set up her vet clinic in Lionel's truck and came all the way around the whole island to check all the dogs and give them medicine if they needed it. I was playing with Picker and my friend Wanda when she came by, and she stopped and gave Picker a full all-over exam—but he didn't need any medicine at all—and she had thiflae in her bag for Wanda and me. She really knew her way around from coming every year to take care of the dogs: she knew to pick the thiflae on the north side and put it in her bag, because she wouldn't find much more over here by our houses. That was the first time she checked Picker, and then I took him to her again when he seemed to have weak legs one day, having trouble getting up the dunes after us when we ran up there.

I knew where to find her because my cousin Lionel was staying with her in her hotel room, that little tiny inn on the bay that used to be open, too, but isn't there anymore. It wasn't like the resort because you could just walk right up. There wasn't a gate or guards or anything, so you could knock on people's doors and talk to them. At the resort—I know because Mom works there in the kitchen, and my brother works garbage, and my daddy used to, too—they go around telling all the tourists how nice everyone on the island is and how you can just stop them in the road, and they'll tell you anything you want and give you directions and help you. But then how come they have all that guard business keeping everyone out but the tourists? Anyhow, I brought Picker there to Dr. Amerie, a real vet from the capital, and she gave him a look all over and found a little something stuck in his paw, and once she took it out and put some liquid stuff on it in case of infection, he was jumping and running just normal like before. And he was healthy as can be. And didn't even try to lick the stuff off his paw because he was a really smart dog, too. So that was two times he'd gotten checked up by Dr. Amerie.

I was playing out by the landfill, but my friends weren't with me because they'd gone home for dinner. I knew I should be on my way, but there was such a nice breeze and a few dogs had come round, running after me and letting me run after them, and Picker was doing the thing he loves, which is brushing the backs of my knees with the side of his face whenever I ran a little slower, so I didn't want to mess with the spell by going home. Figured just a few more minutes, just a few more minutes. Then the sky started turning all pinkish, and I knew if I didn't get home for dinner both Mom and Daddy would agree on something.

I started walking, and Picker and another dog, Henry, were walking along with me, which was usual for dinnertime. I had my bike with me, but I was walking it because I didn't like to worry about the dogs getting too close to my spinning tires. I'd had my bike since the resort sold off their old rental ones down by the snack bar, and Mom got me this green one and fixed it up for me.

We were coming out where the landfill road curves to the main road, and I heard these tourists, a mom and a dad, I guess, crying at each other, and I saw their rental car with the resort sun painted on the door over on the side of the road with a flat tire. I saw a girl sitting in the backseat with her skinny legs hanging out the open door; she just looked really bored, probably a few years older than me.

I was about to tell them if they kept walking they could ask Mr. Bayard either to fix up the tire or they could call someone, since that was the closest house with a phone. I knew Mr. Bayard was home, too, because I'd been playing with his son, Manny, and Manny had just gone home for dinner. But before I could tell them anything, the dad was running toward me, saying all kinds of panicked things, and he put his hands around the handlebars of my bike and started pulling it toward him. I got scared and didn't even think of telling them about Mr. Bayard then. He was leaning over me, yelling, and I was just trying to hold on to my bike, but that made him pull harder. His hands and arms were so tan they were darker than mine, but in a different way. His voice was getting angrier, saying all these things about being stuck and needing to go for help and needing to get his daughter back to the resort for dinner and what were they going to do if it got dark and if his daughter missed dinner. I saw him see the half-rubbed-out resort symbol stamped on my handlebars, and his eyes said the bike belonged more to him than to me anyway. His mouth said I better just let go of the bike so they could use it or, or, or...

His daughter looked fine to me, not even sweaty, and she had a can of something she was sipping slowly, so not even thirsty. And like I said before, it wasn't even that hot because there was a nice breeze and it was getting closer to being night. I don't even think they'd been there that long because it's not a part of the island where cars won't go by and definitely people on foot going home for dinner. They couldn't have been stuck that long if they hadn't seen anyone else go by—but acting like they were so stranded, about to die of hunger. But I wasn't thinking all of these things in my head like clear thoughts the way I'm saying them now; I was just all a jumble. I don't want to keep hearing the man's angry words in my head so I won't say them to you. What he called me is not what I am.

Finally I couldn't hold on anymore, and I fell back, and the dogs just started barking a lot more than they already were. Not jumping or anything, just barking. And the man was so mad by then he started swinging the bike around and yelling at the dogs. Henry ran into the brush, but Picker didn't. He kept on barking, and the man turned around and started walking back toward the car, and I figured he was going to make his plan then, and I got up and looked where I could run past them to get home without getting too close to those crazy *people, but before I even got to my feet, he stopped and turned around and swung the bike right at Picker, and Picker got knocked toward the side of the road. Just lying there whimpering. I'm not embarrassed telling that I was crying more than that mom, and I ran home, and Daddy drove me back to get Picker, and I kept yelling that I wished it was Dr. Amerie's time to visit, because there was no other animal doctor to take him to and what were we going to do, what were we going to do? When Daddy and I got back there, the man and daughter were still sitting in the car, but the mom and my bike were gone, and the man kept waving his hands at us, like telling my daddy to stay away from him and his daughter, but we were barely even looking at them, we just wanted Picker.*

Eventually we got Picker in Daddy's car, and we took him to the clinic connected to the resort, because we didn't have Dr. Amerie or any better idea. Mom was worried they wouldn't even look at him, but the nurse named Shelby was nice and told us to bring him in because there weren't any people patients waiting. At first I was in the room with him, but then after just a little while Daddy said maybe we should wait in the waiting room so Nurse Shelby could do her job best.

After everything, no matter how sad I was, we had to sign papers. We weren't the owners, but Daddy told me it was OK for us to write we were on the papers, since someone had to be called the owner in the end, he said. I can still see his back at the front counter out of the corner of my eye, even though I was looking down at my feet swinging, swinging off the edge of those plastic chairs you wait in. Daddy's back and the top half of Nurse Shelby and the top half of some other guy working there, wearing the resort sun shirt and a superclean white baseball cap. He was just standing there, not making eye contact with Daddy, while Shelby told him the whole story. Daddy asked about my bike but mainly talked about Picker.

"The parvo file?" Daddy asked. Except he didn't say it like he was really asking but pointing out some kinda stupidity. Mom called parvo the worm that hates dogs. "The parvo *file!" He sounded mad. I decided to just squinch up my eyes.*

"We're keeping track of the dogs on the island, mister. For when the veterinarian care team comes each year," the guy said in a bored way.

"Yes, I know all about that. We know her, we know the vet who comes. But this dog didn't have that. He—I told you what happened. A guest at your resort."

I looked up but just a little bit. Daddy kept talking, but the man put the papers we'd signed in the file he'd first picked out of a drawer and then he just walked right out the room—my daddy still talking and Nurse Shelby standing there looking like someone should do something, but she didn't know what.

So if people say Picker died of that parvo that killed some other dogs, they are lying. Even if they're grown-ups saying it. Mom tells me not to go around calling people liars, but Mom and Daddy both say you can't go around not calling liars liars.

When we play Arrival and stand up there all important with our chins in the air and our voices reaching out into the wind, we call this island all kinds of things and make up all kinds of stories about where we are and who we are and what belongs to us. But none of it is true. When we play Arrival we are just saying things belong to us, but nothing belongs to us. I never got my bike back either.

Chapter Four

O vertime meant they kept me as *Maid* into the night: cleaning various parts of the resort that I was sure could've been fit into someone's schedule during the day. But it became clearer why they needed more staff on garbage duty: they were planning to renovate the pool area with new furniture, a new tiled path to the boat dock, and a refreshed reef mural on the bottom of the pool. "Exploding with color," Claudia's assistant told me.

So once I'd put in all my full hours as a maid, I was to report to the truck area and assess how much extra garbage there was from the renovation and what could or could not fit in the regular dumping schedule. I had to strategize how to get all the extra garbage over to the landfill without exceeding the trucks' gas budget for the week and without interfering with the crew's regular duties. It was a puzzle, Claudia told me, but figure it out.

Thing was, the pool deck already had the nicest furniture on the island. Thing was, the path from the boat dock to the hotel was already straight and smooth; the grounds crew kept it that way no matter what kind of storm tore it up during the night. Thing was, refreshed or peeling, the painted reef on the bottom of a pool was a dumb idea. The dumbest idea. I wasn't one for dipping into a cold ocean, beautiful reefs around here or not, but if the tourists really wanted to see one they could go stand on the rocks near town where the water was clear and see at least a little bit of one, or they could wriggle into their neoprene skins and really see some beautiful coral out at the barrier reef. The resort's boats would take them.

If I'd been getting paid it would've been one thing, but I wasn't. So how to explain to Mother why I was working so much and so long if I wasn't getting paid?

And how to keep to myself the under-skin itchiness from not going up inland after work? Since after overtime it was so, so dark, and I was so, so tired. How to soothe that itchiness just enough to get by?

Puzzle: figure it out.

I convinced Lionel to help me take a few loads over during the week, promising to pay him back for his gas. Didn't know when that would happen, but I guessed he didn't either and was willing to help me out, interest- and guilt-free. He knew helping me at work indirectly lightened his load taking care of Mother. And he was coming by the resort to give that American woman a tour anyhow. We'd see how that went, taking a tourist to your house in the dump. But who was I to say stop doing something that might get you stomped on?

I didn't know how Lionel was really going to work the dump into his tour, but he'd promised that he'd drop me and my garbage at the landfill while he and the American woman went around the island. I was worried he might drop me at the entrance where you can't even see the landfill yet; I'd have to make multiple trips up the road to get all the bags there. It was hard enough moving them way past the truck entrance to where no one would see him parked. Still, better than figuring out another way to get them over there on my own.

Counting the bags made me swear under my breath. I knew Lem, as the most senior custodian, knew how to arrange the bags on the truck so none would topple over the side the minute you got on the crappy road. But we were always a little stony around each other, even at work, so I hadn't checked in with him the way I was supposed to. Lionel and I just started heaving bags into the back of the pickup.

"How'd they expect you'd get over there?" he asked.

"Don't know. Walk, I guess."

He laughed. "They want you to walk back and forth all day or they want you to work?"

"That question's too smart for me to ask them. Just gotta get over there and dump the stuff and fill out all these forms so they can start planning for the renovation."

"*Another one?* Dammit! There's no way I can handle them dumping even more. They just redid all those rooms, what, a year and a half ago? Man."

He kicked at one of the bags, then bent over to make sure it hadn't torn. The black plastic seemed to stretch in the heat. Probably melting, too, longer we stood there.

"Well, you can note something on the forms, but I guarantee you I'm gonna be over there with you dealing with garbage from the renovation anyway."

"Not garbage just because you throw it away," Lionel said.

We finished loading the bags. Lionel jumped up to make sure they were settled enough not to flop out along the road, and I got into the cab. Giving up on the conversation, I thought.

"No overtime?" he asked as he climbed in.

"Asking lots of questions got you fired, right? Just drive and don't comment. I know you're doing me a favor, but I'm already in trouble." I leaned out the window for fresher air.

"Why didn't you have me pick you up earlier if you're in such a rush, Your Highness?"

"Didn't want to get in more trouble."

"You're gonna have to wait another minute. And you're gonna have to scoot over."

"Sit in the middle of this tiny thing?"

"Well, there are three of us. Can't get paid for a tour if I put the tourist in the back with your garbage bags, can I?"

"More her garbage than mine." But I slid over. Leg against Lionel's leg like when it was his dad's truck, and we all piled in as kids. Lionel, me, Troy.

I almost didn't recognize B3 when she rapped on the passenger window. Her eyes were smaller behind thick glasses, and she wore what looked like a man's old undershirt, paint-splattered, over sweatpants cut off at the knee. But she still had that huge bag with the palm tree, held close like a baby bundle.

"This is my cousin Myrna. Myrna, Jasmine Manion."

She sort of waved at me as she got in the truck, and I was glad the quarters of the truck cab didn't lead to shaking hands. Kept my eyes cast down like I was a puppet of the employee manual all of a sudden, even off the premises. Just nodded.

"Working," he said to her, nudging his chin toward me, as if she didn't see my uniform plain as day. "I've got to drop Myrna off along the way."

The truck started up noisily, and Lionel turned left onto the road. Sitting so close I knew he could feel me tense at his turn. I moved a touch closer—made sure he could. Right would have taken us to the landfill more than twice as fast. He raised his eyebrows at me, daring me to question the fact of his tour in front of his tourist.

I felt the antsiness of this garbage duty worse than my usual day's last hour, knowing my machete was waking up for me. I put my water bottle between my feet and held on to the dashboard, above the tape deck lined with road dust, trying not to jostle against her. She smelled like soap—one she'd brought with her, not the resort's floral; I could tell by the smell, and I'd seen the thicker bright white loaf in her tub. Her hair held a whiff of chlorine just from sitting by the pool she told us was "heavenly"; I knew she'd never swam in it. I also knew Lionel and I both smelled like garbage. She didn't seem to notice. Filled with her own scents, I guessed. She and Lionel started talking about how good the food was at the resort, compared with the meals on a cruise she'd taken last year. I knew the couple of gourmet magazines in her room sat on her husband's nightstand. Out of tourists' earshot, Lionel always cursed the mounds of food the resort trucked over and flung in the dump. *The waste,* he'd brood. Plus rats coming round.

On our right the brush was occasionally interrupted by a house painted peach or white or deep green. On our left was the ocean. Black arrows of birds in the distance seemed to race us. Jasmine Manion stared by me—through me—to the ocean view that just kept on and on. Lulled. She clicked her tongue against her cheek, a tiny *glub-glub* that sounded like a clock ticking down. Her eyes scanned through the windshield, but I didn't know what she was waiting for.

"My great-grandmother was from Quickly Island," she said. Lionel and I seemed to nod in unison: sensible reason for wanting a tour. "But we couldn't find a resort or anything there, so we decided to come here."

"American resort? Nah, beaches aren't so nice there. Mangroves all over and whatnot."

She'd probably never seen the tangled nest of a mangrove, but she nodded at what he said. All three of our chins bobbed up and down. My thigh squeaked against the seat as I shifted to unglue it.

"Have you ever been there?" she asked.

"Nah," Lionel said. "Not to Quickly. Called that 'cause it's closest to Florida, you know. I've only been to the ones closer to here."

Lionel's first trip off the island as a kid was when his mother took him to the capital to see his father, who'd moved there for work. They'd decided to make a surprise trip a month earlier than expected for his dad's birthday instead of for Christmas as they'd planned. Lionel's eyes couldn't even blink, he was taking in so much. New faces, new houses. Seemed so busy. They ended up surprising his dad, really surprising his dad, who had taken up with another woman. His dad stayed on in the capital, eventually with a whole new family, and Lionel never went back there. He'd been to Grand Isle, where his ma's people were from and the island closest to ours, but he had to fly to the capital and then take another plane back to it. Told me he'd almost wanted to hold his breath at the airport in the capital during the wait-over to avoid breathing the same air as his dad.

Jasmine Manion was asking Lionel to list all of our islands. I remembered running a dry rag over the laminated map that hung in her room. Flat, easy to clean compared with the woodwork running behind the beds that tourists always eye-checked for dust. Thick pinch through my left hip when I folded to reach back there.

"In this archipelago? Mercy Isle, Grand Isle: those are the two closest. You'll find lots of folks round here been to both, have family. I've been to Grand, not Mercy. Then there's Strip Isle." He ran his finger in a straight line. "It's called that because it's like a strip, longer and thinner than this one. Cruffey, of course, and Wells—that's where the capital is. The farthest away from us is Quickly. And there's Flat Island. My granddad was from Flat, but I've never been. You know," Lionel continued in his almost-captain's voice. "They sometimes call Quickly the—"

"Isle of Mysterious Birds," they both said in unison and laughed. Another place with two names. Did she believe in "Furnace Island"?

She pulled out of her bag a children's book, cracked at the binding and grayed with handling. Not the book Lionel had pushed away at the Jamboree. In her room I'd seen only glossy magazines.

"My great-grandmother used to read this to me every time she visited. *The Isle of Mysterious Birds.* I used to have dreams of all the magical birds that lived there. They could fly across the entire ocean. At least in the book they could." She began describing the kids'-book version of Quickly. A specific purple bird that lived only there. She turned to a page where the watercolored purple went from a deep puddle of color to just wisps as the birds leaped off branches and into the pages' white skies.

The way her finger traveled in the air: as if she saw it moving north-westerly to Quickly and farther and farther northwesterly back to her home. As if she believed the birds could fly all the way there. Lionel always said about any tourist he took around, they saw only some painted version of the island anyway.

Maybe the book meant the frigates, who could fly and fly and fly without sleeping. Or maybe those purple birds *could* fly the entire ocean. How would I know, landlocked on an island as I'd always been?

"My little boy likes to hear this book. My husband will read it to him, too, but when he says, 'That little one jumps into the sky with them,' I just can't keep from laughing till it hurts! *Them!* He tries, he really does, but if he tries to say *dem,* it's even funnier to me." Her voice sounded sad, not laugh-y, though.

"*D-eh-m!*" She lowered her voice to, I guessed, her husband's, but her *dem* had sounded pretty much the same to me: the vowel pooling out into a lake. The *ehhh* of hesitation. Even facing straight ahead, I could see her shake her head clear of whatever was making her voice sad.

"Will you say it?" All smiles. I pretended she was talking only to Lionel, my eyes on the road. She cajoled and cajoled until Lionel gave in.

"*Dhm.*"

Smile as wide as her *e* when she heard him say it. *Just* like how her great-gran—and probably her gran and maybe her own ma— must've said it. Mouth barely opening to let it out, like we swallowed up our word for everyone around us.

"Do you see them here? The purple birds?" she asked, still smiling but with that bluish tone slumbering in her voice.

"You'll see them flying around here sometimes, but they only nest and mate back on Quickly, I think," Lionel said.

Even I looked up at the throbbing screech of a frigate, as if on cue. And like that the truck dribbled to a dead stop, stranding me and my garbage duties. Metallic crack of the driver's-side door.

"Frigates," Lionel said, pointing to the birds swooping out over the water. "Come, let's check if we can see any purple birds along the shore."

They both hopped out. But I kept my knees pressed together to stay in the narrow slice of the bench that was mine.

It wasn't the pool deck or the resort's beach where she was standing now. The sand would be slightly rocky in some places and bumpy with branches in others—and, in still others, smooth and soft like the resort's sand. The air might be fuzzy with insects. Soon enough she'd alternate between waving her hands around her head to scatter the mosquitoes and slapping at the pinprick stings on her ankles to kill the sand fleas. The ocean was still clear, like a turquoise jewel, but thick grasses would sway below the surface like long hair. And we were still just on the calm-beach side.

"Oh, hey, look over there." Lionel pointed at a yellow bird flying in a straighter line than the swooping frigates. "You see that yellow one? The littler guy?"

"I see," she said.

"You can find *that* one on Quickly, too."

They walked far enough down the road that I couldn't hear the next part of Lionel's bird tour. The salty air blew into the car, then died down. Against my cheek and away, like the tide. I calculated in my head, at this rate, what time I'd get off work: too late for the inland. I hadn't moved from the center of the bench seat. Their left-open doors like deadened wings.

The birds swooped and squawked over the water, coming and going as they pleased. I watched one move out farther over the water and take a turn. Returning, I guessed, to its home beyond where I could see or hear.

Lionel's voice grew closer. "We better be moving along," he was saying, "if you want to be back for dinner."

She looked at her watch. "It's five fifteen now?"

"They really told you it's five fifteen? Ha! It's *four* fifteen."

She shook her watch and, when no water or sand fell out, shook it again. Lionel laughed and explained that the resort didn't want tourists coming from farther east to have to adjust so much. They'd invented a time zone.

"Man, resort," he said. "Forget how crazy it was since they fired me."

"*Fired* you?"

He laughed at that, too, and Jasmine Manion looked confused as she climbed back in the truck. She must've noticed the AYS on the pool deck weren't the people working behind the fence—and that Lionel would've been one of the people working behind the fence.

Lionel's voice bloated with the bravado of his fake boat speech as he pulled back onto the road. His audience turned to follow his pointing arm. I was in the way but with nowhere to go. My body a mountain, my nose a ledge between them. I leaned back.

I kept my eyes on the road as we passed the trailhead I'd made, where my machete slept during the day. My trail started behind a lignum vitae tree. I'd done my best to cut at an angle so no one would see the break in the brush as they were driving by. Chosen a tree that was big enough to hide, small enough not to stand out. Stooped strangely enough so I could identify it even in the haze of dusk.

When Jasmine Manion gasped, I felt the clutch of exposure in my chest. "Look at that!"

One of our dogs, which looked like three different breeds tacked together, had jumped out of the brush. I let my breath seep out slowly.

"That's just old Eppie. She's harmless," Lionel said. He returned to his narration: rounding onto the north side of the island; his ma's house; Thiflae Bar. I shot him a slitted eye in case he was thinking about stopping. Made sure he saw me peeking over my shoulder to check all those bags.

I resisted the urge to duck as we passed Hebbie's house. A relief to see no car there, no sign of anyone home. To know there'd be no invitation to sit at the kitchen table next to Hebbie, who could look into a cabinet and see her brother's favorite beer glass waiting for him to come back sometime, any time, to use it. No invitation to sit there while he, visiting, drank from it.

Town seemed quiet as we drove in. An extra-hot day, so no one hanging around outside after work or before dinner. No Straw Market or other planned goings-on today. Lionel slowed for the narrower street, and all we heard was the ticking grumble of the tires over gravel and the singing from Miss Wayida's church: the doors that circled her building all flung open to the air; every pew empty.

"Is this town? The AYS told us there wasn't anything to buy here. Or to do really."

The truck stopped, and the only sound seemed to be that singing, which I'd long ago learned not to hear. Last time I was this close to her church was months and months ago with Lem, looking for a private place. A place we knew no one else would be, between her porch and the church cemetery a little ways back. We'd spent most of a night keeping quiet: Lem using his shirt to muffle the pop of bottle caps; neither of us with shoes on, feet soft against the path.

B3 begged Lionel to stop so she could see the church. He finally ran out of excuses. (The realest excuse—that I needed to get to the dump already—never came up.)

I could see glimpses of Miss Wayida twirling around inside the way her voice was twisting around the air, and then she was on the wraparound porch, dress swaying about her in the breeze, chin regal, motioning for Lionel and the American woman to come on in. The way her posture worked against her folded skin reminded me of Miss Philene all stiff with weathering everything that'd happened to her. Two trees, those two were—but poisonous to each other.

Whatever hymn Miss Wayida was singing made Jasmine Manion smile, but I could hear the notches in the lyrics, the gurgle of her throat stuck against its chain mail of necklaces.

Caught Miss Minnie out the corner of my eye, though it wasn't one of her days in town for the market, and Miss Patrice trailing behind her, though these were store hours. (Hand still to that cheek! Though her smile reached all the way up to her fringed, almond-shaped eyes, betraying no pain.) Feet quick, faces still. Felt like the wind coming up to blow this American woman—and us—in a different direction.

"Hello there, ma'am," Miss Minnie said. I thought she was calling out to Miss Wayida at first, but from the way she gestured to Lionel, I realized she was addressing Jasmine Manion.

"Isn't this a beautiful church building?" Miss Minnie said, inviting the American woman to follow around to see the four sides of its exterior and the views of the ocean from the side yard.

Lionel shrugged at me. Came back to lean on the truck without looking back at Miss Wayida.

What would a tour look like that took people into that church? Drew you in by the singing, led you to the path to the cemetery where Minister Callaghan had heard Miss Philene's Jimmy and his friends' raucousness move up the path and then not come back. A tour that led you to the dark spot where those two had found each other. And where Minister Callaghan had left Jimmy behind. And if you were willing to go deeper into the haulback, you'd find the path I'd been cutting to the piece of a building so blocked up with cacti it wouldn't let me in. To the wall that ran alongside and didn't ever seem to end. To our house where I wrapped Mother's hands in humid towels to deswell from the all-day braiding and braiding of sisal. To the airport, where we said good-bye to those who went to the capital, and to the cemetery on the other side of the island, a cemetery of limestone and brambles, where we welcomed some of them back. A tour that left you at the dock to wait in the sun as long as it took for the mail boat to come in. That took you to the school, into the corner where the roof still wasn't fixed from the last hurricane. To the dump, where you might recognize pieces of your yesterday's self. To Junkful Beach, which lived up to its name, and you wouldn't be able to take any of the luck with you; you'd have to leave it here with us.

Flinched back to myself when Lionel's door slammed, and his thigh re-adhered to mine. He sat so still his hair, which had been so animated by the wind as we drove, now stood like bow-legged pipe cleaners on his shoulders. The women had completed their circling. Hadn't let their tourist even one step off the path they created around her.

"And for your baby." Miss Minnie's hand tucked a piece of double-braided sisal rope in Jasmine Manion's hand, which opened as a flower, then closed tight as a clam. Miss Minnie's voice silkier than I'd ever heard it, ironed out by the upturned bend of her lips usually straight as the horizon. Helping Jasmine Manion back into the truck and directing us to back up onto the road. Like the truck was steered by her waving hand.

A bit of rope Mother might have gotten twenty-five cents for at the Straw Market.

Jasmine Manion's face had gone soft and gracious. Island alchemy burbling, catalyzed by the nice womenfolk sharing their postcard-perfect views and their church singing. Their handmade rope worth nothing and also too much. She'd tell people about them at home.

She took off her sunglasses to smile at Miss Minnie. Her gray eyeliner had melted into fat stripes, sitting beneath her eyes like saucers under cups.

Lionel turned the key: nothing. He looked over at his charge with one finger raised to say, *Just a sec, this happens all the time.* Uniform sticking to my back in the stillness. Miss Minnie and Miss Patrice standing by, faces placid but bodies tense with an undertow. I watched his hand turn the key for the fourth time, then the fifth. Finally the engine grumbled alive. Saw their bodies relax now that we could haul our garbage away from town.

"Well," Lionel said, spinning gravel as he pulled back, "let's keep on. I'm taking you over to Junkful Beach."

The American woman stroked the rope like a rosary. Then she slipped it into the bag at her feet.

As we rounded onto the east side of the island—past my house and everything else—Lionel explained in his tour guide voice the two different sides of the island. She'd soon see that despite the island being under four miles across, the landscapes on the west and east sides looked almost like separate countries. One the paradise she expected, where the resort was. One mangy with brush, shore scalloped with choppy water, and flotsam she wouldn't believe washing ashore from across the Atlantic.

"The east side of the island is much rougher because it faces the open ocean."

"Like two sides of a coin?" she asked.

Not really. But I remained silent. Lionel shook his head.

"Like when one person wants plain pizza, and one person wants their side with everything?"

"Actually, maybe a little," Lionel said, chuckling.

Jasmine Manion smiled and stuck her head out the window, looked up at the birds.

The truck turned away from the ocean onto a wide dirt road that cut through the brush. When we got to the sign that said *Dump This Way*, Lionel slowed. Jasmine Manion perked up and said she wanted to see it, really. A tourist who ran a junk shop back home wasn't the usual tourist after all. Could be the impossible tour I'd imagined stirring up. Next stop: the dump. We came to the newer, bigger sign that said *Landfill* with its hours of operation, and Lionel even turned into the entrance. Saved me some long walks with all those bags.

Lionel told me he'd show her his house and then Junkful. Her black flip-flops became the color of the blond dust almost immediately as they walked away. His voice carried out over the landfill, telling the story of the shaggier, unkempt version of the beaches we'd just driven by.

"When I take you to see Junkful Beach over there, you'll understand why as kids we called this place Scruffy."

I heard two laughs echo against the walls of the dump's basin. Their voices faded away as they made the turn toward Lionel's small, square house. The inside tour wouldn't take long at all; they'd have to step around each other across the branched shape of floor made by the hodgepodge of furniture. Unframed prints tacked up along the wall, some missing corners or stained by a seepy yellow. Only seat the plastic lounge chair that looked like an older version of the ones at the resort pool with some slats missing. Almost every single thing in that one-room house had been picked out from the dumped loads at the landfill. The furniture, the bedding, the lamps, the mirror over the dresser, those prints: it was all close enough to her hotel room to strike her with déjà vu. The whole house, even if it was a one-room place: built out of the resort's garbage. Just rearranged, as if Lionel had shuffled a deck of cards. She wouldn't believe it at first, and he'd laugh a big laugh that folded his cheeks back toward his ears. Wasn't his crazy. Was their crazy.

And Lionel continually rebuilding it with more garbage once the sandy, salty air had worn things through. Must be paint chipping all around the exterior, though, without Troy to touch up for him.

If Jasmine Manion looked around Lionel's room closely enough, she'd find the piece of paper, postcard-sized, taped on a window-pane. A drawing of the sunset, looking west from the rocks by the Straw Market. Just drawn in pencil, but expertly, with more grada-tions of gray than seemed possible. Drawn by Amerie, the vet who came once a year from the capital. (Usually stayed with Lionel right there in that room, too, or him at her rented place. Wondered what Amerie would think of Lionel taking around an American woman.) Could a tourist tell it was drawn in the white square from the back of a magazine, in the space where the address would be if Lionel had been a subscriber to the magazine instead of the Land-fill Manager who fished magazines out of the garbage? The space that was blank because it hadn't been sent from somewhere to him, but just came in a pack on the mail boat with everything else, already outdated when it sat on the rack at Miss Patrice's store?.

Wondered if Jasmine Manion in her shop looked like Lionel scaling the plateaued rims of the landfill. Climbing over and sort-ing through and salvaging from her shop's junk-pile landscape. Lionel recirculated the resort's barely used items; the recipients, us, making things our own through needing. Even his own home imprinted with the resort's handling. I pictured her, late at night, scrubbing away the smudgy fingerprints of previous owners. Days later, her customers' curated mantels.

I headed toward a three-walled shed by the entrance to the landfill: Lionel's office of sorts. Queen Isa came to greet me with her barking, all nosing and wagging. Lionel had named her that for prancing around the landfill as if she owned the place. I drummed gently on her sides, and she turned and walked back with me where she'd come from. Lionel was the only one who could fill out my forms properly, but Claudia wanted only my amateur assessment of the landfill's capacity—and there was only one answer to give her. Island alchemy solved all puzzles with *yes*.

Lionel hadn't processed that morning's local dump yet, and it was small enough that I could settle my bags in that pile, keep them out of the way of tomorrow's resort dump. A slit in one of the local bags released the scent of fritters someone had for dinner last night. And then, like a reverse exile from the capital, another scent that my memory had on tap. Hadn't actually *smelled* this one, though, since Troy left the island that day after Dad's funeral, and Mother said he had really gone back now that his big bottle of cologne was off the counter. The cologne he'd worn since about fourteen. Always smelled liquory to me—like adulthood, like freedom, like traveling to the horizon.

The cologne Andre wore, too. The story of the two of them wafting up from yesterday's spilled trash.

When I didn't find anyone at Lionel's, I went around the bend and crossed the street to Junkful Beach. Lionel and Jasmine Manion stood just a bit down from the path I'd come through, facing south. His shirt filled with wind behind him, her shoulders skewed by that bag. Bare feet so flat in the sand her knees popped out back above her calves. She was one of the only outsiders to see this mucky side of the island. Even her own family and her own nanny—the woman who worked for her—were just hanging around the resort on an island beautifully landscaped, low on bugs, relaxing. Sitting by the pool thinking this island had one time zone and one name.

I sat down to wait on the disk of a rock breathing out of the sand. Above me a female frigate hung in the air with her shrug-shaped wings. I watched for a male throbbing his red throat toward her, but I didn't see one. Just her, longer across than I was tall. Tried not to let the angle of the sun make me anxious to get back. No turning off Lionel when he had an audience. A woman new to the island who was also a paying tourist: his best kind.

The brochures called the resort the most beautiful spot on the island. True, the scrubby east-side sand was dark, strewn with sea-weed, a little fishy smelling. Flotsam all around us, some of it iden-tifiable and some of it not. But looking for luck in a big old mess: that was a much better place for me. Stinking of garbage duty and overtime as I was, threads frazzled up and down. My uniform the topography of this beach. I opened my nose to the scents strong enough to block out cologne.

The wind brought their voices to me. Lionel's tour continuing, even here amid the world's refuse.

"Around here people believe it's good luck to go collect it. And see out there on that little peninsula sticking out from the beach? Down there. See it?"

The spot Lionel pointed to seemed very far away but also like we could all just walk to it if we wanted. The ocean could always trick you with how close we seemed, how far we were.

"Yeah. What's out there?" she asked.

"For hundreds of years they thought that was Columbus's land-ing spot. Out *there*. That's the *east* side of the island, on the Atlan-tic."

"But they were coming from the east, so..."

"Yes, but there's no way a boat could land out there, especially those big ships," he said. "They'd wreck on the reefs before they got close to shore. They had to land on the west side. Harbor's still over there. Always has been, always will be."

He pointed again: the water breaking then sealing itself in a white seam over the reef we couldn't see. We watched it split and heal, split and heal.

"What's that?" She pointed farther down the beach.

I let my eyes go unfocused, trying to see it through the eyes of someone who didn't know what she was looking at: a lightning-struck tree or maybe pipes, painted black and roped up in what almost looked like the charred remnants of a flag on a pole. Then refocused to see it for what it was, as Lionel began to tell her about Troy's sculpture.

"There used to be this giant sculpture of a white cross right there, easily two times as tall as me." Lionel jumped up, hand raised to emphasize how high. "Someone took it down in the middle of the night. No one knows who. Or if anyone knows they don't say. It was a monument to where he supposedly landed. But once it was gone, my cousin gathered some stuff that had washed up on the beach and built that in its place—like a distorted one."

"A distorted cross?"

"A distorted monument. My cousin, man, he was a great artist, and it was amazing how he got all that junk to stay together in that sculpture you see there. No matter how rough the weather gets over here: stays just how he wanted it." Lionel picked up a broken branch the size of his arm and flung it into a wave, which heaved it back again and again.

I closed my eyes. Didn't want Lionel talking to tourists about my brother, but there was nothing I could say. Jasmine Manion was telling him she was an artist, too, but I already knew that; I'd lifted her bag of paintbrushes up, careful not to spill them, each time I'd wiped off her dresser.

I jiggled my water bottle to see how much I had left. The sun felt as though it had chosen to sit specifically on my shoulders and upper back. Dripped down like melted wax from a candle. Tried to think of the sweat through my uniform as letting the resort ooze out of my pores, along with the anxiousness of needing to get back. Nothing I could do about that either—couldn't get back from here on foot without a couple hours to spare.

I scooted off the tippy rock and let the sand mold around my body; it was packed hard beneath me so that I fit in it and was held atop it at the same time. The rhythm of the waves had unexpected turns that pulled my mind away. I kept my eyes shut. Felt a sinking: how I'd always thought of the sadness that would envelop my brother for weeks at a time, in between when he made something new and found his baggy smile again.

Maybe they were still talking, but all I heard was faint barking in the distance, an occasional squawk, and the sounds of the water. The crash of the waves was amplified by the absence of the pool sounds at the resort: the pocking beat from the speakers, the scraping *shoo-shoo* of the brooms.

My fingers pushed crude horizontal brackets of birds in flight into the sand around me. But when I looked down, the lines looked like boats, arriving and arriving and arriving at my feet. With my palm I wiped them back into the sand.

Same sand I sat on years ago when Troy, Hebbie, Andre, and I tended to be a foursome on lazy evenings. Charades on the beach —only props allowed were stuff we found washed up. Too much beer fizzing in my head, leaking mischief through my veins, I found a piece of a filthy gray tarp, caped it around myself, and bugged my eyes to be the ghost of Jimmy Cruffey; turned around, and before I even started, all three looked at me blankly. No idea what I was up to. I'd let the tarp drop and had told Troy to take his turn instead.

Finger found the sand again. Made the four slashes of a diamond.

I watched Jasmine Manion pick up objects that had washed into the tall grasses just back from the shore. Wondered if she was here on a quest for ghosts, digging for what her great-gran had never told her. But she didn't seem to be looking for anything—just looking because she wanted to and could.

She held up a knitted mitten. Yellow soaked in mud. Half unraveled by the wrist, missing a thumb. "It'd confuse people if I sold this in my shop, right? A mitten found on a tropical beach?" She laughed.

A plastic bottle—shampoo, looked like to me. She examined the print, bringing the thin bottle close to her thick glasses. "Portuguese!" she said to Lionel.

"Hey, Myrna."

I flinched at the hand on my back. Turned around to see just Manny, carrying his shoes and wiggling his toes in the sand. Had Bayard told his kid about what the students saw when the boat came in? Me in my sheet? Drew my legs into my chest, as if he couldn't tell what I had on. The uniform that was always telling something to someone.

"Oh, hey, Manny."

Lionel and Jasmine Manion turned around at our voices, finally seeing that I was there.

Manny ran toward Lionel, kicking up sand as he went. I knew he was a kid who couldn't sit still in class. Ran around in the afternoon, at the landfill or down here on the beach. The way Hebbie and I used to. Now he stopped and stared; could've been the first black American woman he saw come to this island. Might've been the first tourist on this oval to talk to him, too. Certainly the first one turning up on Junkful.

Jasmine Manion reached out her hand to him. "I'm staying at the resort. From America."

Manny laughed outright, thinking the same thing Lionel and I were: Did she think someone'd mistake her for one of us? On this island where we knew the number of steps between our houses? Lionel's forehead moved back, like he was both surprised and not surprised at all. I froze. We both waited for her response to Manny laughing at her.

She just shrugged. Her shoulder blades sharp enough to puncture the tension. I stood up and brushed sand from my behind. We left Manny standing where the sand had been rubbed smooth by the tide; he waited for the water to creep closer and closer to his feet and watched his toes try to hold on to the tiny islands of sand when it pulled back out. Way Bayard was so upset about kids seeing the arrival on the beach, couldn't imagine he'd be happy to hear from his kid we'd brought one of the tourists to this side of the island. Not the chattiest kid, though—maybe Manny wouldn't mention who he'd seen at Junkful. Doubted Miss Minnie or Miss Patrice would chat about our visit to town. And Miss Wayida's voice sloshed only around her empty church, coming back to echo in her own ears.

The three of us back in the cab, sides of our thighs stuck together with island glue. Couldn't balance myself without touching her if I tried. Talking a mile a minute about what she'd picked up on the beach, her shop back in Wisconsin, where she got her own junk to sell. She'd made an easel out of some varnished fruit crates that turned up in the shop—*PPLES* still visible down its spine—and said she'd pluck from donation piles some kitschy sculptures and random objects to paint as still lifes. Then she'd display both the objects and their paintings in the window. She sold more items when they were displayed like that.

"How long have you been painting?" Lionel asked.

"Oh, a long time. My grandmother used to paint with me when she watched me. Always beach landscapes. Now I wonder if they were Caribbean island landscapes—of Quickly—that she'd learned from *her* mother. Anyway, most of my customers are women in the neighborhood, and a bunch of them started taking group cruises to the Caribbean as a reprieve from the long Wisconsin winters. I started keeping an eye out for anything Caribbean related—I had a few things anyhow, because of my great-grandmother—and displayed it in what I called the Carib-bean-of-the-Mind Nook."

"Caribbean of the mind!" Lionel leaned into the steering wheel, a mix of honking and tittering. I tucked my lips inside my mouth to keep from joining him. *Swallowing laughter is just choking,* Dad used to say.

The way she described it, the nook sounded like a simple plywood bench she'd built under a window and topped with pillows, a bookcase with relevant books, and some shelves with this and that. Imagined her putting the junk from the beach on those shelves, neighbors coming in, like the resort's Jamboree tourists beguiled by broken glass labeled *sea*. All of them sighing over pictures of turquoise water, glossy brochures about places like Furnace Island, where it was already an hour later than right here.

"In harder times, which are almost always in really grim, sunless winters, that nook really keeps things going for my shop. When people are planning cruises and especially when they aren't. Helped fund this whole vacation! Though don't tell my husband I told you that. He—we..." She trailed off.

The truck dusted the air around us; we were farther from shore now, using the landfill access road to cut back to the western side of the island instead of circling the southern tip. Jasmine Manion studied out the window; I thought maybe she'd complain about not getting the full-oval tour, but instead she seemed intent on the tangly hill rising up alongside us. Inland.

The top of her bag gaped like a screaming mouth, and there it was: the book that had shuttered Lionel's open face at the Jamboree. It was broad but not all that thick. Almost the size of a record but heavy. Plain gray cover with a black title at the top and nothing else.

The Cruffey Plantation Journal: 1833.

If management could check on me in this truck, in my fired cousin's truck but "at work," they'd find me staring straight ahead. Not reaching for the book or even looking at it directly. Not talking to the guest. Not matching up the snags on my skin and clothing with all the sharp points of the word *slavery*.

The truck never lost speed, Lionel's leg never lifted from against mine to hit the brake. I could even see out the corner of my eye that he faced the road, nowhere else. But a line of sun coming through the window striped across his ear, then his cheek: head moving just that tiny bit to shift the light. Eyes looking. Still we moved toward the resort on the road we'd traveled all our lives.

"This is from the nook. The same one I showed you at the Jamboree, Lionel. I don't remember who donated it, where it came from. But it's the only thing that's come through the shop from *this* island, see?"

I let my head turn a second-hand's tick. She opened it, flipping pages that looked like copies of typewritten pages, their serifs prominent and cluttered. Each page number bounded by hyphens. She stopped at its center, the left-hand cover and pages sitting on my right leg, the other half of the book on her left leg.

A hand-drawn map of the entire estate spilled across the centerfold. Her hand that'd been gesturing out the window toward inland now came back to the plantation marked out in our laps. Her pointer finger slid over the dipped horizon of the book's binding. Bluish, veiny ink.

"Where do you think we are now? In relation to this plantation?" Her voice bluish again, too. Deeper blue.

While most of the points on the map were marked by blue dots—*storehouse, kitchen, well, lockup, office, slaves' quarters, cotton gin house*—the main house was as big as the pad of her thumb and drawn so we could see what it looked like: two stories, pointy roof. It was perched close to the hill that sloped down to the shore; the key—a dot in the ocean—and the harbor on the west side of the island where boats arrived even now, as Lionel had just explained. In the upper right-hand corner was an insert of another map, a small drawing labeled *Archipelago*. The estate just a speck in the scattering of islands that looked like they'd crumbled off Florida. She connected the dots from one simple shape to another, all those islands flattened against the roundness of her finger. I felt grim, sleepy. The book's weight on my knee like a fallen boulder. The curves of the blue lines on the map blurred until I might have been looking at water.

Her question about the plantation—as if anyone on this island had ever seen this map before, knew where the hell we were in relation to its points.

Her next question: "What's wrong?"

She leaned into me more to hear Lionel's voice, which had broken itself into a slow, low gravel: "Just never saw a map like that before, that's all."

The book pulled off my knee in a *thwuck*, closed against itself. *The Cruffey Plantation Journal.*

My voice: "That's his last name."

Cruffey. Cruffey and Wells: only two islands still named after old-time plantation owners. A name that couldn't be scrubbed off, left to decompose on the inland the way other words had been.

Jasmine Manion, B3, put the book back in her bag and pushed it down under everything else she was carrying. Book of mysterious birds alighting on top of it.

Finally Lionel said we'd better be hurrying back to the resort, and I felt the truck pick up speed.

A bang against the driver's side, and we came to a dusty halt, all three of us boomeranging back against the bench.

"What the—?" Lionel looked pissed but stopped talking when he saw the tourist in the road tipped off his bike with one foot on the ground. Dusty shirt and shorts, gray hair like half a splayed mop, arms skinnier than the rest of him. As far as I could tell, he'd banged on the truck with his hand, since we clearly hadn't hit him. Started explaining to Lionel how he'd tried to ride the whole oval but realized it was going to get dark and he was nowhere near getting around. Took the cut-through but wasn't sure where he was. Voice was full of bile, but I couldn't tell who he was angry at. If he turned down the landfill road, the only one that cut across, the only second road there was, he hadn't even been halfway around. I didn't see a water bottle anywhere on him. Even his eyes looked dry, grayish and flat. A gutter of skin ran down the center of his neck. Lionel picked up the water bottle from the cab floor—my water bottle—and handed it out his window.

"All right, we'll take you back. Headed there anyway."

Compared with the cyclist's English, which sounded droopy as an old hammock, Lionel's words felt taut as a clothesline.

I didn't think the man heard the second half of what Lionel said. He was already around the passenger side, lifting his bike over into the truck bed and grunting. I could see that his face was younger, despite his gray hair and eyes. I didn't recognize him— must be staying in the D wing, which I hadn't been assigned to lately, and out biking around instead of sitting by the pool. His T-shirt said *Sanibel Island* with a sun not unlike the resort's logo, but something—what?—signaled a rising sun, instead of a setting one.

Dad told me that when the worst dark thing was cultivating itself in someone's throat, when the sickliest gray was marbling someone's tooth, his dentist hands couldn't stop feeling out the nothing-est cold sores. And now I was occupying my mind with little details, the tiniest sand crabs skittering along the edge of the grass, instead of maps I couldn't touch even when someone put them in my lap.

Once the bike was in, the cyclist came around to the door. I knew what was coming next. Couldn't collect on tours if Lionel put tourists in the back of a pickup that'd been hauling garbage all day. Took me a second to collect my voice to say a second thing to Jasmine Manion.

"Excuse me."

She got out of the cab, pulling her bag in front of her. Away from me. I climbed into the truck bed and tried to resettle the bike so it wouldn't fall on me. Leaned over the side, ready for some fresh air in my face instead of the leftover garbage scent all around, cologne and old book scents in my nose. The D-wing man and Jasmine Manion were still standing next to the passenger-side door, open like a waiting arm. In the late-afternoon sun, the paint splatters on her clothing took on a sheen. Then he got in the front seat and slammed the door closed.

Jasmine Manion just stood in the road, her face inches away from his through the open window. But he faced forward.

After a long pause of just staring and staring, she said, "You and your wife had dinner at my table last night,. Anthony." She sounded pissed, even with her lazy midwestern vowels. Pissed about being taken to be "at work." "At work" with me.

Lionel was leaning over, but I couldn't hear what he was saying. Whatever he said, eventually the man got into the middle of the cab, and Jasmine Manion climbed back into her seat by the window. Grimy window between me and that book felt as solid as the brush between us and the inland right now. I closed my eyes to the air off the ocean pushing against my face.

We dropped the cyclist at the bike rental shack, where he jumped out and got his bike without saying anything to any of us. Lionel offered to drop Jasmine Manion off a bit closer to the gate. (Guessed that cyclist could be a good alibi if anyone saw us, as though we'd just happened to pick up two tourists who nearly missed dinner. Helped out those two and the resort's meal schedule, too.) But she said she'd just go from there. Handed Lionel some bills rolled to the size of a cigarette. Walked away without saying much.

Lionel pulled around closer to the truck entrance to let me off, and we could see her meeting up with her family on the path. Her little boy pounced away from the nanny and flung himself against his mother's legs. I couldn't tell if her hands were caressing him or straightening him up—worried, now or still, that he could be lumped in with us, too. Keeping him closer either way.

I climbed down and walked over by Lionel's window. Evening now, the color of the sky changed in front of us. Counting up what I still needed to do for overtime garbage duty. Hovering there, even though it was as likely Lionel'd unfold into a mysterious bird as talk to me about that book.

B3's husband had joined her, and I tried to imagine them sharing either a joke or a murky secret. Wondered whether she'd tell him about the cyclist. And if she did, would she do it in front of the kid? In front of the nanny? Or just in bed at night, hedged in by stacks of magazines and paintbrushes on their nightstands, awaiting my morning dusting. Had the book been in that pile and I just never saw it? Or was it tucked away, even from her husband?

"Well, let me go change first, and then we can go to dinner," she was saying.

"Change?" he whined. "You're *fine*. It's a million degrees outside."

"Al."

She seemed agitated, looping the shredded cutoff end of her shorts around her finger. My own finger went to a looped snag on my skirt.

"You and Nathan go ahead. I'll be quick."

Her husband stood waiting, for a capitulation or for more of an explanation.

"Later," she said.

She walked away alone, alone with the book, and her husband looked at the boy, nervously taking the little hand to keep him from following his mother. The nanny left, too, passing through the gate without looking back and without the guard glancing at, let alone in, her purse.

And then we were us, and the truck, just like last night, just like always. Not talking about the plantation book. Not talking about the plantation.

Sun leaking out of the sky, garbage paperwork to file: my machete would have to sleep another night. Glimpse of a map or not.

"I'll wait here till you're through. We both need a drink." Turning that roll of cash in his palm.

There was no way I could argue with him. I'd have to explain where else I'd had to go after work.

When we got to Thiflae, there was the nanny. Taken me so long to finish up she'd beaten us on foot. I was glad we hadn't seen her on the road. Didn't feel like having to scoot and squeeze for another American woman Lionel'd picked up. Who'd told her about this place? Maybe she was just a wanderer.

Considered for a second whether Jasmine Manion could have sent her out to explore for the things her great-gran had told her—

or for the things her great-gran had never molded into words. And maybe this nanny, stumbly with beer five feet away from me, had been sent on a nocturnal quest. Knew something about the book.

But she didn't seem to be on any sort of mission, her limbs looser and head swiveling on her neck; at the resort, I'd seen her making only quick, defensive movements: reacting to a three-year-old. When her purse tumbled off the stool next to her, a toy car clattered against the tile. In her face a mixture of guilt, affection, and relief—parts of her lighter, glad finally to be away from the Manions for the first time since arriving and parts soaked through with missing. Counting up the owing. The same way my face must be when I went inland instead of going home to Mother, and she'd come into my mind like a mosquito in my ear: so close before I even heard it. Tethered no matter where I wandered. The nanny took another mouthful of beer.

She was telling Nelson about Wisconsin winters. He and some others were leaning in for every word. If a black American tourist was a novelty, her white nanny was like a comet we might never see again in our lifetimes. Others had deserted to the porch as soon as a tourist walked in, I was sure. Ones left wanted to hear.

My brain itched to huddle around something small and fluffy as a thiflae bud. Just like Dad and the cold sores. Lionel beat me to it. Shouted a tourist question in her direction.

"How cold was it the day you left to come here?"

"Negative sixteen with wind chill!" She looked pleased by the shocked looks she got, the impressed whistles. Smiled so wide the tip of her nose twitched up. Only Mr. Ken lost interest, rolled his tongue across the inside of his cheek. He had friends in North Dakota and plenty of his own stories to tell about visiting them in December weather. Only time of year he closed the bar. He never spent Christmas on the island since he and Miss Philene split up, which was pretty much as far back as I could remember.

"I mean, it might have got up to plus ten or so later in the day, but it was way below zero when we left for the airport."

Encouraged, she described the whole neighborhood. The Manions picking her up on one of those mornings after New Year's, she explained, when vacation kept the racket of school buses off the streets, and the only sounds owed to garbage day with its dark green dumpsters trundling down the driveways. The crusty snow crunched underfoot, and the discarded Christmas trees lolled on the curbs like drunks.

Garbage day? Lionel mouthed to me.

The strange mix of weather she'd described them having this winter—air so cold it froze the inside of your nose one day, the next day sunny and melty—had left small islands of snow holding on the soggy lawns, littered with shriveled locust tree pods. She traced the shape of a pod in the air: parenthesis shaped, as if everything we were talking about was beside the point.

She leaned her head forward to show those nearby the gritty white patch of frostbite on her forehead. As I'd expected, the taut skin between her braids was the flashy pink of cinnamon candy.

"This was the part of me not covered by my scarf or hat just when I walked between the car and the airport!"

Lionel pointed out that she was both frostbitten and sunburned at the same time. The few interested laughed and huddled in to look at her bitten forehead and her scorched scalp. Her gums revealed the whole time they looked. Lionel was grinning, too, at me. Like it made him happy I was being social for the first time in a long time. Like it made him happy we were away from that book. Or that the focus was on the topographical story of her skin, not mine. The marked skin that had an explanation he could stand. Or maybe he was just happy he'd made extra money today.

I tried to give him a smile. But like I didn't know how to swim around the talk of a crowd anymore. When was the last time I was on Junkful, at Thiflae? And today I went to both. (Bags and bags keeping me from where I usually was after work, machete in hand.)

Turned back to the bar to find Mr. Ken noticing the scrabbly mess of my uniform. A new sweating bottle next to the one the light was already shining through. Soon enough the new one was full of light, too.

Leave it to Lionel to have the American at our table after just his second drink. She shook my hand longer than I expected—kinda felt like my arm being yanked back into the resort when the rest of me had already passed through the gate. I knew she used whitening toothpaste and wore two-piece bathing suits and contacts; that she had pills for air sickness; that she'd packed three pairs of identical black flip-flops, all worn thin under the big toe and that she kicked off anywhere in the room. Even with my uniform, she thought she was just meeting me. But that was for the best anyhow.

I sat there not talking as Katelynn chattered about how funny Captain Columbus was, and Lionel chimed in with good-natured, semi-neutral jabs about the resort. Every time Lionel said my name I kicked him under the table until my leg hung, the nudges I gave him weary instead of cautionary. When the nanny finally slipped *Murna* into something she was saying, I ordered another drink without even looking at him. Excused myself with the beer in one hand and a glass of water in the other and went to stand outside the front door for some fresh air. Freddy, the blondest dog on the island, nosed into the jellyfish-soft place behind my knee. I bent down and put the glass on the ground, letting her stick her tongue down into the water. Gave her a good scratch, and she skittered away from my hand. Whimpered. Even in the pitiful light from the entryway I could see something by her shoulder: a tick. Side ripply with ribs. Been too long since Dr. Amerie had come. For Lionel, too, I guessed, from the looks through the hanging door: his stool scooted up next to the nanny's.

A few more gulps, and I'd be too sleepy to walk home; I'd have to go back in to get Lionel to give me a ride. They slid down my throat, led me back to the table.

"I mean it was so *sad*," the nanny was saying when I got close to the table. "Mrs. Manion practically begging her family to come over for Christmas. And Mr. Manion stomping around the house going on about how *his* family wasn't the biggest fan of their marriage either—big shocker—but *they* came for Thanksgiving. And how he'd stayed in that house long after the divorce from his first wife, a house big enough for hosting a whole bunch of people on holidays, because he thought Mrs. Manion would want to live somewhere like that, like Tehawkee Bay, when her family had only lived in Milwaukee, blah, blah, blah. And it is, like, a huge, really nice house. Nathan has this massive playroom in the basement. And kind of another one, too, upstairs in the room Mrs. Manion uses for painting. But anyway, that was the only time I saw them really fight in front of me. Sometimes they seem to make each other laugh about random things that I don't really get."

"So no one like her family lived in this bay, huh?" Lionel was drunk. *Like her family*: not treading too carefully around tourists. But the nanny was drunk, too. (How many drinks would she need before I could ask her about the book? How many for me to do it, how many for her to forget I'd done it so I wouldn't get in trouble? How many would *I* need—to forget not just the trouble but all the folks in earshot hearing me ask? Far too many.)

"Nah, she's pretty much the only one. First time my mom went to buy stuff at her shop, she just thought she worked there, had no idea she was *Mrs.* Alvin Manion—or that's what my mom called her. My mom goes to that shop all the time now. We live, like, two streets over."

She drummed on the table with both hands, and Lionel's head seemed to bop along to the rhythm. I tried to catch his eye. I was ready to go. But he was rapt as Katelynn talked up her spring semester courses, her roommate troubles.

"You look like my ex-boyfriend," she slurred, one eyelid drooping. (Maybe *that* was why Jasmine Manion trusted this girl with her kid: that ex-boyfriend.) Then she flicked Lionel's braid, and it bounced against his face. When he laughed, I knew he was too drunk to drive me home.

Didn't even try to hide my rolling eyes. I'd lost count of the women Lionel was interested in first minute they stepped on this island from the capital or from the States or from the moon. Tomorrow I'd probably hear about his truck being parked off the road someplace between Thiflae and the resort gate. Nighttime tour, no fee. I told him I was leaving to walk home. They barely looked up from their conversation. Both halfway put up their hands: one full wave good-bye between the two of them.

Freddy was nowhere to be seen when I exited and started down the road. Walk seemed longer when I wasn't coming from or going to the inland. And after a day of double duty. A day of the word *plantation* across my lap.

Could hear the water as I walked but couldn't see it. Reminded me of the way Hebbie used to hum everywhere she went, so you'd hear her coming round the bend before you saw her. Been just me and the inland so long now—if I found myself walking the road with Hebbie like we'd always done, I'd mistake her for my shadow. Now I expected my shadow to be a rectangle with soft edges, like all of me was a thought of that book. The book my shadow— even touching me, I couldn't touch it.

Bench Story No. 6: Mr. Quentin "Q" Cruffey

On my right I have the sack I always wear low across my back, bang-ing against my backside when I walk down the road, which makes a lot of folks laugh, given what they tend to say about me and my Wil-son. But let them. This sack has nothing you would want. Nothing you could relate to money. Nothing you could relate to meaning if you do not dwell within my mind. Inside the sack is a violin bow, big enough only for a child, and it pokes through the sack, makes me look, from afar, as though I have a tail. More laughing. Let them. I carry this with me all of my days. Wherever my destination, whatever my errand.

Ever look closely and extensively at a bow? It will look from afar as though the strings were a solid strip of hide or a similar material, but then close up you will see the most delicate of hairs strung tight and close, end to end, one right next to the other. Both silky and tough to the touch at once.

My bow is warped. My bow is rubbed round in places the wood should still have corners. The wood of my bow is smooth as sea glass and the color of the foam on the waves instead of the delicious color of wine or coffee or Miss Hebbie's mud-and-auburn hair. As most bows of fine craftsmanship would be.

I am not a musician. This is not a confession of a secret musical talent, a knowing way with a violin at night inside my house when no one would hear or suspect. Neither was Wilson a musician before he went back to Miami and passed from this world. Neither is this a relic of my parents or any ancestor in my past whose life centered on violin playing. I will explain how this bow came to travel with me.

Before Wilson returned to Miami to receive medical care he could not receive here, he requested we walk the entire island, not on the main road. He did not want to drive in a circle, as surely we had done before. But rather he wanted us to walk along the coastline from our home until we found our home once again. Many times over the years when we would walk along the southern beaches near our home together, when he was in health, we would wonder at how long such a venture would take; once we walked about a quarter of the way, clockwise, for many hours, deciding to turn back for dinner around where the resort now has made its home. He requested that in this instance we walk counterclockwise because, as he said, that is how we have always lived together on this island and in this world.

I told him, as he already knew, that he was not well and perhaps this would be much too hard on him. Indeed, this would be quite an endeavor for anyone, and I do not know if it has been done many times by even the young and strong. But no, he insisted, we must try it before he leaves in case he does not come back. He must be sure our feet had felt the sand of our home, together, in an unbroken oval.

We planned quite a bit. I would fill this sack with essentials, of course, and we planned to borrow the baby stroller Miss Minnie had that went well over sand, so we could push supplies we might need with minimal effort. I considered a wheelchair so that I could push Wilson or perhaps he could manage a moped that at times they rent at the resort—or perhaps we both could, as I was not such a young man myself—but Wilson insisted on walking. Our feet in the sand, he said. Marking out the oval of this island side by side, he said.

The problem was, as I saw it, if by some miraculous confluence of, well, miracles we were to be able to walk together the full oval of the island: at some point we would arrive at the fences where the resort had made the beach private. How would Wilson react to our needing to circumnavigate these fences, arriving on the road he did not plan to walk on, for quite a spell, as the resort is somewhat vast, before we could descend to the coastline again and continue our journey? When I brought this matter to his attention, he reminded me that we could buy day passes and be allowed into the resort for 350 dollars total. And then we could walk along "their" beach. (He made ugly, crooked quotation marks with his fingers when he said this.)

He asked his brother for the money, but his brother said he should save the money for what Wilson needed more urgently. "Care," he named it. I thought perhaps we could manage one pass, and he could walk the beach while I walked the road and waited for him on the other side of the resort. But when I brought the orange card that was the pass home, Wilson refused it and sent me back the next day for a refund. He said the money was too great without his brother's help. And the point was walking side by side. We would walk around the fences and on that stretch of road together. I could see disappointment in the way his skin relaxed around his eyes, however. Because the fullness of the plan was being eaten away, little by little, as if by ants. Any mention of the resort or the private beach by someone else made his face move in such a way as to confirm each hint he had of a wrinkle. Nights when he was very tired or feeling his pains he would forget to uplift his face for my sake and would say it made him angry to think we were not allowed to walk where we used to walk freely.

I never told Wilson—nay, anyone—what happened the day I returned the day pass. (Perhaps returned is not the right term; they did not take the orange card from me but instead slashed through its words with a thick black marker before handing it back.) I decided to leave through the staff exit, because my nephew was working at the resort, and I had a message for him from his father. Nothing too important, but it seemed no great trespass to leave the resort through the truck bay. Lots of boys back there, both American staff and island boys: some playing cards and smoking; some hosing down what needed to be hosed; some working repairs on equipment in the garage; et cetera. All looked up at me, laughing eyes suggesting I didn't belong there. Expecting I took a wrong turn, though I had chosen my path *of exiting the resort. I didn't see my nephew, however, so I proceeded toward the gate behind the trucks to be on my way.*

Some of them were silent as I passed; some muttered names—you know what kind of things they call a man like me. Bungy. And the like. Me, a man as old as their fathers, and yet some of their hands found their way to me—nudging me enough to try to provoke but not enough to cause me to leave my feet. And I continued to approach the gate to exit. Until one young man I'd never seen before on this island took a piece of pool equipment, a long pole with a net at its tip, and got it caught up in my ankles. I did fall to the ground. And what happened next, well, I will just say that it was a good thing that the dumpster had not been emptied yet that day, so I was not hurt by their throwing as I might have been, and it was not as difficult to climb out as it might have been. I was able to walk out the gate myself.

I went home and was able to continue my plans with Wilson without any physical ailments to make our endeavor all the more impossible. Today is the closest I have come to entering the resort since that day.

As for Wilson and me, we made it as far as Junkful Beach. This location is not so far from our home. But also this location is not so close to our home. No matter how you want to think of it, as far or near, that is the distance we walked. Wilson became weak, and even after resting for an extended period on the rocks at Junkful Beach, he was unable to continue. We were unable to continue. I had, of course, made arrangements for such a possibility by scheduling with another of my nephews several locations to which he would drive to see how we were faring. As it happened, we were at Junkful Beach for quite a while before his arrival for our eventual, and last, ride home. We sat in repose and talked and didn't talk about everything and nothing for the better part of the afternoon in that strange mix that is Junkful Beach: the scruff of the weeds, the band of sand washed soft by the water insisting on coming in over and over again, the stretch of the water to the horizon, east to all sorts of places we have not seen with our own eyes. Africa, Asia. England the only faraway place I have seen, when I went to study a spell, long ago.

Wilson gathered some energy, in our final half an hour or so there, to meander a certain stretch of the beach and examine — marvel at, more accurately — what we found there. What had found its final resting place on our little island, he said. The most unexpected object we uncovered that day was this child's violin bow. How strange that the wood could be rubbed nearly colorless by the sea but that its strings could remain so wonderfully, relatively intact. Not all of them had hung on, but some had. In addition, how wonderful, Wilson said, that we found it among weeds so close in color. So that we knew there had to be something special about the way we used our eyes to find something that so many others would have mistaken for another ribbon of weed on the most unkempt beach of the island.

His last days on the island before the series of planes took him to Miami, to his brother's house, to die, he would recline on our front porch, facing the ocean, and wave the bow like a conductor's wand. Wouldn't it be the way, he said, in that way he had of saying such things, if we could direct it all. He moved his hands in concert with his eyes, in concert with the waves, as if he could catch up to and even overtake them. On the day of his departure he handed the bow to me and told me to keep it raised in the air, keeping him aloft even across the water between us.

It was so very difficult to get off the island, in those days when the resort was flying so many in and out without the number of flights having caught up. I wanted to go with Wilson to the capital, to be with him at least for the two days he would be waiting for his flight to Miami. But there was only one seat to be had, for a stretch of months it seemed. We could not wait any longer, and I saw him off from the dock as he floated, seated backward on the boat, waving, to the airstrip to go and wait alone. In the capital for his flight, and then in Miami.

The bow does not work, my friends. You may laugh at it, of course. It is powerless, in its way, against the ailments that overtook him. It was, in the end, powerless to conduct me through the visa channels in time to arrive for the funeral. I carry it on my back. Slung low on my back, against my spine. It is powerful in its survival, tossed in the sea, in the memories with which I've strung it taut. It reminds me, my friends, of the way we had to see to discover it. It reminds me, from behind, that I am not leading the way on my own.

Chapter Five

T *he Beach Blanket Blog* said, "The House and Lovers' Lookout Tour. Great views! Magical views!"

Going inland in broad daylight: the real magic trick.

I had a bunch of big greenish garbage bags Lem had given me. I'd convinced him part of my garbage duty could be collecting litter during the tour. I didn't want to ask him for any favors, didn't want to do anything that'd have him dogging up to me all the time again—all the time still. But Lem agreeing to the extra garbage duty I'd invented to do during my *Maid* hours meant I could walk up the path—the resort's way inland—for the first time. The bags stuck to my hands in the heat, shimmered, as I slowly caught up to the tour group.

I knew the Manions had gone up with this group. Maybe Jasmine Manion had taken her book up there, to compare what she saw to the map. As if I wasn't drowning in the inland already—now that bag of hers was something I couldn't stop tracking. Eyeing how squared-out its edges seemed.

Getting inland through the resort's path was so much easier than getting inland anywhere else on the island. They had dug into the hillside to make an evenly graded slope paved smoother than any paved road around here. As far as I knew, not a single one of us local folks who worked for the resort had ever walked this not-too-steep path, each serpentine curve the shape of a machete blade. It was as off-limits as swimming in the pool or sitting down to feast in the dining room. Drinking with a guest, island-glued to another in Lionel's old truck. None of us had ever witnessed the AYS giving the tour: the storybook version of the inland, with its concocted Lovers' Lookout.

I shook one of the bags out to its length. It filled with air and my pretense of litter duty. Pulled a wisp of paper out of a bush. Realized the plant I was reaching into was landscaped haulback posed, almost unrecognizably, in carved circular sculptures along the path. So it could be tamed. Pricked me just the same.

I knew I was getting closer when I caught bits of conversations. Even closer when slices of tourists flashed in between the landscaped foliage. A glimpse of a man unfolding the legs of his sunglasses and wrapping them around his puffy pink face, then wrapping his arm around the waist of the woman next to him, who seemed not to mind his sweat. A glimpse of a kid with thick white sunblock puddled in the valleys around his nose, the divot below his mouth, the swirls of his ears, and the creases of his elbows. Squirming away when his mother tried to rub it all in. Glimpse of his mother: Jasmine Manion. Glimpse of his nanny stooping to take the boy's hand, her dark eyes probably bloodshot and glassy behind mirrored lenses. A glimpse of an older woman in a broad-brimmed straw hat batting absentmindedly at the camera strung around her neck. Strolling up to the Manions too casually to be casual.

"Where are you from?" she asked. "We're from New Jersey. Central."

"Wisconsin," Mrs. Manion replied.

The woman leaned back as if a wind had come up out of nowhere. "Wisconsin? Really! Bruce," she called, waving to a man nearby. "These people are from Wisconsin! Have you ever met anyone from *Wisconsin?*"

"I most definitely have not! Wow." His T-shirt stuck to him in shapes of sweat that made his torso look like a map. It was definitely the hottest day since the last boat came in and the farthest any of the tourists had gotten from the resort's air-conditioned interiors; even the pool deck was speckled with fans.

Jasmine Manion morphed into a streak of orange until I came around another bend in the path and saw her more fully: crisp white capri pants and a shimmery mango top that flowed around her. Full makeup. Matching earrings, bracelet, and necklace. Her hair was still pulled back in a tight, short ponytail, as it was during Lionel's tour, but tiny ringlets were popping out along her forehead from the humidity. She was overdressed compared with the other women in their swimsuits and cover-ups or tank tops and shorts. Holding up her hand as a map of Wisconsin to show the other couple where they'd come from.

Around another slight bend in the path, and I could see her son badgering her husband until his father handed over his sunglasses. Purple lines left on his nose. His grayish-brown hair was plastered to his forehead, drips of sweat migrating from his ears down to his chin. The boy looked up at his mother, showing off his oversized glasses. His cap of paper-bag-colored curls had tightened in the humidity, making his face look rounder and babyish. Jasmine Manion took a handkerchief from her palm tree–stamped bag and handed it to her husband. I couldn't see inside the bag.

I finally emerged from the landscaped path to the outlined clearing. The gray of the stone was brilliant in the sunlight. They called it the House, but it wasn't a house. Really just three walls still standing: the taller wall connecting the lower longer ones was two stories high and pointed at the top so you could imagine the roofline. Still, much more of a house than anything stone I'd found. And so much higher off the ground—lift of importance. What house? Views of what? The blog hadn't said, and neither did the AYS leading the group.

There were open rectangles where the windows had been. A stone slab came away from the front door at an angle; the AYS called it the veranda. Steps had been built up to the second floor from behind; I heard the AYS say the original steps would have been more like a ladder through a hole in the floor, which made everyone gasp and laugh. Both kids and adults were scampering up and sticking their heads through the empty rectangles, making goofy faces for pictures in the empty spaces that had been windows. The ocean *whoosh*ed somewhere below. The way people pointed from the top of the stairs, through the upstairs windows, I assumed they had a tremendous view out to sea. Only me staring at stones instead.

I hovered around, sniffing for the excuse of more garbage near the Manions. Her bag looked bulky. Had to keep my eyes down. If Jasmine Manion recognized me and said anything, the AYS would hear. If I hovered too close, the AYS would feel the change in one of their flat-eyed maids.

"Alvin, let's go up there and take some pictures," Jasmine Manion said, nudging the boy toward Katelynn, who was snapping pictures of the ocean. I stayed at the nanny's back; now that she knew my name, she was another hazard. Fire coral in murky water.

"I think I'm going to find a chair," Jasmine Manion's husband said. "Are there any damned chairs around here? I'll wait for you if you want to go up."

"No, come with me." They stood facing each other, not saying anything for a minute. "I'm not going alone, and you know why. What happened by the truck?" She whispered *truck*. Her forehead stretched back, as if her point should be obvious. Then I saw her eyes dart around, maybe looking for the mophead cyclist.

Her husband ticked his head to the side, an assent, and flicked the screen of his phone before sliding it into his pocket. "What's the way up to the top? Steep?"

She scoffed at him. "I don't think so. The AYS said I could make it up all the way in my mules." They both looked at her feet and, despite myself, I looked, too.

Some unidentifiable string appeared nearby for me to pick up, slowly. A loop of clear plastic, slow again.

Another couple had joined the conversation as well, smiling and nodding as one. The wife stood very close to me without seeming to notice I was there. Her hair hung in a blondish drape around her face; I was close enough to see the dark gray roots.

"Isn't it just gorgeous up here? I can't get enough of this blue sky," the husband said.

"Yes, but it's just so *hot* today," the woman with the hat said. "When I was a girl, we used to go to the movies in the afternoon because it was air-conditioned, and we stayed there as long as possible in the cool and in the dark. I wouldn't think there's a theater around here, though." She shielded her eyes from the sun and hunched her shoulders with a grimace.

"When I was a girl, my mother used to drive around on the hottest days with all the windows rolled up so that people would think our car had working air-conditioning!" Jasmine Manion let out a half laugh, half whimper.

Her husband looked annoyed, his hand swatting mosquitoes or the air. He turned toward the House. "Don't talk about that now, Jasmine," he said. "Let's go up."

Whether she was following his command or just wanted to go, she quickly looped her arm through his, leaned into him, and stretched her leg in an overstated step toward what had been the doorway of the stone house.

I stepped back as the AYS motioned for the group to turn away from the House facade and down a narrow path. I stayed a few steps back, not wanting her to see me watching but wanting to see Lovers' Lookout.

A few steps in, the tidy brush opened up to another small clearing with a railing built out from either side of a thick pillar of wood wedged into a base of stones. A balcony overlooking the sea. The tourists stared and stared; nothing they had to do but respect its beauty. The water out toward the horizon had been mesmerized into ruffles, but near the shore it lapped peacefully.

The AYS, in her pink resort T-shirt and crisp white shorts, propped herself up on the railing and waved to get our attention. The sun caught her slicked-back ponytail with white stripes. Beneath the sleek plane of her sunglasses, her nose looked skinned, with a raw pink patch that matched her shirt.

The group stirred when the Manion boy decided to scramble up an embankment toward some baby palms, slipping from his nanny's grip like a thief. Heard one of the snorkeling women murmur, not that low, about where that boy's mother was. The others just stared, silent and wilting in the heat.

"Nathan! Nathan Manion, you get back here!" Katelynn's eyes darted up toward where his parents were, worried they'd see she couldn't wrangle him.

It was so quiet except for the ocean and the nanny's yelling. Nathan was sitting, laughing until she reached him, and she pulled him down alongside her, with both of them scooting through the dirt on their behinds. They were both filthy by the time they were back standing with the others. The boy's laughing had turned to crying as he fell against her legs. The other tourists looked at them with some mixture of disapproval and pity. I was glad no one was looking at me.

When the AYS started speaking, her voice boomed out above the sound of the water, got their attention. "This, ladies and gentlemen, is Furnace Island's own version of Lovers' Lane. We call it Lovers' Lookout. It is said that this is the most beautiful and the most romantic point on the island, and any two people who stand together and look out on the gorgeous sea from here will—be careful, now!—fall in love. Proceed with caution, ladies and gentlemen, boys and girls. You know how hot furnaces can get! And it is said that any two people who *kiss* up here will be bombarded with good luck for a *year!*" She wagged her finger around, head tilted to one side.

There was a confluence of quiet laughs, and I could feel everyone around gravitating into pairs. Arms stretching around shoulders, cheeks and lips finding other cheeks and lips, the spaces through which you could see the sun between bodies thinned out more and more until they disappeared.

The most romantic point on the island? Felt like I was on some other island with some other inland. I turned back away from the lookout and toward the House. Had a good view of it from the cleared-out space where we all stood. The sun had seemed to multiply in the sky, but I could see it all now through my squint. Its state of partialness—the doors and the windows just blanks of nothingness squared off by stone—made it resemble the crude triangle drawn on the map. The biggest point on that map. The Main House. Master Cruffey's House.

A handful of tourists were up there climbing around on the House, pointing and bending their arms to take pictures of themselves. They posed with the ocean at their backs, but that meant they were facing inland. What could they see? Maybe from their perch their today-view was my everyday-view—but bird's-eye. Master's-eye. Walls of stones swallowed by haulback, glimpses of buildings rising up from the brush like shark fins. Any sign of a diamond, with its bundle of sticks, just an accidental scribble in just another crumbling wall. Maybe they could see my path—I couldn't calculate how far away it might be from where we were— but I doubted they could cipher what that was either.

The Manions were still up there, and I saw the gray square come out of Jasmine Manion's bag. More furtive about it since our reaction in the truck. She opened the book, closed it, pointed toward where I'd just left the group by the lookout. Scowled all the way down into her shoulders. Her husband put his hand on her back, then turned away. It was hard for me to imagine the two of them whispering at night in their shared resort bed about the book, the name Cruffey, the landfill. Or maybe he was just shouldering out anything with the word *plantation* on it just like everyone else on this island. Except her, great-grandbaby of a woman telling tales of island birds in Wisconsin. And except me.

With that map, maybe she could see more than any of us. First time I ever wanted to have tourists' eyes. See what one of them saw.

When I saw the AYS coming back up toward where I was standing, and me with the almost empty bags to show for my invented litter duty, I ran back down the path just slowly enough not to be noticed.

When I went to put the empty bags back, I saw Lem behind the fence getting lectured about something by Claudia's assistant. I saw him notice me over the guy's shoulder. Swimming in his eyes the mix of resentment and interest and willingness and maybe pity, too, I'd gotten used to. Like I was one of the bottles he managed to empty during slow days behind the fence: clutter he made himself. Clutter he both regretted and didn't. Worse than useless—bringing Claudia's assistant. Regretted, then, this time. I rolled and rolled the garbage bags together until they were compact as a fist, easily hidden in case the assistant spotted me, too.

When the guests came back down, I waited for them to change and head out to the pool before I got started cleaning the rooms in the B wing. Took just a few days for me to figure out the guests' schedules enough to know when to clean or not to clean their rooms. Once this new group went to the pool, they seemed to stay there until the next meal, so I could get the whole wing done without sneaking in and out.

But: a thud as I was scraping the sheets from their edges in B4. Almost made me jump onto the bed. When I turned around, Katelynn was standing there crying, with the little boy wrapped around her like a backpack strapped on the wrong way. Reminded me of the way Christine's little Jamal wrapped himself around her after she'd worked a shift at Miss Patrice's store immediately following her maid shift.

The nanny was definitely crying, not just watery-eyed from a hangover. The boy was dropping crayons through his fists and watching them fall. His shorts still dusty from sliding through the landscaping. With her sniffling into his shoulder, face red as her scalp, couldn't even detect the pink triangle on her forehead anymore. Her whole storytelling face absorbed by this crying one.

"Sorry. Excuse me. I was just coming in—coming back, because... Excuse me."

I could feel my eyes stretching toward her. "It's *me*. Katelynn, it's Myrna."

"*Oh!*" She half laughed nervously. "Yeah, oh, right. Murna. Hey. How's it going?"

The door to the room was still open, and I watched for anyone else in the hallway. Talking this way with a guest, in her room when she was there, too, of all things. (Let alone that eating feeling inside me, wanting to ask what she knew about the book.) But she was sobbing now; seemed all I could do was ask her what was wrong. I walked around her and sealed the door first.

She put the boy down, and he busied himself collecting the stuffed animals I'd just tossed off the bed. His eyes were his mother's eyes—their eyebrows had exactly the same arch and the identical taper you couldn't help but notice; his soft curls dark like her hair but also streamed with a lighter toffee brown: the only sign of his father I could find in him.

"The AYS—she said the word I don't think I'd ever heard someone called outright before. Definitely not a kid. And she said it to *Nathan*." Crying his name.

The story I heard later from Lem, who was in the storage room behind the gift shop when it all happened, mirrored just what she told me. Kid wandered from the lobby into the gift shop, knocked over a stack of hats before she could chase him down. AYS working the gift shop muttered, but the nanny could hear her.

Lem told me what he'd heard: *Who let that little nigger in here?* When I told him how Katelynn had stepped around it in telling me the story, we both half snorted, half shrugged at the shock that had deepened her eye sockets. "B4 was *crying* shocked," he said.

Katelynn's flip-flops rolled backward over a crayon, and she plopped onto the naked bed. I handed her a tissue from the box on the dresser. Other hand reached to square the new awaiting tissue.

"I was gonna buy my mom something from that gift shop. But now there's no way I'm doing that."

Kept eyeing the door, my voice hushed below the humming of the air conditioner. Pulled the curtains closed, just in case. Thought maybe through the wall to B5 I heard the *chirpity-chirp* of other guests talking and the *cling-clang* as someone lifted closet hangers on and off the rack.

"Nathan," Katelynn said, and he popped up next to her knee, bopped a stuffed parrot in her face and *caw-caw*-ed. A chuckle in her crying. She hugged him with one arm and swiveled her fingers through his curls like it was something she always did. He picked up his blanket and put one corner over her shoulder, a comfort. Made me see how long she'd been caring for Nathan. Not just hired for this trip.

Did she know about the book? Had Jasmine Manion told her about it, even shown it to her? Had she read it? Soon as I sat down on the opposite bed, ready to find a way into asking, I jumped right back up as if I'd been burned. Like my brain had tilted for a minute—from "at work" Maid who could touch guest beds only with working fingers to inland scavenger incubating questions. Thought I saw a silhouette pause behind the curtain, out by the path to the pool, and held my breath, hoping Katelynn wouldn't choose now to say my name.

Management had their way of asking guests how they were being treated by the staff that let them see if the AYS were getting to know the guests enough and if the custodial staff was getting to know them too much. If someone mentioned me by name...

"Don't tell Mrs. Manion. Promise?"

Took me a second to realize she was talking to me. I shook my head. Of course not.

"Could you—I don't know. Talk to the AYS from the gift shop?"

I wanted to stare at her until she talked herself out of that question. "OK" was all I could say.

I turned, but just halfway, eyes down the way I'd been taught. "Would you like me to finish cleaning the room now or when you are through?"

She seemed a little calmer now that Nathan was distracting her and didn't seem to notice my ending the conversation. Color draining out of her face like the tide retreating.

"Huh? Oh, now, I guess. I guess Nathan's OK, so I'll take him back out to the pool. His mom's in the art studio painting. Until dinner, I think."

Art studio? Claudia kept one guest room empty so she could invent whatever space a guest asked for. Resort promised dreams just waiting for the dreamer. Sleeping island awakened by their landing on the key.

"OK," I said again. My chin moved as if it would bore a hole in the carpet. I didn't know if I'd get another chance to ask about the book. Ghosts slithering back into the densest haulback. I kept looking down until the door slapped into place. Stood like a stone listening for footsteps outside the window. Remembered the weight of the rag in my pocket.

I started hearing around the resort that the renovation would begin for real after the banquet the next night. I didn't know yet what that would mean for me, but I was already exhausted. Waited for Claudia or anyone else to fill me in on what else my late afternoons and evenings would turn to.

First thing I had to do while the guests went to dinner was clean up the art studio Claudia had set up for Jasmine Manion. Her canvases lined up against the wall: A painting of the Portuguese shampoo bottle she'd found on Junkful Beach. Another of the mitten she'd found, that one with a backdrop of the sand, the sun: everything a blinding yellow except the muddied mitten. A painting of the magazine-square-turned-sunset-sketch from Lionel's house. And a crosshatching of black lines that I looked at for a while before I recognized it was a close-up of Troy's sculpture. My brother's re-vision of someone else's monument re-created by this woman's memory and paintbrush: layers and layers of unsettled sediment. (Could I fit that canvas under my skirt? Drop it at the landfill or file it facedown with the discarded books under our table?) No paintings of a map. No evidence of a quest, inland or otherwise. *The sensibility of its maker?* I didn't feel like an art historian who could figure that out. Just someone who'd been at Junkful Beach with the maker because we both needed Lionel's truck that day.

Before I got back to the clipboard of banquet chores Claudia'd left with Lem for me, I was to clean this space. Tomorrow it might be a pedicure and massage room or a yoga studio or again an art studio with blank canvases, pristine.

The door opened, and Hebbie was standing next to me. Sent in with a mop she handed to me. She nodded at the canvases. "Guess one of 'em biked all the way to Junkful, huh? At least they're not painting postcards."

Hadn't let myself be alone with her in I didn't know how long. After school we used to lie on our backs at Junkful Beach squinting at the sky together.

Her hair was striped more than usual, the maroonish highlights pinker than I'd ever seen them. The sun had made her more girlish, while the shade of the inland had scraped lines into me like the swelling veins of an elder. But an elder going in instead of keeping out. We talked only about the banquet.

"I don't know—they want some of us to be acting something out with the boat staff," she told me, packing her bag. "It sounds really, really weird. We're supposed to wear sheets but not like the usual stuff. They want us to run around the pool wrecking everything and screaming and stuff."

Sometimes Hebbie could be a little bit naive. It all didn't sound quite right.

She pulled one of the canvases toward her to see the one behind it: something brown and bony lined with snow. "You know what that is?"

A voice behind me: "It's a pinecone."

With her glasses dwarfing her eyes, it was as if Jasmine Manion were looking at me from down a very long road. She picked up the cloth bag of paintbrushes she'd left behind. Her other bag, the palm tree bag, was slung across her body like armor. She considered her canvases, altered their order, switched to her storytelling mode.

"I used to make these paintings of parts of our house, and then we'd find places to hang them where'd they'd sort of show you what was waiting for you around the next corner of the house. That just seemed so funny to us. I'd hear my husband laughing from downstairs when I'd hung a new one upstairs. We stopped showing them to other people who came over, though, because they didn't get it."

The way she described their house with all its corners to turn, it sounded big as part of a hotel: mazelike hallways, stuffed furniture the size of cows parked all over. Pretty much all I knew of her husband was the pinch-of-salt motion he made at the screen of his phone, his clove-and-talc aftershave, the way any time of day he was yawning and stretching, his hands almost reaching the ceiling. Figured he spent his days slumped in their overstuffed chairs. Tried to picture them laughing together. Maybe he did things to surprise her, was the one who'd set up the sideways bookcase in her shop; maybe he'd watched her walk it with half his mouth smiling in the same direction as his cowlicks.

Hebbie laughed but not her real laugh, and Jasmine Manion smiled and then was gone again. I'd taught Hebbie that "at-work" laugh, back when she was still thinking she could hum inside the gate.

"Anyway, Myr," Hebbie said, gathering her non-maid voice back. Her lids sunk heavy with the day behind her. Voice sleepy and young. "You know my brother's back on the island visiting?" She waited for me to say something in response, anything. Then she quit waiting. "All right, then, just telling you. I can't help it if your ma sees him." And she left.

The end of her day but not the end of mine. I wiped my sweaty palms against my apron and felt an itch to have my waiting-for-days machete in my hand. That night after work, no matter how tired I was, I would get back to it.

When the late shift finally came to an end, I distracted Lem as he locked up the maintenance supplies so I could swipe one of the flashlights from his crew's stash, and I found a way to bind it in my apron, so the guards wouldn't see it when they checked my bag. Someone had left a bottle of bug repellent on a table by the pool, and I'd snatched that, too. No matter how bleary-eyed the chemical cloud made me feel when I sprayed myself, I knew I'd need it this time of night.

My heels knew exactly how much ache there was between the exit from the resort's gate and the entrance to my own path. But before my feet had logged even close to the number of steps, a car rumbled to a slow crawl next to me. Sunset insignia spray-painted on the door. I kept facing the direction I was walking.

A prickly voice through the open window: "Hey there. We're practicing for the banquet."

Even just out of the corner of my eye I recognized the driver and the passenger: two members of the boat staff who each took turns as Columbus when Max was sick or on vacation. I could picture them both pulling on the undersized felt hat and the oversized gold rings. Gleeful backup captains. I wasn't positive of their names. Matt and Taylor, I thought, or something similar. I was sure they knew only my uniform.

"Don't know anything about it," I said. Walking, walking. "Off duty now."

"But we need maids to *run* from us," one of them said, laughing.

It was hard to see their facial expressions in the darkness, but I didn't want them to see my flashlight was swiped from the resort, so I kept it rolled up in my apron. I kept walking, knowing just where my inland trail would be when I got to it, where my machete was planted. Awaiting, expecting. The car kept rolling alongside.

Then it stopped, and they got out. I heard a bottle shatter against the ground and smelled the beer pooling out. Wouldn't be the only bottle on the ground around here.

They walked along next to me no matter how quickly I moved my exhausted legs. I tried to seem calm.

"What's going on with this banquet?" I asked, keeping my voice high and innocent. My pulse felt fluttery; it couldn't decide between being anxious and being annoyed.

"We're taking over this island!" Their voices were filling with the bluster of the boat script I'd heard a thousand times, and they were giggling a little, sounding like kids. Just stupid. But I didn't like how they were also sort of circling around me.

"Run, native! We will be plundering!"

I tried a laugh and a dismissive wave of my hand. I tried the tipped-up chin of wonder the boat crew seemed to want us all to show during arrivals. But I picked up my pace a little, to keep them from getting real close to me. If I could just make it to the stooping lignum vitae tree—my marker—which was coming up around the next bend. I'd slip away before they could figure out where I'd vanished to.

One of them started sputtering synonyms for *plundering* while the other seemed to be pounding on his chest.

"Run!" he said. In a low, low voice this time.

At first I thought they were trying to grab me, but they kept getting too close behind my heels, without touching me, and calling "Run! Run!" at me, trying to make me let them chase me. Kept my fast walk still a walk, deciding what to do. Kept walking. Kept walking more quickly but still not giving in to a run.

But then one of their hands swooped close to my stomach, and I bent away, spinning. Cuss-cussing like my mouth had never done before. Another car pulled up, and when the two looked back at it I was able to duck into the brush and come out with my machete.

"What the fuck?" one of them said, backing toward their car, opening the door.

I stood in place, weaving the machete in a figure eight around my head, no matter how my shoulders burned from mopping and dusting and lugging garbage all day and night. The handle fit right under the notch of callus on the inside of my thumb, as it always did.

The other guy was planted in the road, cautious but smirking, deciding what to do.

I recognized the car that'd pulled up as Hebbie's mother's car. And sure enough Andre got out, yelling at the boat guys till it was all mayhem, and they looked at him and looked at me and looked at the machete and finally climbed in their car and sped off with a silly shriek of tires.

Car door still open, one frayed backpack strap hanging out like a dead man's arm. Standing there alone in the road, staring at me: my brother's best friend. Andre was a tall stick and bronze, while Troy was stouter and shiny colored; Andre was always wearing T-shirts so hip you might not understand the phrases they told you, while Troy was always done up a little dressier than anyone else, button-down shirt tucked in, always.

Still: looked like a single bookend missing his twin side when I saw Andre by himself, without Troy. Not sure if the dark was playing with my eyes or if that broken strap had been red. If the night was playing with my imagination or if I should've smelled ginny cologne on its way five minutes ago. Nose filled with it now.

"You OK?" he asked.

My only response was to let the machete down from above my head. I passed it back and forth between my hands as he was talking, rambling about being back on the island to check on his elders, how Hebbie told him I was still working at the resort, how he'd heard Mother was doing, and on and on and on and on. Streak of words that never slowed down just like always. Never let me catch my breath.

"Also wanted to come talk to you while I'm on the island. You and your ma. Tell you all, you know. What I know."

"Don't tell me anything else," I said and ran back in where I'd gotten my machete from, fumbling for the flashlight and the feel of the path under my feet. My legs were so tired I had to check the ground with my hand to keep on. But kept on, waiting for that moment when I was far enough inland the sounds from the road couldn't reach me, but the pull of the stones and their ghosts could.

Andre's voice caught up to me, but I knew he wouldn't chase me in. No one from this island would.

What a damn hypocrite I was. Running in to find out what no one else would tell stories about. But running in to escape Andre telling stories about what had happened to my brother. Bloody stories all.

"I'm a bigger ghost to you than those two ghouls?" he called after me.

Got a machete for them.

Bench Story No. 3: Mr. Harper Cruffey

My favorite dinner is fritters, any kind of fish, freshly caught and fried right before I put it on my plate. And a mixture of tea I make myself from the jumbled mess of bushes that grow behind my house, all hunkered in one area of the yard as if they knew they'd make the most delicious tea for me. Some people are real particular about what they pick for tea, what different leaves are good for. I think: if it grows together, it goes together! I tell you this stuff because people will come and look at me rolling up the road in my wheelchair or digging crutches into the gravel or sand to come sit with you, one leg on and one leg off, and that will be all they think about my life. The life with one half-leg. But my life, when it's good, is about fritters and tea, and if I'm really lucky and have a woman sweet on me, whatever vegetables she pulls up from the garden and brings to my table.

My father was known for the boat business he ran that most folks around here called a genius thing. Before his business idea people either fished just for themselves and their families, or even if they were going to sell their fish, they had to invest in a boat or negotiate with friends who had a boat. But then they were kind of competitors, you know, all going out to the same spots together, but then all trying to sell. So my father had the idea that he would spruce up this old boat that had wrecked out and beached up on the east side. No one thought they could do anything with this thing, and it sat there getting beaten by the wind and all for months until my father and his brother hauled it three miles just with their hands and their feet to our house and spent a month building it all up good as new and ready to go. Then they took contracts for all the fishermen around. I was still too young at this time to even go along in the boat, since they didn't want to have to worry about a little pip like me.

You could reserve your place for a certain number of days per month, and he had all sorts of priced-out deals for making up bad-weather days or how much you hauled or not bringing other people to your sweet spot and that sort of thing. He knew all about fishing, so he knew just what the fishermen would be concerned about and interested in. I should say fisherwomen, too, since there were plenty of women who used his services and did really well. Did so well, my dad's business did. I remember my mother just sort of walking a little more relaxed, once he started doing that business and the task of feeding a family wasn't so hard on her anymore. So relaxed her bag might swing all the way to the dust like a schoolgirl's instead of being all clenched alongside her hip.

I love the smell of sisal rope when it comes out of salt water and somehow holds the hard, twiny scent. Sharp like it's rocket-propelled to your nose. That's what it feels like when it gets to my nose. Most people can't stand that briny shit, but I love it. You'll smell that only around here. I've traveled to the capital and to Florida and to South Carolina and to Haiti to see my mother's family there, and I've never smelled quite the same thing. My late wife used to—when I was coming home after a long spell, which happened all the time before I lost my leg, especially when I was traveling often to Haiti to help my mother's family—my wife, she would dip some rope in the ocean the day I was coming home and would tack it up on the door to our house so I could smell it right when I was walking up. Right when I was thinking, I'm home! I would smell that and know I'm home.

Now: how did I lose my leg, that's what everyone here who isn't from here is wondering. And maybe some who are from here, too. And I'll talk about it because it has to do with this resort here. It did not happen in Haiti, though people have asked that when they hear I'd spent time there. *They have some idea that things are so peaceful here and so harsh and violent there—like it would just make sense to come back from Haiti without half your leg!*

The resort had all these papers saying they're buying all that inland land in addition to the beachfront strip. I don't know who the devil they think they bought that inland land from, since it didn't belong to anyone. And if you really go back to how the land was given out at emancipation, it "belongs" in its way to the families here anyway, not the government or whoever claims to have sold it. Even if those families don't want it. Even if not a single family stayed up there. Still theirs.

And when the resort was first opening up, they had all these "blueprints" of the inland, along with their "land deeds." For all I knew these blueprints were just a mess of guesses about what might be under this giant mess or even a complete fake. Used to build the resort, not unbuild the ruins.

But anyway, I was telling you all about my leg. We all knew this land-deed-and-blueprint business was bogus—those of us who talked about it hushed up in kitchens—but who could do anything about it and what difference would it make anyway, most of us said, because we didn't want anything to do with that land anyhow. How'd it get so full of brush never tended to? That's how. Nothing at all to do with that land. That's why it's like that.

But anyway, they wanted to clean up the area of the Cruffey Main House, because that was the one building you could tell was a building, and it was closest to the main resort space on the beach. So it made sense for them if they're going to try to take tourists up there— that's the spot. They needed some men to help clean it up so it'd be accessible: both the ruins of the house and the path up to it. Get rid of the crumbled piece of wall and all. And they said it might lead to more work, if they decided to go farther in and clear out any of the rest of the site. So a bunch of us took the work, you know, we were always looking for work. That or leave the island, and I still had my mother here after my father died, needing me. So how'd I end up with half a leg when I was born with two strong legs? Strong enough that

I was one of the ones they hired for this kind of work: not to just clear out the brush but really landscape it out, so it wouldn't just grow back each time it rained, and also to haul out the extra stones or the loose stones that people shouldn't climb on and also to fix up the path so it wouldn't wash away or become dangerous in any way? People who aren't from around here, they don't know what to look for when they're navigating a path such as that. Around here we can sort of tell when a big boulder's not quite steady in place. Sometimes, anyway.

So: my leg. It's not that I remember everything that happened, play by play. Because there was part of it that happened very fast, and I didn't quite know what had happened, and then there was the part that happened so, so slow. Took maybe almost a full day once it had finished happening for them to get me out and airlifted to a hospital in the capital. But you know some about that now.

And so, you see. It is a crushing literal metaphor, the damnable weight of those ruins waiting to fall, fall on me, with just the slightest nudging out of the places they've been settled in, covered with dirt, for so many years. And now, right now, me sitting on some of them, them holding me up like I held them up. You have to laugh, don't you? Taken down by the thing we don't want to speak of. Yes, I guess we got to laugh. We got to go right ahead and laugh.

After, when I had come home and gotten a little used to things, I spent my days watching my neighbor's kids for her while she worked cleaning up hotel rooms all day. She had just two, and one was at school, and the other little one was very well behaved, so she figured I could handle him, and I could. He wouldn't run away from me if we went outside for a walk, him ambling alongside me with my crutch-es—crutches when I was still young enough to haul myself here and there.

And this boy's favorite activity, all afternoon, was to collect every-thing that was in one trunk and take it to the other side of the room and put it under the table, and then do just the opposite, taking it all out from under the table and putting it deep in the trunk. I think his mother would specially fill that trunk because there was so much in there: shoes, books, marbles, a dried pepper that rattled if you shook it, an old sack with only one handle left, unusable bits of rope. I can still see it all now these years later. And all day long I just watched this little boy, Harold. You never saw such concentration, just dismantling one life of objects and creating a new formation on the other side of the room where it all looked different and then picking that apart, ever so carefully not to have an avalanche, and reassembling it in the bottom of a trunk, like a city's remains on the bottom of the sea. But he's grown and left the island like a bunch of the other boys. Off, off to the capital.

Who could have known that the way all that house stuff got moved around, that people would get moved around, too? And stones getting all moved, then and now. Me sitting here, the stones holding me up. You do have to laugh at that.

Chapter Six

I'd never been to a resort banquet before or any other kind of banquet. Only the AYS were allowed to serve at them, and I'd seen only the aftermath that needed to be cleaned up. Pounds and pounds of untouched food that started in careful displays and got bulldozed as if the long table were a conveyer belt ending in huge garbage cans. Bags of it sitting in a dumpster nobody was allowed to fish in. But this wouldn't be like any banquet I'd seen or hadn't seen. *Banquet* just a word to involve us all in the renovation. Speed up the demolition process. Create garbage and the need for new stuff that would become more garbage soon enough. Lionel was right, of course: no need for a renovation. Though there would be soon, once we made a big enough mess out of things.

AYS dressed up as Columbus and his sailors had circulated all day, letting the tourists know that tonight's banquet would be a "special opportunity." They'd be given characters—some sailors, some stampeding wild cows—and would "embark on the adventure of discovery and settlement." The cows were even supposed to wreak havoc all over the pool deck, upturning anything they wanted. Guessed sailors could and would, too. I'd kept my distance from any of those sailors since last night, but the script spelled it all out. Natives, bring your sheets.

The banquet hall—the meal would take place after the rest of it—was a tent set up alongside the pool deck, encased in plastic with air conditioners noisily inflating the whole place. The tourists were lined up in front of it, waiting. I watched their open faces, wondering what they thought *banquet* meant.

I walked along the line, eyes down, handing out the cards that gave them their characters: if one card said *sailor*, the next one said *stampeding cow*. Miss Philene followed behind me, handing out plastic swords to the sailors. I knew I would've held those swords too tightly, my fingers remembering machetes. With each cow card, I handed out a bell, too; every step I took an alarm until all the bells had been distributed.

"Discovery and settlement." The words dribbled out of my mouth as I handed the *sailor* card to Jasmine Manion's husband. The nanny was looking away from me. Seemed she was enthralled with the boat crew trying to lure the *Pinta*, gussied with balloons, closer to the pool deck.

"And what are *you*?" the husband asked me. His face, usually pul-led more taut by indifference than even sunburn, seemed almost amused.

"A native," I tried to say. He squinted as if he couldn't hear me but laughed anyway, head drooping toward his left shoulder; his two cowlicks veered right as if trying to straighten him. The pool deck was a din. Even to my own ear I'd heard myself say, "Taken." Katelynn seemed to wince at that. Nathan hovered just below her hand, smiled up at me in his T-shirt with a picture of a tie. No sign of yesterday's tears. I didn't know where his mother was, but her husband seemed now to be looking around for her. Or maybe he was just checking out the bizarre scene setting up around us. The wind came up around him and flattened his hair across his forehead. Looked monkish or boyish.

Out of cards and bells, I crossed the pool deck toward the entrance to the hotel. Through the glass doors to the lobby I saw Jasmine Manion sitting at the bar, though I didn't think anyone'd be serving inside during the banquet. Her ivory sundress was crisp and bright against her skin; maybe she'd gone inside so no one would mistake her dress for one of our sheets. She didn't have on any jewelry but still looked a little fancier than the other American women. She picked up the white rectangle in front of her: the book of mysterious birds. Hands picking it up and putting it back on the bar. Nervously? Her great-gran's book, kept away from the madness outside that couldn't possibly line up with any island memory her great-gran had ever shared—while her husband and son lingered in anticipation of the banquet, taking on the characters handed to them. (What were those island memories told to Jasmine Manion when she was a girl? Would an elder from Quickly ever dip into history, let the word *plantation* tumble from her mouth? It seemed maybe so.)

I imagined her arrival here, stepping out onto a key with the sun pushing down, head buzzing with expectations for her first trip to the Caribbean. A book-heavy but summer-weight "Vacation, Resort" bag pulling her sideways to look at the island in the distance from a new angle. Now, on the barstool, in her lap only a small clutch purse the size of my apron pocket.

I'd never seen the deck empty like this, the pool water like glass, and I leaned slightly toward the edge and looked down, my nose scrunching away from the chlorine fumes. There was no reflection in the water, but I knew the sheet hung on me like a hospital gown. The wind had left us for other islands this week. Even inside these gates, where they sprayed and sprayed against them, insects hung easily in the air.

Looking at the bottom of the pool through the water was like looking through fire, with the way the colors waved, sometimes clearly and sometimes not. But I could make out the painted floor, its fluorescent mural and scabby patches of blue where the paint was gone, here and there. The handlike plant shapes rough markings of coral, the brightly colored egg shapes tricking your eye into spotting fish.

An appliance like a giant vacuum cleaner sat on the bottom, snaking out corrugated blue tubes. I followed one of its arms to the break in the fence and half tripped over the forest of wire brooms it had knocked over, just within reach as they always were for the crabs. Even without bells, my body couldn't help giving itself away. Watched or heard. Lem was getting the pump ready. He and B3 the only ones not dressed up to play. His back was to me, but I hovered near, hoping the fence hid me a little. Knowing that when the pump went on, all the tension on the pool deck would crescendo into the kind of waves boats steered clear of. He turned and noticed me, and we both stared offshore to the line where the ocean went a darker blue.

"So Andre's around," he said.

I responded with a nod, but he wasn't looking at me.

"Them guys"—he pointed at the boat crew, the two backup Columbuses who had run last night—"came into Thiflae last night. Sounded like they saw you two talking on the road. You and Andre. All private, sounded like."

Couldn't tell if he was trying to suss out if Andre had told me something about Troy or if he knew something himself. Wished I was heading up my path with my machete—hands finding the diamond and its bundle of sticks that wanted to loosen and tell me something—instead of waiting here for what other hells might be let loose. On account of the banquet or Lem's throat. But I hovered with him like the fence was our fortress, watching the tourists starting to shift their weight back and forth.

"Two of 'em said they had to get going, you and Andre had so much to talk about."

I realized he was jealous of Andre and me; boat guys painting a picture that left out their plundering, sprinkled in what was never there. Shook my head something fierce. Nothing I could do but change the subject.

"Look, the thing with that kid in the gift shop the other day? Do you think you can talk to the AYS about it?" Nonsense question, I knew, but if Katelynn checked up, could say I'd asked, kinda.

Lem turned to me, blocking my view of the pool deck. Eyes pink, forehead sweaty. Face twisted just like my question was:

asking him to get in trouble for no reason—me as the reason—and not for the first time.

"You and Andre messing around or what?"

Sourness again. A feeling to dump out because I couldn't stand the touch of it anymore.

"You drunk or what?"

Lem's lips looked shriveled, everything about him smaller and clutching. Sucked in, old-man-like.

I stepped around him. Couldn't hear what he said next as Max rang a huge bell that'd been strung up on the *Pinta*. The pump kicked on with a *whir* and a *boom* at once.

All the hotel guests who'd been lined up flung themselves into a run, screaming wildly and even knocking over chairs and kicking at the fence. Burnished bronze in the sunset except for the insistent pale stamps of their palms and their toothy smiles. AYS, all dressed up, were waving play swords, running in circles, too, and kneeling down to rummage and scatter the boat path in a din of ricocheting gravel. Some were dragging tubes from the pool down toward the ocean. The pump's growling only partially drowned out the screaming.

Looked back at Lem. Wondered if he could smuggle me out the way he smuggled pallets of plastic bottles back in. Had to force my mind to race to the finish line, though: what leaving the resort meant for Mother. The features of his face had slid apart, like he was chaos, too. I couldn't tell anymore, with men, when their eyes were sad or their eyes were mean.

I knew I had to go out into it. Only thing between me and other people a sheet labeled *nakedness*.

All around me: shrieking and jostling. Some of the others ran by, their sheets flapping with their zigzag paths. The saggy, almost bored fear on their faces: Was it part of the show or for real? In my toga sheet, I was supposed to be running like a frightened native, running for my life. Men baring teeth all around. Wished for the wind on the shore that would billow the sheet out so much I'd feel more covered.

I turned around and almost ran right into Taylor, same look on his face as he'd had on the road. But now something extra. Sneer a little higher on one side, like, *Here you are without your machete.* But there was no way those boat staff guys would recognize me, not really. All they'd seen that night on the road, I knew, was the uniform on my body—and the glint of the blade. My blade. Besides, half the maids were draped as natives, and half were draped but labeled *cows*, and no one seemed to be keeping track of the two halves. All was chaos, blind: no one could see what I was doing versus anyone else, with or without a white sheet all over me. Same sneer all the same.

He jumped on top of a pool lounger, arms thrown up in triumph above me, but the strips of the seat buckled under him, and his feet fell through, tangling him up enough for me to back away. Feather hat skittering to the ground.

I backed away slowly and more slowly. Felt the cool aura of glass behind me, reached back to turn the handle, and stepped backward onto the tile of the hallway. Looked out. People running around every which way. End of the world, looked like. But no one looking in: made me feel ghosty in my sheet.

When I heard a thud behind me, my veins felt like steel rods. Turned and saw Katelynn had crept inside, too, Nathan in her arms again like a twiggy bird. His face wet as a wound. Couldn't blame him in This Storm they were creating. He twisted the broken hair, crisped white, that had fallen out of her braids. His face contorted into a question mark, tiny O mouth. She just looked nightmare woken up.

To my left: hallway to the B wing. Figured she could follow me and would never tell, looking at me like I had the tools for draining the terror from the pools of her eyes. My own fear seeped out of me, replaced by a hunger in my hands. Like fear could be a cloak when it was someone else's.

Found myself in front of B3. Key card for cleaning still around my neck. Katelynn and the boy stood in front of B4, looking at me. Me: like I could make the storm outside wither to an innocuous drizzle, or make the AYS forget words. I realized she didn't know I'd lied about talking right away to the AYS—of course she didn't know how I couldn't, even if I'd wanted to. I'd only asked Lem knowing he probably couldn't either.

Everything we did got done by hands the tourists never saw. Rooms came apart by invisible forces. Put back together the same way. All the evidence the guests left of themselves scoured out of the rooms—without any evidence of us doing the scouring. Beds unmade and made by the wind. The turquoise-and-beige curtains torn back toward the walls, muslin-like layers left behind, fluttering like a spirit had been there and gone.

Everyone was outside. Not a body tracking where I was.

Doorknob in my hand, then carpet under my feet. Room coming apart, coming back together. Until.

The Cruffey Plantation Journal levitated for an instant while my other hand—instinctively folding around an imagined rag—made an efficient swipe across the dresser beneath it.

When I came out of the room, B4-one and B4-two were still standing in front of their door, eyes still on the spot where I'd been.

My ankle turned on something, and I couldn't keep my footing, with so much pool water messing the deck and the corners of the book poking my bare thighs. My sheet good for something, hiding the shape beneath my skirt. I regained my balance, looked down to see I'd stepped on a crab, the crushed stones of them scattered everywhere.

Christine's face—"at-work" smile—came flying toward me. Her speed creating wind in her sheet and in her hair.

Someone called, "Christine," and she turned around, and her cheekbone smacked against the knuckles of Captain Columbus. I gasped, and my heart pounded up in my neck. The chaos kept on and on around us. A pile of girl and sheet against the ground. Her eyes catching mine.

Book knocking at my kneecaps as my legs went as fast as they could to the path.

Getting inland on the tourist path was just like being a tourist anywhere, open walk ahead. Or open run. (Not like last night when my cutout trail felt like a hiding place to get off the road. When I'd sat up in the brush, covering my ears until I was sure Andre'd be gone.) Even with a maid knocked to the ground behind you—an easy way up. I could feel the pounding of my feet in my knees, my chest, my forehead. But my only way up—away—was on their path.

The book bulked out the corners of my skirt. Only book I'd seen in my life with *Cruffey Island* written on it—its cover thick and dull, its pages bookmarked by its last reader with a Furnace Island brochure that was slim and slick. I told myself I'd put it back when I was done with it. Borrowed it. But that wouldn't matter if anyone saw me with it. Or if Katelynn told anyone. Or if the Manions reported it gone before I could put it back. My name would be on the week's room log. I'd be gone. Mother sitting at a barren table.

My feet just kept moving, though.

The brush was a growing beast that overtook anything in its path. Once I was away from the resort's clearing, it closed around me as if it had a vendetta. But I knew I couldn't be *that* far from the path I'd been cutting myself to the corner of those two walls. How to reach that path without Dad's machete or anything else? Under my uniform my legs were bare, so instead of crawling I put my head down and pushed forward, with the book's back cover held up to protect my eyes from swinging-back branches. I had to push through the brush so long I thought I might get stuck, but if I could make it back to that corner, I might be able to figure out where I was in relation to the House on the map. This *map* that had turned up in my hands—couldn't quite believe it yet. Finally I sensed my arms meeting less resistance and looked up to see the clear sign of a path wandering diagonally away. My path.

With no machete, there was no way to make more progress. I was left with whatever was already cut away. But at least I had some sense of direction between here and the House. I brushed the fire ants from my legs, sent them racing around the ground as I lowered to my knees, shooed dirt away, and put the book on the ground. Leaned at an awkward angle so I wouldn't sweat or bleed on it. Opened it to the centerfold where five tiny stitches seemed, against all odds, to be holding the whole heavy thing together. I smoothed the left page to the left and the right page to the right. The map was rough, and out of sight of the resort's clean path it was hard even to orient myself north, south, east, west. The buildings were an archipelago of blue dots labeled *storehouse, kitchen, well, lockup, gin house. Slaves' quarters.* If I could figure out which building my corner of two walls was, I might be able to map out most everything else up here. Know which way to head when I returned, with my machete, to find the rest. Felt it skimming in my blood that I could find it all, see it all. Like all my skin was seeing. I stared and stared at the map and back at the walls, worrying I wouldn't make any mental progress either before it was fully dark.

I hoped I'd start seeing the map transposed on the land. But that wasn't what it was like. Neglect, nature, tricks of the eyes. No sense of the whole estate once my eyes left the pages.

I thought about Dad, describing how he matched up the smoky X-ray pictures to the cavernous mouth in front of him. The rocks of teeth half submerged, hiding their pains. As he explained this to me he'd closed his eyes and fiddled his fingers in his food, lining up whatever chunks of vegetables we were eating.

"That's nasty, Horace," Mother had said. "We're at the table now."

And Dad, smiling: "Yes, Daphanie, so just look away from my messy fingers."

And Mother—smiling, too—closed her eyes and continued to eat. Mouth seeking food like a blind baby bird's.

Running into the brush the other night, feeling Andre's voice, my eyes were Mother's pinched-shut eyes. But there was no smiling for me: thief who stepped over a girl on the ground.

There were some loose stones along the foot of the wall, and I decided on something I'd never attempted before: climbing through the window. Thought of Mr. Harper's leg. But the danger of not naming the stones' ghosts seemed worse than the danger of the stones, worse than the danger of stealing and trespass. Couldn't let the past alone like Dad couldn't leave a bad tooth to rot.

I perched the book in the crook of the cactus and felt with my foot until I found a part of the pile of stones that wouldn't shift with my weight. Closed my eyes. Next thing I knew I was on the floor inside the building, not remembering the fall. My knees bloody, my arms pricked, my face burning. But the book had stayed safely lofted in the menacing green arm.

Branches taller than I was grew up through the floor, but there was room to move around a little and to see. On the far wall was the open mouth and throat of a fireplace. Nothing else it could've been. Tears of gratitude came, silly perhaps, for something just presenting itself as what it was. A horizontal beam of lignum vitae running across higher than my head. Leave it to our vitae: the only wood that would outlast vicious nature and neglect. I could even see two holes where nails had been. Blackened stone lined the three walls of the inside. Swaths of monkey fiddle and cacti choked it. But there it was.

I returned to the ground with the book. *Kitchen.* I *must* be in the kitchen! I put my finger on the *kitchen* dot and inched left and right on my knees, all the way around in circles and back again, trying to orient myself. It took a while, but I figured out which direction I'd come from—from the only building on the map I could find without question: The Big House. The Main House. The Owner's House. Cruffey's House. The only time the word *house* was used on the map.

Like an all-gray X-ray clarifying itself into black and white, separating teeth from skull.

I ducked inside the fireplace and found myself facing a nest vibrating with paper wasps. Slowly I lowered to my knees. Around me the walls were swathed with black, the scorchings still here after all this time. And then, tucked in the corner by my knees, another diamond my fingertips could fit in. The bundle of etched sticks again. But in here the lines had taken in the black, which made their shape clear.

A ship.

I pulled my fingers back. Crawled out of the fireplace so I wouldn't disturb the etching or the nest, shuddering with wings and legs. I was shuddering, too, standing still in the kitchen with the fireplace and the nest and a drawing of a ship.

All of a sudden I could picture, really picture, the estate. And could picture myself walking on it, from building to building, tracing the steps of the ancestors. A day in the life of ghosts. Who might speak to me.

I knew I was going to have to copy the map before returning the book. This was going to take a long, long time: lots of machete clearing and lots of daylight needed. Smacking against lots of overtime. Depending on garbage and the rain, could take months and months or more.

Once I'd climbed back out the window of the kitchen—in the process reopening old scrapes on my knees and deepening new ones—I went down to the road by the trail I'd made with my own hands.

Cars were steadily zooming down the road. And more streaks of headlights. Maybe because of what happened to Christine. Maybe something worse.

I wrapped the book in my sheet like a bundle and clutched it to my chest. Stayed just inside the brush all the way home. Could barely see for the scratches on my eyelids by the time I got there.

Mother already asleep, I could sit at the table with a flashlight. Sat in her chair at the table, since that was where the moonlight and starlight came in. Pedestal of books against my shins.

The opening pages had lists of first names that I read over and over, playing spooky rhythms in my ears. *Wilton, Lloyd, Betta,*

Joon, Vack, Pittman, Warrant, Mort, Tildy with one arm, Missy, Old Grebba, Nilly, Divvy, Suma. They were listed in columns with their ages, and Xs next to some of them under the column heading *Africa born*. The dates listed next to some of the names were, as far as I could tell, dates of purchase. The names without dates, I guessed, were born on the plantation.

Pages upon pages of lists, made by Master Cruffey himself: each entry dated, listing what was done by which "hands." Who was in the field, how much was planted on planting days, what was brought in from the field, who gave birth (just coming in from the field), what and who came in and out on the occasional boat, which calf broke its leg and got turned into dinner. What his wife, Martha, was doing; what his son was doing. What or who they were doing things to. As I read I figured out some of the relationships among them. Owner doing the writing. Martha, his wife. Son. All three of them Cruffeys, I had to remind myself. I turned back to the column of names and connected them with my fingertip. Finger traced a line from Mort to Tildy with one arm. From Tildy to Divvy. Another family of three but not listed together. Mort and Vack: maybe brothers. Their mother maybe Grebba.

There were a few diagrams of structures being built: mainly new walls but also what the author labeled *NEW BETTER FOR WHIP. POST.* In the ink drawing it looked like a thin pen of stones with a tall stick shoved into the center.

And then, days and days in, more than lists: something *happened*. Recorded only in the broken-off sticks of half-sentences. As if that surveyor of the plantation, that list-maker—hard for me to call him by name—didn't know how to account for those hands he thought were his acting *not* "at work."

'33 Feb 20

Martha in kitchen & call Tildy with one arm to move pot of hot water   Tildy with one arm say, Need help with pot, call Betta   Martha say, No, dinnertime, hurry   Tildy with one arm drop pot all over and Martha call me & Son   Son pull Tildy with one arm to wh. post   Give her 4 strikes with stick & count more   Mort come back from guinea corn field, put his hand on my back & push me out way to stop Son   Martha scream & I tell her, Back in house   Mort hold switch from riding, stand behind Son   'Fore I stop him, Tildy with one arm pull Mort's arm down & say, No   Outside all hands (male—female—littles) gather round   Son yell, Get back to quarters   All stay standing but go after while

Place on my back where later still feel Mort's fingers   Martha say, A long time Tildy with one arm been too slow adding food to pot, too fast slipping food to her pocket & how she track blood in kitchen sometime, not keep any leaves under her feet   Old Nilly come ask for cloth for Tildy with one arm—for burns from water pot   Martha say, Back to quarters   'Fore sleep, bring switch to hold in bed   Feel real thick like when my hands tired from riding   Wrap both hands to hold strong   Mutiny Day, say Martha

'33 Feb 21

'Fore first call every hand, even old women barely walking, stand round the well with sticks   Don't listen when counsel them get to work   Still standing while Son ride on horse 'mong them   Finally go to work but some carry sticks all day through field, stable, storehouse, around stock   By night put sticks down but no knowing if more to come

'33 Feb 22

After Mutiny Day sent Son on more rounds to make sure all hands working   He report back, Stones   Ask him, Stones?   Son says, Stones for new wall now by livestock's water hole   Not there last time Son near water hole   But now put in pile   Told Son, Keep eye on   All male hands take corn to storehouse when I round 'fore dinner   Female hands, 'cept Old Grebba, come in from weeding field   Son on last round 'fore dark—Warrant not at stable, he sitting on stones pile Talking but stopped when Son come   No more hands near   Told Son, Report next day   Warrant never trouble 'fore but since Mutiny Day not sure what not seen or not heard by us   Dinner, Son comes and

says, Betta now on stones   Same—talking 'fore saw him   Martha
says, Stop worrying, but we remind her of Mutiny Day   Colder,
Nilly not keep fire good overnight

'33 Feb 23

First round, Son see Joon on pile but still talks when Son come,
'bout time punished in stable   Warrant stand near, watch Son   Son
say, Stop   Joon leaves, Mort sits on stones   Look Son in eye   Where
Mort, Tildy with one arm & little octoroon not far

Go with Son next round   Tildy with one arm on stones by stock's
water hole   Like bench, as Son say   Her feet wrapped by rags from
barn   More hands round water hole   Betta, Warrant, Mort   Betta
water stock like Son say to   Told Tildy with one arm check if Martha need her   She stayed on stones, not talking   Look Son in eye
Son go for her & then she go toward Martha quick   Son kick stones
over   Told Warrant and Mort, Spread stones along two walls far
apart   Send Son to check Tildy with one arm in kitchen   Son fast to
see about Tildy with one arm, always fast to see about her   Rubbed
out lines where stones been with my own foot

'33 March 1

All hands in big field 'cept 2 women and 1 little in house with
Martha (Tildy with one arm & Nilly & Tildy's octoroon Divvy)   Call
Divvy Loitering Boy—he stands near walls, not fetch quick enough
Martha call Divvy Boy Whose Eyes Look Like Son's   Always tell her
not to say so in front of the hands   Martha say, Octoroon gone soon,
no matter   Tildy with one arm slow again, so post octoroon myself
Tie to post all day   Weather dry, wind low for boat in   Send Son down
with 1 horse, 2 hands (Herold and Vack)   Letter come on boat with
prices of wood, send notice of sale out with boat

'33 Apr 8

Next boat in, bring Martha's fabric and payment from N   Boat out
take back mutineers to capital for sale—Mort, Divvy the oct, Tildy
with one arm   Tildy belly swole 'gain—lose her new little but send

anyway, raise sale   Take Vack with down to harbor, transport fabric
back to house for Martha   Vack stand too long looking at boat sail out
Have to get going with stick   All other male hands weed new cotton
field 'cept 2 at stable   Amount weeding typical this time of year

I couldn't take in any more right then. My filled-up eyes blurred the words. *Mutiny Day.* I'd call it something else. Wondered what those enslaved would have called it—what they *had* called it.

Once we'd watched satellite images of the eye of a hurricane hanging over our oval, as if the storm were only on a TV screen and not all around us. Water so furious turned the image opaque; we were looking right at ourselves without being able to see anything. How the named people moved in my mind without me hearing any of their voices. All those people sitting on the bench of stones, but I didn't get to hear their words. So much for them to tell: made my brain sag with exhaustion, just seeing it with no sound. Waiting for the slow, slow eye of the storm to shift someplace else.

The moonlight was fading, the stars screened behind the clouds. The flashlight dulling. To read it all I'd need to keep the book longer, not just copy the map out. I couldn't imagine letting the book go out of my hands at all, even to hide it as I knew I should. It was heavy in my lap, didn't fit there. Uncomfortable. But like it was supposed to feel like that on top of me.

Still, I knew I needed to hide it to keep at it. Like with the brush and the stones.

I crept into the bedroom I shared with Mother and slid the book under my pillow. Pressed my head down hard so I could still feel its edges. Too-thin pillow let me. Bringing that book into the house was like inviting in a wild animal: something that could bite, dismantle. If she saw it, what would happen to Mother? She'd already stopped speaking since Troy. If it touched her, would her skin pucker into blisters? Split like haulback snags? Streak dry and raw like hands held too long in the ocean or in the resort's soapy buckets?

Closed my eyes even though I knew I wouldn't sleep. The rush of Mother's whistly breathing was steady at my right ear. Wall steady at my left. My body felt like it was holding itself up uncomfortably. Like I was on top of the pile of stones that propped me up but also shifted beneath. A pile of stones that called for careful movement not to tumble away. A body finding a way to be still and to speak: that's what my body was trying to be. A body trapped and a mouth free. Somewhere, couldn't place it, pictures formed themselves out of shadows. Not in my mind exactly, not on the screens of my eyelids either, but also not in the room, not way out there in the world somewhere.

A stranger day at work. But I was stranger now, too. The other maids were scarce around, moving through the day with their heads down. I wasn't the only one with scratches anymore. Everyone looked torn up like the pool deck. I didn't see Christine, but I didn't ask anyone if she was at work. No one was talking about anything. As though the whole day were a Jamboree—we didn't stand still for eight seconds or trade more than a few broken-off words. The book the only thing on my mind anyhow. No word of it being reported missing yet, but I couldn't have much time.

At the end of the regular day, stiff from bleach to my wrists, I checked in with Lem about garbage duty. I was supposed to take another load to the landfill to help clear the pool deck so the renovation of the actual pool, which had been drained completely last night, could start.

He barely looked up from the clipboard when I found him behind the fence.

"Lionel sent a message he could drive you to the landfill. Picking up an American girl soon anyway. B4, that nanny." Chuckled, muttering about Lionel's truck parked outside Thiflae Bar x nights in a row with her, just as I suspected but no longer cared about.

"I can't— Why is Lionel going around with her?"

He shrugged. "What, you pissed he's hanging out with a white girl? Or you just pissed at everyone lately?"

I hadn't talked to any AYS about the gift shop the way I'd said I would, and if Jasmine Manion had told her about the book's disappearance, she knew I was the one. But if I tried to walk all those bags over and come back for more, it would take all night.

Lem was still eyeing the clipboard. I looked down, too; saw a tiny constellation of bleach splattered on the toe of my shoe. I told him the litter up by the House had been awful the other day. That I thought I should go tackle that before any of it caught wind and blew down, got in the way of the renovation. That I knew where I'd seen the garbage gather, so I could take care of it quickly. If he would just take care of dumping that load.

He gestured around, arms and voice flailing. "You see the mess went down here last night? House litter worse than *this?*" The fragmented images of the banquet mayhem pieced together in my mind. He knew I knew my garbage duty was all about this banquet-turned-renovation. But I just turned away without answering and headed for the truck exit. The stones were pulling me.

"I'll just do it quickly, and then I'll be back for the other chores." Tossed a vague promise over my shoulder that I'd do both our jobs the next day, swore to it.

I didn't turn back to see which kind of eyes he watched me with this time.

I didn't take the resort's path to the House, though it would have been much quicker. I went all the way around to my path, my machete hiding spot by the stooping vitae—where I'd hidden the book, too, wrapped up in the sheet and covered in branches—and made it back to the kitchen without reopening any wounds on my knees.

Didn't look at my watch as I was standing there, in front of this place of fire, of food, of sustenance, of labor. I imagined how big the cauldrons were that could sit inside this fireplace. I imagined how hot the heat of the fire must've been. Whether Tildy was allowed to step back from a surging flame. I imagined the smells filling this small area. Working to make food that wasn't ever yours. I imagined the lines of sight in the room, how to sneak morsels into the folds of an apron.

What did it feel like to stand so close to the fire, being watched by a man with a switch in his hand? Looking down at your own feet, torn up and cracked against the crispy edges of moldy leaves. Moving just so to keep the blood from your feet off their floor. Fire at your face. Master at your back. Feeling what it felt like to move the side of your body with no arm there. Other side, moving the pot would take flexing the fingers of one hand and pulling in the biceps of one arm. The rush inside as your fingers couldn't hold it upright, the clang of the pot on the floor, the sear of the water on bare skin. The kind of burn that burned deeper over time. (Like tonight when I'd feel that bleach work itself down inside my hands?) To feel the waiting at your back. I watched my own hand reach toward the vitae beam, finger the air beyond the nail hole that might have held a hook. Imagined taking a poker down that was hot as the fire, swinging around and flinging it behind me at whichever ghost was there.

I stooped into the fireplace and let the wasps hover near my face while my hands hovered near the diamond. Imagined ducking into the heat to get the boat from your mind into the rock. Let the flame out of your hand, safely covered by the fire. But then get sent in a boat to the capital. To be sold? To a worse prison than the estate?

Bodies off now to the capital disappeared. Came back to our oval only as ghosts. Sometimes left their artwork behind.

My feet followed a bed of rock in the ground that had kept the brush from growing in a total wall. I reached a small area where brush didn't seem to grow. I opened the book and looked around. In front of me, the sun was just beginning to sink on a gorgeous view, I had to admit, of the ocean in the distance, aqua light as a dream. Looking from afar, the green brush below looked soft and decorative, thorns invisible. In front of my feet: an oval crack in the rock, almost a bowl, half filled with rainwater. I moved my toe in an oval. Looked back at the map, traced from the kitchen. This had to be the watering hole. The livestock's watering hole. All around: more walls running as far as I could see into the surrounding brush.

Despite those walls and more walls—how free the animals must have felt, watering with a view out to the sea. What *they* all must have thought: how free those animals must feel right here. View of the land spilling down to the sea. The sky above you and the sea below you just kept buzzing blue like beauty could matter. Once in a long, long while: ships in the distance.

My brother used to show me how to trace simple shapes in the sand that turned into boats with just a line here, with the correct angle there. Half-circle base, triangle sails. Frailness of the lines laden with dreams heavy enough to depress into rock.

Making their bench right here on this spot. Making it out of took-apart walls.

I walked toward the Big House to get a better sense of direction, figure out which way to slice next. Gravity leading inside and out.

The diamond cut into the base of the House was clear, even in the running-away sunlight. I could see it and feel it, too. Same shape and size I'd been finding. But inside the diamond: smoothest rock in all the inland. Felt like the pool's tile edge, a screen in the lobby, a platter at the buffet, a guest room mirror. Sanded to facelessness. Limestone wasn't the only thing on this island at work dissolving. My hands felt so empty I picked up the book as quickly as I could. The pixelated grain of its cover, the serifed graves of its title.

I stood on the veranda and studied the map. Just off from the House, toward the shoreline, a small line like a hash mark. The map told me: *Wh. Post.* My feet plodded, one in front of the other, the path to the lookout. The path to the hash mark. One finger holding open to the page with the diagram labeled *NEW BETTER FOR WHIP. POST.* And then I looked back at the drawing of the post and realized why it was familiar.

I stared and stared before sunset threatened the sky bloody, not sure, looking to and from the map to the pillar of penned-in stones in front of me. Remembered Jasmine Manion standing on this very spot, comparing to the book just as I was and sinking into herself. It was clear from where the plantation border dropped off, where the water was drawn along the edge in simple little waves as if a kid had drawn them. Lovers' Lookout: right there on the map as *Wh. Post.*

Stared and stared. Tasted like bile in my mouth. Feet sparked from numbness, and my fingers around the book's cover felt like hardened clay.

I knelt, felt the stones against my knees. Let my hands move slowly around the pillar's back. In a space between the pillar and the cliff's edge, a wedge only a child could crouch in, my fingers found the grooves of a tiny diamond. The shallower etches of a piece of a sail.

Post octoroon myself. Tie to post all day.

Divvy.

Felt my feet finding nooks to stand on, propped myself up until I was draped over the top of the post. *Proceed with caution, ladies and gentlemen, boys and girls.* Could feel it pressing the air out of me. Too dark now to make out the nearby harbor below. The bundle of my sheet disappeared into the opaque water. Seemed so easy just to slide over. Become a ghost of the inland myself.

When I was a little girl and my brother would create art that was strange to me, I'd try to see it as if I were him. Stare at it for hours trying to make my eyes his eyes. Is this what he saw staring at the ocean for the last time? His own scent covered by salted air and fear? *Loitering Boy.* Felt a post against his chest?

When the voices were close enough for me to identify them as Claudia and Max, it was too late: I turned around and faced them.

Bench Story No. 12: Mr. Vitman Whylly

I the oldest person on this isle, male or female or what have you, white or black or anything. I left only a few times in my life, so I have seen all the changes and all the sameness for going on ninety-four years now, come November. You meet someone on this isle doesn't know Ole Mr. Vit? That person not from this isle, don't know his nose from his bum, says I. I outlive my two wives and one-third of my children. The other two-thirds make sure I taken care of. That's how we do on a small isle, everyone knows everyone. See in one another's windows a good and bad thing, *my great-gran used to say.*

I hear from my *elders what it was like just after emancipation. Can still say that word—*emancipation—*without creepy-crawling on someone's skin. Say its opposite, and people leave the room. Maybe even leave the isle. That's the way it is in a place like this. Every summer celebrate independence festival from the old Brit motherland with music and beer and such, but don't talk too much about what it all means. (Even some of the people younger than I am, many of you surely old enough to remember when we were all Brits, of some sort, even way long after emancipation. What a thing!) Talk maybe about what it used to be like when everyone kept pigs or when water started coming inside the houses, or maybe,* maybe, *some words your great-great-great-gran say, like: he know about* slavery time *or that was daughter of* Africa born. *But tread lightly in the isle of your mind.*

Don't get too far inland, you know, where it all overgrown and pain-
ful to dig out. Haulback get you every time.

So I going to say things go creepy-crawly on some people's skins.
If you one of those people can't take it, I invite you just take a walk,
come back for the next storyteller. But maybe, just maybe, you stay
and listen to Mr. Vit. 'Cause you want those resort staff to stay and
listen, thinks I, even if they have to and they holding badges against
the listening. You want they ears opened up. Can't get the mollusk
so's you can enjoy that fritter till the shell get opened up.

Miss Daphanie, Miss Patrice, Mr. Harper, Miss Minnie, Miss Ver-
nie, Mr. Q, Miss Philene, Mr. Kenneth, all you others not as old as me
but getting to be the elders on this isle, I sorry. I know your lips tight
for reasons. Ears, too. But now I speak.

Speak what it's like when the resort come, build on the Cruffey es-
tate. The estate. Inland. The ruins. The plantation—there, I'll say
it—we've all not talked about to our children or nieces or nephews
or neighbor children. But that's what it is: the plantation. What we
mean is the place where the people almost every one of us was born
from was enslaved before emancipation.

We all practical minded here. Got to be when life about making
do, scrounging 'cause the soil won't grow no more, taking care of old
ones and young ones. See clearly why the government opens up so
much for foreign companies, wants to welcome tourism. Seems like
the only thing we have that people will pay for is warm land, beauty
in the views. Yes, we do have that. We have more, yes, but I mean
what from-afar people think they come here for and willing to pay
more money than any of us on this isle ever see in a life—even a life
long as mine.

So no doomsday talk from me when the resort coming. Seen it be-
fore, sometimes companies come and go. Sometimes say they going
to build, instead tear up and run away. All kinds of things. We lived
through it. Not all good, not all bad, but that's what we do. I never get
to ninety-four years next November without being a forgiving man.
No, can't be here this long without that.

I forgive three things:

One, you say you hire all people of this isle for all of your wait-ressing jobs and security and front desk jobs. Strike a tax deal with government saying that. Then make them all maids in silly costumes and maintenance working to the bone and fly in your own people from elsewhere to do those other jobs pay more and talk to customers. We know why, none of them dark at all. Say you worried about staff speaking "perfect English" for tourists' sake. But this isle a former British colony and certainly speaking English for the ninety-four years I been on it, so: two, I forgive ignorance. And that related to three. That nonsense you think you can change names, let alone the time of the earth. Don't matter to me you think that. What is is.

Here what I worried about for you. Here what I having trouble for-give. Here what makes no sense to me, old wise man as I am, lying in bed at night worryin' it in my ole mind. Showing up here, clear you know what you looking at, what land you claim: slave plantation. That's what isle is ever since Columbus wash up here, kill or work them out of being and set the way for hundreds of years of slave ships. Slavery time until too, too recent history. Lot of trouble to bring all them people all that way to this little dot on a crease in the map — sprinkle of dots we call our country. Isle be so small and plantation be so big only one on this whole isle, that why so many of us got the same name, the name of the owner. Owner of the plantation. (No one owns people, says I, no matter what they say.) Not lucrative, you know, since they just kept ruining the soil worse than it already was, whoever wash up here. Couldn't make a good buck or even handful of coins after a while. Owner and family gone to capital long before emancipation, and folks already set up here got a little land and then finally, when couldn't take no more of their own memory, descend to outskirts of island, brave more storms, the almighty ocean, in ex-change for a road to get to one another easy now, and letting all that memory get all covered over.

So why I can't forgive you when no one want to look anyway? Why I can't forgive you when no one using that land, no one even want it? Here is number one of no forgiveness. Whole list: one thing, says Ole Vit.

Only part of plantation left in a way you could see what it is, not just piles of rocks and such, is the Big House. Two stories, some walls standing as you know. Plantation set up with owner's house next to whipping post. You got land deeds tell you what that whipping post is? Ground around it full of nicest plants and flowers on the isle. Fertilized by blood. Best view on the isle, that post, so everyone could see who being made example of, thinks I. Made that post your lookout point, your lovers' lane, your Columbus storytelling gobbledygook, your spot for happy people to go get happier and sad people to go get minds full of beauty and peacefulness and feeling like they on top of the whole damn-and-heaven world. Not everything is to be walked on, even with shoes willing to pay.

Here's what I do day I hear what's been done. Heard what's been done with my own ears from so many people not usually willing to even mention thing like post—that I know it must be true! Painful for them to tell me, like the words glass shards in their mouths. Here's what I do. I tell my granddaughter Serena who with me that day, little as she was, take me over to the cemetery where my ma and pa and their ma and pa and their ma and pa buried. And we just sit there all day long till the sun go down, her picking up trash blow up from somewhere, put it in her purse to dump at landfill later. While I just sit. Feel older that day. Feel like maybe I won't make it to the next birthday. Feel like maybe my granddaughter should go far 'cross world to somewhere else, find someplace in this wide, wide world where whipping post don't make people fall in love.

Chapter Seven

T he room they put me in was not Claudia's office, with its yellow slips and windows facing the pool deck. The room they
put me in was a collection of counters spread out from a center
chair, where one of the security guards who searched our bags at
the end of the workday sat. His face slack with disinterest, pep-
pery with stubble. The room they put me in was a room I didn't
even know existed, without a single window but with a grid of
screens showing what was happening: by the gate, by the snack
bar, by the pool, in the lobby, by the trucks behind the fence, in
the main hallway, in the dining room, in the kitchen, at the boat
dock. The images played continuously in their boxes, black-and-
white stories stacked on one another, but the sound filling the
space kept switching among locations, like when Lionel drove me
crazy with his hand never leaving the radio dial in his truck. The
guard looked at his watch, glanced from Claudia to me, and left
the room. Claudia pointed to the chair, and I sat. Then she and
Max stepped outside. I could hear sounds of at least one of them
staying just outside the door.

The guard appeared again, this time on the screen that showed
the front gate. I saw the other maids lining up to check out, but I
heard the pocking of the pool deck music, then the low din of the
lobby setting up for happy hour. As I sat there waiting, three dif-

ferent AYS came in, none of whom really looked at me in the metal chair. The room was small enough that no one could go about their business without coming so close their calves brushed mine or their smell got caught by my nose or their hips chucked my chair an inch this way, an inch that way. When Matt, from the road the other night, came in and brushed by me, elbow near cheek, I turned away. Curled into my apron some.

A poster against the wall in the corner. Pictures of all the maids and maintenance staff gridded like the screens but the pictures not moving a fly wing's twitch. Not pictures we smiled for. Frozen images—must have been from the security cameras while we worked. Didn't recognize myself with my chin tucked toward my shoulder; and there was Hebbie with her hair on fire in the light; Christine with her cheekbones like a baby's balled-up hands. Christine.

This was the room I'd heard about. The mug shot room. Now the firing room.

Saw Lem on the screen by the trucks. Claudia there, too, along with an AYS who worked the lobby and gift shop. Happy hour sounds all around me. Was she just going through the clipboard of the night's garbage duty with him? Did they know he knew where I'd gone and hadn't gone? That he'd, in their view, signed off? Had he been trying to talk to that gift-shop AYS about the nanny and the Manions' boy because I'd asked him to? When the sound finally switched to the truck area, Lem was there alone. Walked offscreen. Just the sound of him opening and closing a door. The *beep*-pause-*beep*-pause of a truck backing up.

Even in black and white, the ravaged pool deck was mesmerizing to me, like watching a storm from inside. Its emptiness. Yet it was littered with signs of the banquet's destruction. There were plastic cones by the steps to the pool: single caution of all the resort's hazards.

The security camera, wherever they'd nested it, was perched high enough to show that the pool itself had been emptied, and an assortment of AYS were in various positions inside: all fours to standing erect, like a diagram of evolution. The bottom of the pool was a mix of scabs scraped clear to cement and sections of the reef mural still there, looking sickly. The background's startling electric blue just another gray on the screen.

Claudia and Max came back in. Claudia held the book, Max held a file. He began unloading its papers.

I turned back to Claudia when I heard a *thwap*: she'd let the book drop to the metal counter against the wall. She yanked the cover open, slumped over it. Right foot scratching her left calf. With the tourists she was ethereal, like they could pass through her to go wherever they were going. With us, carrying with her all of her duties at once, all of her family's needs, all the stuff of sickness and tiredness and demands coming down from management. All the weight of dealing with an islander walking across her island.

She ran her finger around the bookplate that I knew said *MAN-ION COTTAGE CONSIGNMENT ~ TEHAWKEE BAY, WIS-CONSIN.*

"Shit," she said.

She flipped through quickly, doubling back here and there. Watching her uncareful fingers touching, I wanted to reach out for the book. Hugged my arms in tight. A stone on a chair.

Claudia looked up at me. Took me in, as though I were bigger after absorbing all the garbage she'd charged me with since our last doomsday meeting. But this book wasn't pennies, and she'd found me trespassing. And now she knew where I'd gotten the book, if it hadn't already been reported missing. Stolen.

Eye of the Arrival Manager, of the House builder, scriptwriter, of the smoother of diamonds, stealer of ships. I couldn't tell if she knew what she was looking at, if she was figuring out what danger had been unleashed. By me.

If they'd just come minutes later, maybe I would've been down in the water, tangle of limbs nobody's problem anymore.

Max's voice just before they had come upon me: "You're getting new mugs for the coffee station in the lobby, right? So smash the old ones, we'll put the shards here, clear that landscaping out over there where there's that flattish space behind the House, just throw dirt on top. They'd just need gloves. Or it could be a kid thing, like a sandbox with plastic shovels. We'll just put the shards in that old sandbox we used to have on the edge of the pool deck. 'Native Tribe Archaeological Dig!' Or something." He spread his hands out in front of him like a banner.

He hadn't seen me yet. Claudia looked straight at me. When Max realized Claudia wasn't answering him, he turned toward me. Columbus hat on his head like a stranded bird.

"You were not here. You were never here," he'd said, when his thumb and forefinger were squeezing around my shoulder, heading down the path.

"Proceed with caution, ladies and gentlemen, boys and girls," I'd repeated to him as he hustled me along. *"No falling. No falling in love."*

"Shit," Claudia said again now, and looked steady now, book dangling by the small clutch of pages between her thumb and pinkie. Letting the rest of the book flop toward the ground. I could see the twitch of her pupil, deciding.

The center pages. Felt as though the stitching holding it all together thinned fragile as eyelashes.

"Tear these out."

"What? But I—"

"Tear these out."

I took the book from her, the cover gently atop my palms, and put it across my lap. I took each page by itself. Each leaf of the maps. Tore as carefully as I could, all the way to the binding so I wouldn't split any of the printing. Line of severing trembly as my hands. My hyphen hands. She reached in my lap and flipped some of the pages over. Turned around and mumbled something to Max. *Blueprints?* Turned back to me.

"That, too," she said. The *Wh. Post* page.

Had I heard correctly: *Blueprints?* Or did I just want to hear that: a plan, some other paper I might find to piece things together. But: *their* plan. Word like a slow tear in my stomach. Slave boy's etched ship sanded right off the side of the master's house.

Resort might not be a stumbling, ignorant storm over the ruins after all. After all, might be an architect.

When I was done she took the carcass of the book back from me and tossed it toward the floor into a box with *Guest Lost/Found* in green marker on its side. Sticking out, askew. Missing its pages that told me where to go. Claudia tucked those torn-out pages in her armpit.

She was gone only a couple of minutes, but Max stayed, fiddling his boat hat and barely noticing me. Babysitter Columbus. My eyes on that box. My body glued to the chair. She came back without those pages and with new ones.

My employee ID said nothing but *Maid*, but my firing papers for trespassing had my full name, stretched way out: *Myrna Daphanie Cruffey Burre*. My middle two names: Mother's first name and born-to last name. Her whole name broke my go-by name in two.

They debated whether they could take my uniform back, but what would they have me walk out in? I pressed my back against the chair until I could feel the bundle of my zipper still in its place.

"Sit here," she said, as if I hadn't been. "A guard has to take you out or you're trespassing again, but as a nonemployee; jail time would be possible, so you want to wait. So wait for him to be done checking everyone out and to come back for you." The happy hour music came streaming in from the security video bay, almost comical behind her pinched face.

She and Max spoke low to each other, and Claudia pointed at my feet. Thought she was going to say something about the bleach dots, pinkish brown now. "We don't want you walking around representing the logo. Give us the shoes."

Max rattled the carton in the corner of the room, and the book disappeared from my view. He reached in and tossed two mismatched flip-flops at my feet. Told me again to stay still, wait for the guard. The door clicked multiple times from the other side.

I stared at the box, but I was afraid to get up. Stayed in front of those screens. Silence from an empty hallway, then the chatter and phones at the front desk, then the sound of a truck shutting off, then the clinking of the setup for dinner, then the tinny bobbing of the music on the pool deck and the clacking on of the nighttime pool lights, though the sun was still up. An unfamiliar whirring over that music I was so used to: sanders inside the empty pool. Then a silence, then the cranky squeak of the opening and shutting of the gate. The voice of the guard calling for the line at the gate to tidy itself up. Then silence. Then voices in a noisy kitchen, indecipherable. Then the pool deck music again, the sound of spinning blades against concrete.

It took me a moment to realize the woman on the screen was Jasmine Manion, in her painting clothes again with that left-behind cloth bag over her shoulder. Almost felt like ducking, as though she could see me, the thief, the way I could see her. Was she looking right into the camera?

She and her son were passing a paintbrush back and forth between them as he kept loosening her fingers from around the wooden handle and waving it through the air like a conductor, and she kept grabbing it back. Then I could see he was swinging against her hip, then over to a broken lounger. She looked harried. (Nanny running around with Lionel again, maybe.)

"Hey you!" The voice echoed strangely from the depths of the empty pool. Or maybe everything I was hearing and seeing warped as it traveled into the cave of this room.

The AYS who'd called out climbed from the pool, tall and sweatless. He looked back down to address the others, pointing his long arm at Jasmine Manion. "That's the lady we're waiting for. The painter."

And then to her: "Come on, come on."

Tried to mind-see the renovation chore list on the clipboard which of us was supposed to help paint. Me? Then the sound in the room took on a new interval: the crunching of gravel as those who parked by the snack shacks left for the day.

Jasmine Manion swatted his hand away, annoyed. I could see her lips shaping *no*.

The AYS put his hand on her back, nudging her toward the pool. Lips moving as he nudged. The sound switched again, what I was hearing matching what I was watching.

"Here. Come on. You're already late."

"No. *No.* Curtis," she said, reading his name off his shirt, I guessed. "I'm not—I'm a guest."

"We need to get this going," another of the AYS yelled from within the concrete grave.

Another one of their voices grumbling: "These people. Always late."

"Let's go," Curtis said, his hand still on Mrs. Manion's back.

From the pool: "We can't keep waiting for these freaking people to show up for work. And then not even get to work."

Sound switched again. The gate. Hebbie leaving, then Della. I heard them say their names and the contents of their purses. I hadn't seen Christine all day and didn't see her now. The voice I heard was Miss Philene's: "Philene Cruffey. Nothing to report."

Jasmine Manion was looking more frantic as the AYS had walked her right up to the edge. Her son dashed nervously between his mother's back and the lounger. I felt weak and floppy. Vision sparkly with not eating or drinking all day, with everything I was seeing. But I kept my zipper against the chair and my eyes on the screen.

I heard the music for happy hour get louder: the shuffle of guests gathering on the screen in the top right corner, their outsized bodies looming behind them on the refracting glass doors of the lobby.

I could see by her waving arms that Jasmine Manion was outright yelling, and the little boy's body tensed up at the sight of his mother pulling toward him but being pulled away from him.

The sound changed to chatting and music, and my eyes moved briefly to the lobby screen. The cyclist with the mop hair. The woman in the giant hat. All just standing there looking at nothing, as if their eyes had glazed over. Jasmine Manion's husband: palm upward, stem of a wineglass growing down through his fingers. Eyes blanked out by his sunglasses, and he seemed impossibly still, surveying his own feet. So still I wondered if the screen had frozen, but the sounds continued.

"*Al—*"

"*—vin!*" I heard one part of his name come from the lobby, the next part when the sound switched to the pool deck.

Then he was on the deck. Right before they pulled her in, and her calling stopped, but the music played, and the sound switched to the boat arrival area on the beach, silent now except for the wind.

Bench Story No. 13: Mr. Ken Cruffey

*In our typical life on this island, I interact with most of you at night.
Folks can wax on about the night coming down like a blanket to cover,
to collect. But I say darkness can shatter. I see it all around me: faces
across my bar a jumble of pieces just barely held together by skin, that
bag growing looser every day. I see those capillaries beneath coming
out sometimes—fissures spreading, warning us. Can't see them in
everybody's skin, can't see them unless we're sitting too close, but
I wait for the shattering nonetheless. Yes, can see it all around me:
how darkness shattered Philene and me—who knew marriage was the
weakest glue? And the falling apart in the middle of the island shows
us all of it.*

*The joke around the island is always that Ken wants ten: convince
anyone to spend ten dollars on three beers instead of four one at a
time. What no one knows is the darkness brewing behind that joke.
Not a joke at all. Not about the money, not really. The bar mostly
keeps me going all right no matter what an individual buys or doesn't
buy one night or the next. Steadier than most around here, anyway.
But I can't keep myself from wanting that little overflow—not of
money; that overflow of emotion. That moment when the beer gets to
the high-tide level and opens your mouth for the flow to come out. I
want to hear stories, if you didn't know that about me. Not looking for
a party as a bartender, not for the laughing and dancing that comes*

along to shake the place sometimes. Not looking for tourists coming in showing off what they'd let the sun do to them. Not even looking for the warmth of the men who come stand on the porch night after night just to talk and talk. I'm really looking for the darkness to come out of a crack, so it doesn't fill up and shatter the whole. A little bit more beer makes it more possible.

Beer even makes it easier to slur the words. Let your tongue soften into it—sllll...—and see where to go from there. If even one time anyone—one of you—had said the word, had let slavery's sl whisper against the roof of your mouth and let your lips push the ver out toward me before the y settled back into your face: I could've talked about losing my own Jimmy. Fifteen years now of waiting for that.

I didn't take on the bar looking for that. The place just came to me after Mr. Gerard's Broken Oar Bar had gotten beaten up by and closed after That Storm. But then something changed.

Fifteen years ago now? My Lord, Philene, can it be fifteen years? But I don't need to ask. I know it. Has been and so it can be.

That night I breathed in and out, in and out, rocked back and forth on my feet—fighting myself to take the first step into the brush. We were going looking for a boy wandering, my boy who never came home the previous night. Never dreamed something'd be bad enough to warrant stepping into that brush. But there I was, first step in. And I came home out of that brush with a lost son, with a body.

Two people were with me that night: Mr. Vitman and Minister Callaghan—covering his tracks, his bloody, bloody tracks. Though when we found him, found his body—I mean, Jimmy'd wandered so far from where the minister first unleashed his rage—trying to find his way out, we must assume—so the minister couldn't have led us to my son even if he'd been willing to own up to what he'd done.

Maybe some won't believe I'd never set eyes on a stone from the estate before that night. But it's true—as true as it is that these stones under me now are those stones. I'd never set foot inland as a boy or man. As far as I knew, no one had. As far as I knew, the whole place was a fog of fused nightmares, a place you couldn't see *for the darkness of it, and that was what I thought even before that night. Monster movies and murder movies and Grimms' fairy tales and the muckiest parts of your awful mind all melted together. A circle of the underworld. All the circles of the underworld. All the tip-tops of all the most threatening mountains in all the legends of all the cultures of the world, where the combined sums of our fears and our hurts have packed into shapes we call the bodies of goblins and evil wizards. A place where you found the name we invented called* monster.

But I understood differently, when we found my boy and carried him out: what it meant for those stones to contain blood. What it meant when you could see *darkness because darkness meant something else when it wasn't just a concept made up in the crevices of your own brain. Made-up monsters not the thing to fear.*

I became a man whose child was dead. I became a split-up man. I became a man with a bar who comes to work each day, each night, hoping someone would leak and tell me something terrible. That they'd relieve the pressure inside their own heads in a way that would teach me how to do it for myself.

Haulback get you every time.

Yes, sir, Mr. Vit. Yes, sir.

Got to relieve that pressure, else you turn like the minister. Explode from not being able to explain to a child why he had *to flee that demon place. Get so you choose blood over telling.*

So it has taken the stones, someone bringing down these stones, to make the leaks happen. Like taking plugs out of a dike across the world. I don't know how they did it either, whoever did this. *And I know what it takes to bring something broken and precious down from the inland. I'm speaking about my boy but about all of us, too. We know what it takes.*

The sign outside my bar says Thiflae Bar: Something Sweet. *And anyone who's asked me why I chose that name instead of sticking with the Broken Oar has got pretty much the same answer:* a thiflae flower is something sweet. *But that explanation isn't the true one. I chose thiflae because it's tiny and red. I chose thiflae because, if you walk into the brush, it's most likely the only dot of red you'll see among the green and brown and gray. I chose thiflae because that's what it was like when we finally figured out how to get Jimmy—Jimmy's body—down to the road: leaving behind the teeniest splatters of red dots on the stones. All we left behind.*

Stones I hadn't touched since that day, until today.

That same night my son's body was found, which was the night after he died, I became the funereal director on this island. Minister Callaghan himself and Ole Mr. Vit himself both agreed, after consulting Mr. Horace, who was also on the committee, and they passed it on to me. Mr. Vit was getting too old, they said; he was ready to retire from that particular part of his life on this island.

At the time I thought such a thing went right along with the death of your child: the darkest-struck person on the island doing the darkest things for all of us. But they'd had an entirely different conversation about asking me then. Later I knew they figured I'd be the last one on this island or on earth to want to talk about or throw my eyes or my voice toward the inland and those stones with their pinpoint dots of red, literal and otherwise. This was how it went, one generation to the next. Determining the person whose mouth would be reliably gummed up with their own hurting. To keep the unspeakable unspoken. Callaghan had his own reasons for everything he did, of course, and we knew some of those soon enough, God help him. But Ole Mr. Vit and Mr. Horace and whichever other elders they consulted—making the decision of who would keep death and all its darkness to himself, even in the moments of his own heart's deepest fissuring, especially then—they chose me.

Around here we could talk about plenty of historical and geological reasons we use limestone in our burials. Whatever else, it dissolves. Bodies. Even bones and teeth. We could reuse graves every decade if we wanted. It disappears them for us. I knew that putting my son to rest. I didn't know another choice.

Some days I was surprised the funeral committee didn't head inland with that limestone, try it out on the ruins. On the spot my boy was found. On all the red.

And to this day I've been their helper with the dissolution. The kind of bodies that might not even come back to the island, but we pretend to bury them anyway. The kinds of death stories no one tells.

And then I sit at the bar waiting for a leak that hasn't come. Until today on these stones.

Chapter Eight

B y the time I'd walked home, the rubber wishbones of the flip-flops had carved bloody slits between my toes. I should be bloody, after two nights in a row running or walking away from bloody someones. I limped right by Mother on the couch. I put the firing papers down on my bed. The tattered edge of my uniform curled with the wetness falling on it. The blanket was wet where my hands pressed into it. My voice was the soggy sound I hated: getting all low and high at the same time, thin and then thick again with crying. Throat flapping open and closed. I kept talking it over and over, rushing, so I'd be ready with a speech when Mother came to bed.

What I wouldn't tell her: blood on my feet, bruises on my arm where their fingers had been, nothing compared to the last two nights on the road and the pool deck and my running away. I couldn't tell her why.

What I had to tell her:

Mother, I've been fired.

I'm sorry, Mother. I'm so sorry. I'll figure something out. I'll beg Miss Patrice to take me on. I'll ask Mr. Ken if he'll pay me to clean the bar after closing. With Serena most likely going off to study in the States, he'll need someone. Christine needs someone to watch little Jamal some, now that she's working more nights, and maybe sometimes she'd be able to pay. Maybe—if she's willing to speak to me at all. I'm sorry. I'm so sorry. Lionel will help us. Bayard, Uncle Q. Uncle Q's always saying we could move in his place if we need. If we need anything. He's always saying that: anything, anything at all.

Sorry, sorry, sorry. I know that's not what you want, but...

I know it seems like too much to recover from, too much to bear. But I will take over all the moneymaking ways you do all day, and maybe they will hire you to work in the laundry or in the kitchen. Or, or, or, or...

I just couldn't help it, just needed to go up there and see. *You know how Dad would say:* Seek out the source. *I was being so careful, went up there so many times without anyone ever knowing. Not even you. For over a year about. And then all of a sudden they came across me, up on the estate, my manager, and there was nothing I could do. She had it in for me for some other things they— It doesn't matter, I guess, they caught me up there inland. "Trespassing." And they might say "stealing," but that's not how it sounds—that's not—that's a different story. Stories.*

They fired me, but I will figure out something. There must be something, some way to...

I will write to everyone I know in the capital if I need to and find work there. And if I have to go I promise once I'm there to—just so you know that—

I was still practicing when I heard a shuffling in the hall outside the bedroom door. Not a shuffling of a body coming down the hall but a shuffling of a body that'd been standing there and couldn't take any more standing and listening. The door opened slowly. The papers rose.

Mother looked at me a spell that wasn't long or short. Eyes cold brown in the low light. I stayed put: perched on the edge of the bed with my feet dangling like a child's. Then she stepped farther in, pointed me out of the room, and closed the door behind me. With all the doors closed to it, the hallway sat dark as midnight.

Mother and I had not always shared a room. Before Dad died, even when he was away from the island, I slept on the loveseat in the living room. Troy had a room made up in what was meant to be a closet at the end of the hall. I felt along the walls to make my way to it now. I opened the door and sat down on the bed. The room was big enough only for a cot and a nightstand made out of a crate on its side. Inside the crate a clutch of art supplies Lionel had fished for him out of the dump. We used to sit together at the table, Troy teaching me how to draw the shadows in so my pictures wouldn't look like they were floating in nowhere. (So exacting, my brother's fingers around brushes and pencils! Opposite his too-tight hold on the machete, his useless perpendicular hack that left the patch behind the house unchanged and him panting. The death grip, the wrong angle: getting him—us—nowhere.) Mother had left this room exactly the way it was when Troy first left. The only thing that had changed was that sometimes we came in to get a candle from his pile, taking them one by one as we needed them. I lay on my side on the cot, then at some point, still far from morning, I jiggled the key four times without letting it rattle before turning it all the way; slowly, silently turned it back just a tick; pulled the doorknob just so to make the key uncatch; skipped the broken step that would make its twitching sound underfoot.

So many stars out the sky looked dusty. Looked like the sea dried to a crust of its own salt. Looked littered with lint tufted almost imperceptibly into the reaching arms of the Milky Way, pointing us elsewhere. So many stars out the sky looked spangled with broken glass, like pieces of what had been a life.

And then the lights came to make it all look smoky, impossible to see. Constellations blurred to nonsense. Wind all around, but not real wind. Batty, swooping sounds from above sounding like war. And I knew it was the emergency airlift, finally, for Jasmine Manion, B3, the American woman with the white husband. Off to the capital in a helicopter. In whatever shape she was in.

I felt all the dirt that my hands had picked up as I climbed up a trail that I was making as I used it. And I felt all the places I had touched with my hands, streaking dirt wherever I touched: myself or stones or anything. Kept grubbing through the brambles for stones—stones the ghosts had quarried from the clay earth—like how I'd seen Dad coax out stubborn wisdom teeth (slowly, only sign of force the veins leaping from his arm).

No one was with me, but if someone were, we wouldn't speak. I pictured various people walking with me, helping me lift: Lionel or Bayard or Miss Philene or even Lem. By now they'd all heard—must have—about the American woman and the airlift. And heard, too, about me getting fired for trespassing inland. Maybe they thought I was just escaping the banquet ruckus going up there; maybe they'd figured me out with my maps and secret trails and haulback-ravaged skin. Maybe no one was even talking about it, because it would make them talk about the inland, the post, these stones in my arms.

I let my mind go looser and imagined Troy, Dad, or Mother as the one helping me carry the stones. We would not speak, but we would catch the whites of each other's eyes in the dark so we could coordinate our steps, walk smoothly, one of us forward and one of us backward.

Just me, I found ways, after many tries, to be more efficient than I'd been just carrying one stone at a time pressed against my belly.

The wind got harsher, and my eyes adjusted to the settled blackness of the night. I didn't know why I still had on my uniform, but now it wasn't a uniform. Just something on my body that took on streaks of maroon from my skin, rubbed-in dirt, yellowing sweat, scars in its fabric that told where I'd been. I took off the apron, bundled it like a sack I could swing over my shoulder. Even with only three stones in the bundle, all that would fit, I couldn't walk without a stripe of pain from my ears down either way on my neck. And then the apron tore, spilling stones on my back and my stripped feet. Their shapes that were neither square nor round; their rough edges that were neither all smooth or all knife blade. I told myself over and over that there was no hurting, no tired, no too-heavy for me.

By morning I could see crosshatching etched in the palms of my hands, written over my lifelines. By morning I could see the mosaic of the gravel in my legs and knees. Hadn't even realized—between the darkness and the wind and the struggle to get it all done before the first light—hadn't even realized I'd started crawling.

Uncle Q had sent a note that he'd come by later to see about everything he'd heard. *See about*: I knew what he meant, that he expected we'd move in with him. Lose our house since I'd lost my job. More lines on the list of lost things. His writing showed the shakiness of the hand that had inscribed it. The note itself looked so fragile: his own brittleness seeped into the paper, as if it'd washed up on Junkful Beach from another time. Reminded me of how Uncle Q himself looked these days, like a walking stick carved out of an old, old branch. He and Mother like two old pieces of furniture I had to worry I might break but had to sit on just the same.

See about: the phrase Mother's generation always used when they definitely wouldn't *talk* about. Mother pretended she hadn't seen his note, gestured for me to get ready to go with her to search for shells. Didn't see the mess I was, head to toe. Or didn't look.

We stepped outside into the light. Rattled the key four times before turning it all the way to lock the door; turned it back just a tick; pulled the doorknob just so to make the key uncatch; skipped the broken step. But instead of heading to her first stretch of beach, I took Mother by the hand, and we began the walk toward the resort's gate. The long way there she walked with me. Didn't try to pull me in a different direction or gesture to ask where we were going. Maybe at first she thought I'd come up with a plan, something more than selling flowers by the snack bar.

I didn't look at Mother as we walked, but I spoke and spoke and spoke, her quiet thickening my own voice. Almost everything bobbed up from my throat: the inland, the book, the map, the whipping post. I knew she wouldn't say a word in response, but

I didn't know whether she might turn away from me, walk in the clear other direction. Say no to listening as well as speaking. Hail a passing car to pick her up so she could slip the bogeyman that had burrowed in her daughter's stomach and was now coming out her daughter's mouth.

Didn't tell her Andre was back on the island. Did tell her what had happened to the American woman at the resort. She held up her fingers: *One or two or three?* I wrapped my hand around hers so that three fingers had to stay up.

Anyone we passed on our way kept his or her distance. Gave us a half-wave but didn't stop to talk, ask after Mother through me. Wasn't the firing. They knew I'd been tainted by the inland. Could see it in the turn away of their shoulders, the seal of all their lips. Maybe they saw my mouth moving and didn't want to risk hearing anything I might say about what I'd seen and touched. Mother didn't try to go toward them.

Unlike the stones I'd taken from the inland, the bench I'd made from them was not on resort-owned property. Near the gate, near the gravelly snack bar and parking area, but technically just on the side of the road. In the same spot where Mother would sell her flowers. *Tourists: Buy Native Island Wildflowers for 50 cents a bunch. U.S. coins and other OK.* I swished my foot in the dust as if to rub out her words written down for tourists and not for me. I looked at my own feet: barely strung-on sandals that didn't belong to me.

We both stood in front of the bench. I told her about the book's description of the enslaved sitting on a pile of rocks, telling. But Master Cruffey didn't write down what they'd told.

"Mother," I said. "Sit."

She wasn't used to me telling her to do something. I think I surprised her so much that she went right ahead and sat down on the stones without waving me away. She and the stones shifted just so, then found a staying place. I stood close, tall over her, her deep, pond-like eyes looking up at me, waiting for what I was going to say.

It was Mother's long green skirt, and it was Dad's white shirt she liked to wear in the sun. But I'd never seen my mother sitting on a bench by the side of the road.

"Go on," I said. The word beneath my skin somehow crawled up into my mouth, pushed out from under my tongue, until there it was. "Tell."

The word lassoed her head and made her nod. Her own feet shushed through the sand, one against the other. Crabs scuttled out from under the stones, feeling her weight, my voice, our waiting for her movement. Still she looked up at me, and I looked down. Expression hardening to how it always was.

The wind dusted up the ground, blocking my view of my own feet. The wind brought the linen scent of her as she walked away. By mid-day Mother had not come back, but I was not standing alone by the bench of stones.

When Claudia heard I was out by the gate, and that there was something afoot out there, she sent some staff—as security, it seemed. The resort was already partly shut down with the airlift and all, and they made it known this was a temporary wall of staffers while they waited for international management to arrive. With what and for what, we couldn't know and wouldn't be told. They stood at intervals of about three feet. They slumped in their positions with a strange mix of resignation and resolve. Before I might've been looking out for them to be more threatening, but I guessed they knew with everything that'd happened, we'd all be looking out for that. Standing there, I noticed for the first time that day that someone had scratched *Cruffey* into the sun of the insignia on the gate, right in between *Furnace* and *Island.* It was hard to read. Not its own color but chewed out of the sun's yellow paint. The way the *y* had a little loopy tail, looked like Lem's handwriting. The way he used to write the *y* in my name. The island *y*. The sneer.

I'd been standing around long enough to have complaining feet, crusted with dried blood; the staff people Claudia had sent just standing around, too, not knowing what we should do with one

another—and then something else happened. About half of everyone I knew on this island, probably more, started showing up in
the gravelly space outside the gate. No matter the sun was at its
highest standing of the day. The story of what happened to the
American woman at the resort had spread among the maids and
the garbage crew and all around the oval, and seemed worse, I
guessed, after the banquet. I hadn't even known everything that'd
happened. All around me the maids were almost as scratched up
as I was. Christine in particular: usually standing so tall and yak-
king away, now all ducking behind her sunglasses.

"Didn't even go to work today," I heard Hebbie say, bewildered
without her uniform.

Young and old and in-between: so many were there. The elders
who'd been strong and silent all my life. Even Mr. Harper in his
wheelchair and Ole Mr. Vit, the eldest on the island. Even Miss
Patrice, with the store supposed to be open this time of day. (Hand
still to her cheek after all these days since Mother mutely named
her pain.) Even that Wayida Callaghan, owlish behind her glasses,
so rarely, rarely seen outside her own church. Miss Minnie and
Miss Vernie and Miss Philene and Mr. Ken and Bayard—Bayard
always so busy, strange to see him standing still. And he wasn't
teaching at the school if he was standing here, holding Manny's
and Gussie's hands.

Eventually even Uncle Q was there, holding the arm of his sister: my mother. I could tell he'd brought her, not the other way
around.

Even some kids. Bayard's two, but also Angelina—Lem's baby
sister, Miss Minnie's grandbaby—who never missed a day of
school. Some of the teenagers, Nelson and Serena and some others, hanging by their parents' or grans' sides for a change more
than by one another.

Almost all the maids, who were supposed to be at work at the
resort: all stepping toward the bench. Lem was there; Lem, who
might never speak to me again, and I wouldn't blame him. Might
never know if he was the one scratched that sign. I had no idea

what he thought about anything that'd gone on at the resort, after all. Too busy roping him into everything that got me fired, without a word about it between us.

Even Lionel. Wondered if he'd tried to pick me up for another landfill run that morning, what the guys behind the fence had told him—about me or about Jasmine Manion.

And even Andre. He was standing around the corner where maybe he thought neither Mother nor I could see him or catch the scent of Troy's cologne. Made the blankness of my father and brother more solid in the air.

Everyone standing around, looking like the whole wide archipelago—our outer islands and foreign countries spit farther around us, too—huddling in just a little closer to one another. We all stared at the bench found in the stones. Maybe we were all expecting the security line to make them scatter again, float away like they hadn't shown up for the bench, for *something*. Or make us scatter. But security was still as trees. Looking a little nervous, though. Trees, but trees in wind that was picking up.

When I'd first started going inland, everyone had started to seem like ghosts of glass, treading the earth with iron feet. The past the iron. Now they all grew solid in front of me. Glass burnished by the sun. I stepped closer to the folks nearer my age. Andre still keeping his distance—and Hebbie closer to him—so I could breathe in that crowd, didn't have to worry his voice could reach me from where he was planted. Or worry that he'd approach Mother and make it all worse.

Then the older folks started hunching together a little bit. Mother on the edge of this oval of elders. Their mouths near one another's ears, their chins nodding just the tiniest bit. All mouths that at one time or another had held Dad's hands. Been healed by him so they could talk another day. The rest of us waited, silently, for the elders.

Miss Minnie stepped out of the crowd. She approached us and gently removed Christine's sunglasses. Christine had a black eye like purple marker scribbled under her left eye. No one seemed surprised but me. On her cheekbone I could see half the resort's sunset logo, backward, in a searing maroon. Heard myself gasp. Miss Minnie slid her hand gently along the side of Christine's face, keeping away from the bruising. Seemed too late now to *see* about.

Miss Minnie said she didn't know where this pile of stones came from, maybe they gathered themselves of their own free will, and I didn't say anything. But maybe it was time, she said.

"Yes, it's time," she said, looking first back at the huddle of elders and then at the rest of us and then at the line of resort staff alongside. Talking to us all, in our turn. "No use pretending we don't see these stones or where they came from."

Then she walked out in front of all of us, eyes on the staff staring us down. And she sat. Just like in the silent pictures that had played through my head of Warrant, Betta, Joon, Mort, Tildy on their bench. But not silent anymore. Because then Miss Minnie told us the first story.

Bench Story No. 1: Miss Minnie Eldon

Times come round when you have to sit and to speak, whether you want to or not. Who would've known today—a typical sunny January day—would be one of those rare times to do so? But seems to be.

I tell you this—all of you close enough to hear my voice, no matter you my people or people come to this island to work at the resort. I tell you this: I am nearing eighty-two years old, and I never would have thought I'd be able to say the same thing about this island that my mother and father said about it and my grandmother and grandfather said about it. We are in one of very few countries in the Caribbean, in this our little pocket of the world—our island and the capital and the handful of other outer islands in our little country afloat in the sea—that the U.S. never came in to occupy for any reason. Never sent military to. My grandparents would never have believed we'd stretch our luck this far! Just keep stretching it like the last hunk of taffy in a child's hands! Sometimes sitting by the shore, waiting to sell at the Straw Market, I hear all the fore-parents' unbelieving laughter in the sound of the water looping over the rocks. Used to talk about it being so with my late husband, more times than you'd believe we could talk one thing. Couldn't stop my tongue even with kids around—Daphanie and Horace's Troy doing odd jobs for me around the house when he was that young and skinny boy, big smile but most days inside a cloud of sad. My husband would hush me not to talk about such things around such young ones, but I was just so incredulous. Couldn't help but keep asking him, You believe it? Still?

And so you wonder, back when the resort was built, when an American company came down to poke around and not tell anyone what they were thinking of doing—you wonder why we got a little itch in our eye to examine closely what you were doing, and you have to understand this itch, and you have to understand why when you take our kids' bags at the gate after a day's work and say you're making sure they haven't stolen anything, we look right back at you and wonder what your hands are really doing inside there. You wonder why we surprised and not surprised when a girl comes home from work with bruises or scrapes.

You wonder why we keep tight locks on the stories of our own isle, inland, town—wherever you or your guests come round.

But coming home with something like a brand*—like what Christine has here from that damned captain's ring—well now, that is just too much.*

That is all. That is all I am going to tell you, even though I am an old woman who has seen a lot, a whole lot in my time, and I could tell you things that you will never see on your own. But that is all I am going to say. Going to not *speak more because still up to me whether to do so or not. Patrice, we know you've got plenty to tell about this here resort. But even if you want to keep quieter like me, can you come help an old woman stand back up after sitting and speaking here on these stones?*

After helping Miss Minnie, Miss Patrice stood by the stones, looking out at all of us. "I can understand why Miss Minnie holds her tongue about so much. But it seems fitting for me to let mine loose, give some context for this here resort and the many predicaments we find ourselves in here together."

She sat down on those stones herself and told the story of That Storm we all thought we knew backward and forward. But I'd never heard about the resort staff coming in her store to pick up some things when their delivery boat had been delayed, and saying she shouldn't have been living so near the shore, tempting the winds. Never heard the description of lowering her babies out the window, not the way she told it.

Bench Story No. 2: Miss Patrice Lightbourne

...I scooted a chair up by the window for the smaller children to climb up on, all of them wrapped up in some tarps like little squishy jellyfish, and got them lowered down. I had to put one arm under my belly and use the other hand to lower them by one arm, with my oldest boy, Frank, out there first, helping each of his siblings down. Then I looked at that chair and looked up at the roof as if I could see the sky and heaven, asking whether I was actually going to be able to do this with my belly the size of a washtub. They say you don't remember pain, but I do remember when I fell out the other side of the window because I had no balance, nor room to move, and the kids all too small to try to catch me or help lower me down. And then I crawled on my hands and knees, with all the

children in front of me—made them go first even though they were
scared so I could keep counting all four of them were there—and,
thank the Lord, as we went I couldn't see my brother's wife because
of the rain, but I heard her voice coming down the hill, and once
she got to us I knew she'd make sure we got to their house OK.
And we did.

You know there was no phone then, during That Storm, at my
house or at my brother's, and not at anyone's house for a while after
the hurricane, so my husband didn't even know we were OK for
almost a week. Unless I'm remembering wrong and it was more
than a week, much more. And all the while had to imagine him out
there in the capital counting the days of not knowing. I can't now
remember how long, because, well, you know, maybe you can't *al-*
ways remember the pain!

Murmurs of assent traveled through the crowd like a breeze.
Miss Patrice nodded at each of us hovering near before she got
up and returned to where she'd been standing. At Mr. Harper's
request, Della pushed his wheelchair over the gravel to the bench
next, and when he asked, several folks were willing to come near
those stones in order to help him on from his chair. He told the
story of his leg: how it happened, for those who knew the story
and especially for those who didn't. The way the stones—and the
resort—reshaped his whole life. The airlift he'd waited and waited
for.

When he was finished storytelling, a cluster of folks stepped up
to help him back in his chair. Della waving them away when they
told her she was next. When the others had accepted her waving
and stepped away along with her, Bayard stayed and sat down to
talk about his students witnessing the boat arrivals and coming
to him with their questions. I could see Hebbie and some others
cringing at the thought of kids seeing us out there in our nonsense
sheets, entertaining for pennies. Just like I had when I'd first heard
about them seeing in the resort. And Bayard had plenty more to
say about it.

Bench Story No. 4: Bayard Tournquest

...kept thinking maybe we did our students a disservice, not talking openly about the inland plantation and the layers of trauma on this oval and the relation of the resort to how we think about all this island's skeletons.

When I first started teaching, we discussed it once in a while, just a little, among the teachers. How to talk about the past? Should we take the kids inland? Everyone was against it. Even though Miss Daphanie wasn't teaching anymore, they'd remember what she'd said about it: Like looking at the sun. It's there, but...

Most teachers just wanted us to count how many hours we had with these kids before they went out into the big world and how we could prioritize what we should spend time on. And, yes, there's this part of me doesn't want to talk about my fore-parents enslaved and how they got here. And doesn't want to talk about way back when, that there was actually a native people here we know so little of because there's not a soul left to remember, to speak about them.

*And all the teachers agreed: talk of or not—*it's in their bones.

When these students came to me with their questions—well, what these students are really coming to me with is the simple question of why people in the world proceed as though the things we know are not known. Don't guess we'll get an answer to that question today or any time soon, though, will we?

Bayard motioned for his brother, Garrett, to step forward to the bench, but Garrett held still with his hand waving *no* in the air like his wife had. Della put her hand on his back.

From where he stood, he told us: "Been sitting here listening to all of you, kin and might-as-well-be. And I feel uneasy, just going to say it, with all this talking. Mighty uneasy. In front of *them* by the gate. Watching, hearing. Miss Minnie understands what I'm thinking, I would say, holding her tongue on how much life she has to share. You can hold your tongue if that's what you choose to do. OK for the kids to learn that, too, I think. And sometimes got to in open company. Keep to your own. My life is full of joy, no matter what anyone thinks about it or about the problems of this isle. My life is full of joy. No need to say more."

While he was speaking, Miss Wayida Callaghan, the minister's wife, had seated herself on the bench. I didn't know much at all about the Callaghans other than the hazy story from my childhood: Miss Philene's Jimmy beaten and left to bleed up by the ruins and then one fewer minister on this oval. Had never even heard Miss Wayida's voice for more than a few words at a time or from her distant singing. The hush deepened, none of us quite knowing what to do with her other than listen.

"With respect for those who choose *not* to speak. But I guess my speaking couldn't make much of a difference in what all of you think of me," she began.

Bench Story No. 5: Miss Wayida Callaghan

I, too, struggled plenty: many years with my husband trying to set up his church and a couple of kids with us when we moved here from Flat Island and then a couple more once we were set on staying here. I know how you all looked at us then, coming in from elsewhere and setting up our church when you already had your own, but that was our job, to spread the Word around this country on all its islands, and we knew there were plenty of people here didn't go to the standing church anymore. So we picked up and came here to share our church with those who were looking and show it to those who didn't know they were looking and build it for those who weren't looking but someday, sometime, might be looking.

Point all you want, some of you know very well that you came to us when you needed your dead churched and you couldn't do it yourself. Or when your local church couldn't secure any more grave plots for you, and you didn't want to just put them to rest by your home. You know we set up the dead, worked with the funereal committee to help them travel to their resting places, some finding their place up the little path behind our church.

No one really wants me dealing with their dead or even their sick after what happened, but I still run that Sunday service myself, even when it's only me and Miss Minnie. Even most times when it's only me. I sit and look at that gorgeous altar we built with those windows behind it: a view of the sea like God put it there just for us to enjoy. And He has seen fit to bolster up those windows and that altar and that little apartment we lived in—I live in—on the back side of the building through every storm that has come since we set foot here. My children are gone now, off to other islands or to the States. But that building we put our faith in and made a monument to our faith—in Him and in all of you—still stands intact as the day my husband put in the final nail. In spite of everything that was done, that had happened. In spite of the circumstances that lead us to sit here, my brothers and sisters, on a pile of rocks by a parking lot, to talk ourselves to a higher place.

For that's what we're all trying to do, each one of us, isn't it? Whoever built this bench here, makeshift as it is, I believe was touched by the Lord. Because the Lord loves a makeshift kind of life the most: each one of us doing the best we can with whatever pile of rocks we can get our hands on. That's all. That's all we can do. And Miss Minnie and others of you who have sometimes thought about coming on a Sunday—even with the ghost of the boy haunting our church—I know you know of what I speak about.

All of you have heard about my husband. You all knew him as a minister for years—whether you joined his flock or not, he saw you as a part of it. And you all know the shadow that has formed out of the gossip about what he did fifteen years past that has overtaken the man himself, the memory of the man. All of you from the resort who are not from around here, have you ever heard a story about a murder taking place on this island? A minister bringing about the death of a congregant's boy? About a man beating a teenager, then leaving him to bleed and get lost, alone? Up on the inland? Of course you have. But meaning, of course, that you heard such a story of that murder on the inland after you heard the murder stories of Columbus and after you heard the murderous stories of slavery, of course. All the deaths up in that death place, with its demons that can take over a decent man. That bloody demon, slavery itself, that overtook my husband when a boy didn't understand he should run—he refused to run!—from that demon's cradle of a place. I think we all know that particular demon, even if we don't care to say its name. A demon doesn't go running just because you don't greet it.

My husband was the sort of man who was watchful for that demon's approach with both eyes and glasses on, patrolled for it. Stood by the window and, when he saw teenaged boys going too far up the path— and off the path into the brush—to create mischief, went after them to tell them whose arms they were stepping into up there. Got all of them 'cept one to turn the other way, then he and that one, Jimmy Cruffey, met the demon face-on. Jimmy Cruffey—yes, Cruffey still the name, my Lord.

They took my husband off to the capital since the law here doesn't really deal with these kinds of cases. He has disappeared from my life as he has disappeared from all of yours. Though at times, I admit, I wrote him letters. For different purposes, but mainly some feeling that no one in the world was thinking of him but me. Maybe not even the Lord. My husband a ghost in matter of fact, too.

And where did all of that take place? It happened inland. You may have heard when folks dare mention all the details. When it all went down, and we knew it had happened on the inland, when I knew, or accepted, that it did happen: I had this thought I never told anyone before, not in all the many years since it happened. Years more than a decade now. But I will tell this thought now, because maybe it helps explain some things that I with my limits can't explain about His ways. And even with all the things other folks have been testifying to, and testifying to well in many cases, yes, even with all that—it hasn't really been explained to outsiders. Or to us.

My thought: There's a new ghost up there. There's different blood up there now.

Wasn't a haunting thought either. Just a wondering, I guess, about it being so.

Long, long silence followed Miss Wayida's story. Though she was right about that demon: the very mystery I'd been wondering about since Jimmy's death all those years ago. When she got up from the stones, folks stepped aside. To let her pass or to let her back in the crowd? I wasn't sure. No one met the eyes of Miss Philene, mother of the other person made up that inland story. Not even me, who most days lived right alongside her at work.

When the silence finally came to an end, it was Uncle Q who'd ended it. Felt myself sway as I listened to his voice, elegant as his words, always calmed me no matter what he was talking about. Her brother's voice closest thing to Mother's voice there was, I guessed, even with how differently they spoke. Even telling of the sad tale of Wilson's death after he left the island: my other uncle I struggled to remember after all this time. Even telling of what had happened to him on a spot of the resort I'd walked through hundreds of times without any idea what had occurred there, without knowing the pain under my feet.

Didn't know what to think when the next one to settle on the stones was Lem. Looked away when he turned toward me, and I saw one of Claudia's yellow papers poking out of his back pocket.

Bench Story No. 7: Lem Eldon

I've worked garbage at the resort a long time. Long enough, needed a new uniform twice because my ankles, then my calves, showing out the bottom. Been longer hours nowadays, no better pay, though. Miss

Myrna there could tell you. Even if she doesn't want to meet my eyes. Even if she thinks I'm some kinda weak head. But I won't talk none about her anymore, just tell this story 'bout her uncle: Mr. Q.

Thing about working garbage at the resort is garbage full of bounty. So much food there, they throw away half. Got instructions to guard dumpsters like they full of gold. Couldn't even let your own pa take something still good. Still great, in some cases.

Thing about working garbage at the resort is you spend lots of time, when you're not driving to and from the landfill, in that fenced court-yard area the staff use for all kind of things: coming and going, trucks and dumpsters, smoking, chatting 'bout nothing. Place smell like weed and rotten food most of the time. Buzz of chatting rivals sound of the waves. Residents who work the resort be there, in and out all day long, just like rest of the American staff, too, except management, 'less they checking up. Or once in a while smoking. So I spend plenty my time with some front desk staff who smoking while I working back there or waiters and pool deck attendees and even the boat staff come back for various causes. Boat boys even set up an old picnic table back there, play cards. Lots of people in and out all day while we garbage boys haul in and out of the trucks, back and forth to the landfill, hosing down what needs to be hosed, working repairs on equipment out the garage, and all that.

My pa taught me all about how our family always work with gar-bage, even way back 'fore he worked at the resort, too. He and his bred-das swam out to wrecked ships, abandoned on the reefs, went through it all for whatever they could swim back with. But me working that resort garbage brigade, he say, like him and his buddies collecting, 'cept he said swimming better for you than driving trucks back and forth, and he'd laugh away. Garbage not really "garbage," he said, when can still be made use of.

"Garbage grows here, too," he'd say. "Native as Columbus, spit onto the sand like the ocean didn't want it no more." Native as Columbus: always made so many folks laugh away hard and laugh away long.

This day with Mr. Q years ago, when I went to work with my pa one day. Me: still a boy. Don't remember why that particular day but went with him sometimes. Spent plenty time with that fence round me even 'fore working there myself.

That day Mr. Q come on through, and that someone who don't belong there out of everyone. Didn't know how he got back there but came through the staff door. Thought he musta took a wrong turn from the lobby, but I didn't know what he'd be doing at that resort front desk anyway. Now I know, hearing your story, Mr. Q. Now I know.

But that day he look kinda surprised as he come through the door to see us all and the dumpsters and all. Holding a bright orange day pass card of all thing. Kind of keep-quiet guy on the island, knew he's not joining the garbage brigade or nothing, 'cause he real proper. Bunch of boat staff there, smoking and playing cards and talking 'bout girls but get all quiet when Mr. Q start walking through. One of the boys who knew him point to the gate behind the trucks, knowing he looking for the way to get back out whatever he doing here in the first place. But boat staff start in 'fore he can get to the gate. Start saying name like—well, you know what kinda things they call a man like that. 'Fore you know it they pushin' him around, man old as their daddies, and still sayin' all kind of nasty talk, and one of them take a piece of pool equipment like a long pole and get it caught up in his legs so Mr. Q fall to all fours, and they sayin' their shit and like spankin' him with it. Not that hard, so I'm not sure if he can't get up 'cause he hurt or just think it better to wait 'em out.

I turn round to some of the other guys, guess 'cause I don't know what to do and, too, little 'fraid to see what gonna happen next.

But I do watch my pa. See him out the corner of my eye, so I know he's not moving none. But his eyes darting round way they do when he wants to do something real bad. Plotting, like. Waiting to do something soon as he can. His eyes darting to the guy sitting in the corner smoking: his boss, I know.

Pa don't move, and I sit still there, too. Don't know if just boat staff do it or some of our own garbage crew, too. Kind of boy I was then, just looked at my hands when trouble swellin' up round me. Just look to my pa. And knowing, no matter what, I'd end up working there just as soon as I'm old enough. And then until I'm too old.

By time I turn back round boat boys running off, boss finished his smoke and went inside, and I lookin' around for Mr. Q and then some other guys, and my pa, help get him out the dumpster they toss him in. Dumpster still pretty full, since no one'd taken a load yet that day, so that's good, because he not real hurt. Able to walk out the gate himself.

Never told this; didn't say nothing to my pa nor he to me. Didn't tell it even later to Myrna. Never heard Mr. Q tell it neither. Guess this my story, too, 'long with Mr. Q's. Me, Lem, just sitting at that table lookin' at my hands. Pa's eyes racing; my pa's body froze. Every day workin' back there in that fence a day I think about it some. Maybe felt like I owed that family some, owed her on top of how I was sweet for her. Maybe all of us need to be weak heads 'bout remembering all the years' trouble behind that fence.

I saw only the point of that yellow paper sticking out Lem's pocket as he walked off. Lionel stepped up quick as Lem was off the stones. As if he'd been wanting to for years. Then he winked at me and jumped up on those stones—standing, not sitting—and gave his boat arrival speech.

"I have arrived! I am arriving! Bear witness to my arrival and taking of this island! That's right: laugh, clap your hands, stomp your feet, stand up, lie down, do whatever. I will sail in and make my sovereignty known by the amount of alive stuff I rename Garbage in the name of the almighty International Office and with which I fill your landfill at three times the rate it was designed for! I will throw you down if you are late or if I even think I know who you are! I will convince your central government that I will bring so much money—so many jobs, investment beyond the dreams of simple outer-island folk. Yes, laugh if you believed me. Laugh if you believed my claims ever to be true! Laugh, Madame Arrival Manager! You have already fired me and banned me and need not worry about me screaming this on the beach to your customers. I am just on a bench in a parking lot!"

Longer speech he'd been working and working on, seemed like. I didn't laugh this time around, but plenty did. Lionel jumped down and grabbed Angelina's hand, urging her to go next. She looked up at Lem. He patted his kid sister's head and pointed her toward the bench with his chin.

Angelina sat down and told us all the story of Picker and the tourists on the road. Manny and Gussie hovered around her, like they were going to act out their parts. Seemed as though tears were about to seep out of all of us after all this storytelling—a deluge, couldn't be stopped—but I saw lots of folks smiling, just the same, at how smart Angelina was.

When Hebbie stepped up to the stones, it no longer felt as though I had anything to do with putting them there. The stories could go anywhere now, be so many things I—we—didn't want to hear. As Hebbie spoke, Miss Philene came to stand by my side. One of us holding up the other. Wondered if Andre'd told his sister what had happened on the road that night with the boat guys, but she didn't say anything about it. Just told her story about inside the resort's gate. Similar things we hadn't shared.

Christine couldn't stand back while everyone else did their talking, especially Hebbie talking about her. She was up there maybe longer than anyone. My gaze wandered to Mother, still hovering next to Uncle Q. I blinked back to paying attention when Christine's talk wound around to the banquet.

"The captain's ring may have gotten me 'cross the cheek here with all that banquet chasing—he got too caught up in acting the captain. Still, I'll keep this job and not let someone else have it. I can outrun most of them men, with my legs long and them so drunk most nights. Don't feel too bad about it, all of you shaking your heads. It'll fade sometime."

Maybe she finally stopped because Ole Mr. Vit was waiting near her. He took all the time he needed. First time in my life I heard anyone on this island speak the words aloud: *whipping post.*

I felt Miss Philene's touch leave me as Ole Mr. Vit's voice faded. I'm sure everyone, not just me, was surprised Miss Philene would say anything with the resort staff standing so near. She wouldn't even name her kids when she was at work. Always said her life, especially her babies, was no one's business but her own. All this time, did she know about the cameras' eyes? And here she was sitting on the bench. Maybe she couldn't let Wayida Callaghan be the one to touch on Jimmy's story. Or maybe she also had other things deep inside that bobbed to the surface just now.

But before she took her seat on the bench, Mr. Ken was standing beside her. I thought he was just lending a hand to help her sit, but she nodded to him as he took a seat instead. Jimmy's father, after all. Though I never thought of him that way, since no one ever talked of them as a family. Two of them split since I was a kid, and their daughters together left the island years back.

When he finished speaking, Mr. Ken looked over at me as though we understood each other, as though he knew it was me who spent a night of moving stones to let the darkness leak out the cracks into the open. But he didn't know some ways I was bad as the elders with their fortress around the inland, wanting some of those bodies to come home without the stories of how they got to be just bodies. Turned my head away so I wouldn't smell Andre's cologne on the air.

Was Jimmy just a stubborn kid? Wouldn't leave, just 'cause an elder said so? Or was he tired, looking for a new place on this oval he'd rounded a thousand times? Or was he like me, couldn't stop unburying?

Quiet all around as we waited for Miss Philene to settle herself on the stones. First she sat silent. Maybe taking in all Mr. Ken had said. Maybe answering by not answering. Then she spoke.

Bench Story No. 14: Miss Philene Cruffey

What I want to say today is about that woman and what was done to her. Yes, she was an American woman. Yes, I'm sure she was here

because she had money and not so bad off, maybe you say, but let's talk
loud and clear about the fact of her skin. Not her husband's skin or
even her baby's skin, light mix-up as he is, but her skin.

I've been in that woman's room, because some days it was my job to
clean up after her. I never spoke to her once but could tell you all kinds
of things about her. But let us say something that no "Investigating
Manager" or "Claims Adjuster" or no one else you fly down here to
wipe up this mess will say. That woman was pulled into that pool,
that woman is injured bad, because the people who pulled her thought
she was one of us. And thought she thought she was too good for the
job they wanted her to do. And no explanation for that except skin,
skin, skin. Except black, black, black.

Now when Mr. Harper got pinned under that rock, got his leg
crushed under that rock, so help him, those of us old enough to be here
knew the painful slowness of it all. No Claims Adjuster, no nothing.
Just waiting. Finally getting him to the capital for a hospital took far,
far too long.

Didn't take as long for that American woman. And I know all of
you thinking that that woman will go home to the States and see her
fancy doctor and be all set up OK, and maybe she will; maybe she'll
spend every evening relaxing on the shore of a lake with its water so
cold and opaque it'll make our turquoise sheen seem like nothing but a
dream. But still let's all remember that nothing's thrown down quick-
er to the ground than a black-skinned woman.

No one spoke for a long, long time after Miss Philene. Way
things felt right then, I figured the bench stories had come to their
close. Done their part.

But without Mother finding her voice.

After that long silent spell I looked up, and Andre was sitting on
the stones, readying to speak, as if I'd called it all together for what
I was most afraid to hear. Not sure for a moment whether I wanted
to be like the master and order the stones back to their sitting places inland. Rub away this spot with my foot.

Then it was too late to do anything but listen.

Bench Story No. 15: Andre Whylly

'Fore I went off to the capital, spent months of nights wandering the road. 'Fore I left, only one thing strapped to me, nothing else: drum Granduncle Vit made me long time back. Sometimes visitors threw coins when I played.

Wandering the road with that drum like I did, prickly brush against my arm—stepped into it when a car went by. Edge of the inland brush took me in. But I didn't want to stay there.

Lionel, bredda, do you remember once years gone by wind so strong my hat blew off from your truck, all the way inland? Said you: "Inland now. No use trying to find it."

But see Myrna there. Scratches all o'er her face. Old and new scratches. She comes in and out of the brush quick like a ghost but catches in the haulback like a body. Carousing with ghosts, girl, visiting dead. Maybe she wants to stay there inland, not just bring a trickle of it down with her.

But who knows the right place to be anymore? Nah, hard to say what's home.

Out on the capital Troy and I shared a home some o' you would say was no home. Room in a house with strangers. Two beds, two chairs, coffeepot, sink with hot water. Might seem modern to some of ya. No home at all to some. Weren't there that much anyway. Worked. Played, too, at first. Out soaking in all the new. And always looking, hustling, hurry-up-ing for work. Think it plentiful in the capital compared with here. Is, some ways. And lot o' new girls. And roads to walk up never seen before what's at the end of 'em. Not just a circle road, like here, bring you right back. But still a hurry-up life to keep what people take and give somewhere else at a drop of a hat.

So. Troy Burre. Troy's pa helped us out at first get set up with some folks he know. Then we start knowin' folks, too. When Mr. Horace gone all of a sudden, seem like we both been capital dwellers a long,

long time. Like we old, old men. But still hot boys, you know, way we were. But Troy could get shadowy and spook-eyed, too, stuck in his bed with darkness.

A hurry-up life it sure was, when folks barely eating two meals a day need to send money back home. That's what happened once Mr. Horace gone, you know. Troy wouldn't want me saying such a thing to his ma, but it's true just the same. Writing home with money saying he was selling some art at a market here, a market there—but with money he got not buying food for too long. Or some extra dollars in his hand after he spent the day cleaning a house or hauling a mess around town like a mule. And did those things only after I got him out of bed. Lay in our beds laughing some midnights when we couldn't sleep from hearing each other's bellies groan from 'cross the room. But mostly wasn't time for laughing in our life there. More like waiting. Waiting for the whites of our bloodshot eyes to whiten once more.

Could sit here all day totin' news, speculating all the things that would make a guy far away from home, trying to eke out a living—a guy like Troy with fire spilling out all his pockets—could make a guy like that give up. Go to the capital and die by his own hand.

We were breddas to each other, me and Troy, both hot boys run off like we did—and I know what made it so. Only one who saw it, no speculatin'. What I came and wanted to tell you, Miss Myrna. What I wanted to tell you, Miss Daphanie. All that made what happened to Troy so.

Morning after a mad, mad storm, not too many tourists coming into the capital on account of all 'em flight delays and cruises pulled into ports overnight. You know how a morning is after storm like that. Bright, quiet, sense of waiting.

But all of a sudden, when everyone's on the way to look for work in the morning, there's a boat comes to dock and out come a whole long line of soldiers. American. Just a line of soldiers that keeps coming and coming out of that boat.

Yes, I hear ya, Miss Minnie, I hear ya: all you said about your fore-parents. Everybody there that day—and most likely all your fore-parents, too—thinking just what you're thinking: So they here at last. Luck runs out on an island.

Troy and I stood watching, like everyone else was doing. I looked up and down the beach and could see just about everyone there is to see, all standing there. Silent. Frozen.

We waited to see what those soldiers gonna do. Stood there a long while, while their line started to get a little looser, and started noticing that their faces weren't so serious, were even fun-like. Didn't know what it meant. Whether better or worse than we were all thinking.

Troy just let his shirt go up in the wind. Took it off, reached up and let go, not sayin' nothing. It looked like a big white flag floating on the breeze for a second and then swishing down into a puddle. Made me think of all sorts of things, none I want to remember just now; glad they're not all washing around in my head anymore, night and day.

Even when some people gave up trying to figure it all out and went off to work, Troy just frozen there and then like he wouldn't look at me. I stayed there awhile, trying to talk to him. Eerie how he was so still. Not like Troy to be so still, 'less he was stuck in bed. But 'ventually couldn't try to talk to him, get him to get to work like everyone else was getting, 'cause I needed to get to my own work. But I stayed there awhile, Miss Daphanie, Miss Myrna, promise I did. A long while. Promise.

By next morning: gone. Put himself in the waves, meant not to come back.

'Nother day later Troy washed up out of the sea without life in him anymore.

Found out by that evening, like everyone else did, word passing mouth to mouth, ear to ear, that all it was was a boatload of U.S. soldiers on leave, got a special trip to the big Paradise Now resort. A little bit of leave, a little bit of peace. For them.

And that what happened to Troy, how he came to travel from us.

So what about you now, Miss Myrna? You not going to speak on these stones, even with their shapes all bruised into you from the lifting, huh? Nah, didn't think great chance you would. Didn't mean to prostrate you so by telling. It's OK: we all see what your eyes saying, *watering the ground like they are. We'll help you stand back up when you're ready.*

Miss Daphanie, Myrna's ma, Troy's ma. Take my hand here. Sit and rest your feet. Speak some if you will or sit as long as you feel. As very long as you do feel like. We'll wait for ya.

Bench Story No. 16: Miss Daphanie Burre

Thought dem going off to the capital was the worst thing I'd be carrying with me as a mother and a wife. See now, that's what I thought back a ways, before they were lost for good. Wasn't just the estate; all of life got too sad for talking about.

Used to go outside at night, or even just by the window, look at the sky, and try to think which direction they were in away from me, how we all look up at the same stars above our head somehow. Reflection of these islands all up there, glittering down. Each night just look out there, and I'd start counting all the stars. And each night I'd count the same number. And when they did not come to be counted, I'd count the holes they'd left behind.

A hush fell down on all of us after Mother spoke. She remained on the bench, and our neighbors and kin stayed just where they'd been.

Hearing her voice after all this time! My mother's voice! Hearing everyone tell their stories, all those voices forming words that hadn't slipped their lips in years! And knowing now the details of my always-sad brother's final sadness: not just Dad's death and the capital's disappointments, but some fear mixed in with the sadness he carried. Finally pulled him under. Finally saw his tiny, fragile place in the world's busiest ports. All of it made me feel bruised inside layered with all my bruising outside. Like more stones tumbled down from the inland on top of me, on top of all of us. Looked down and saw how close I was pressed to the ground, kneeling.

But also: it felt like everything in my brain that had previously been scattered, like all this archipelago, now had some design, like a constellation. Kept hearing Dad's voice describing those dice spilling out in a scatter and then gathering themselves back.

I felt a body near me and turned to see that Claudia had stepped out of the line she'd been in all day. Last person I wanted to talk to right now, but she was facing only me. I stood up and wiped the streaky layers of half-dried wetness from my cheeks. Started feeling the memory of her hands all over my uniform when we met in her office. Now I might push her off me if she got too close. Would I really? Maybe. Probably.

Her arms were asleep at her sides, though, a clipboard in one hand and a pen in the other, but just hanging there now like props. It was the look she always seemed to have but intensified: ready to call it a day. Unsmiling face showing the symmetrical lines that came down from the corners of her lips, nose, and inner eyes: a kid's drawing of a pine tree pressed into her face. As if the tornado of the banquet had been whipped up inside her and then spun out, leaving her listless and disconnected from its path. Not even watching as it went on its way. Listening, though, to us.

She turned in a semicircle, right and left, looking at me but also beyond me.

"Let me say to all of you, local residents," she announced. "As of this afternoon I will report my resignation to the international management office. I am no longer the Domestic Staff Manager of the resort." Her voice sounded not resigned but relieved and, I thought, also proud. *Domestic Staff Manager* kept repeating in my mind; we'd always called her Arrival Manager because she seemed so focused on our beach theater with the boats coming in. I didn't know what her role was in the departure of the American woman. If she'd stood on the beach when the helicopter alit and lifted off again. If she was the Departure Manager, too.

I wanted to say to her that one person stepping back wouldn't change anything, but I could see in her posture that she would-n't have believed or understood me. Departure of the Arrival Manager. One big step for Claudia, going home and washing her hands of all of it. I saw her pass a folder to her assistant, smudges of inky blue along the edge: From the handling of the blueprints? The assistant slid the file into his bag, zipped the top, folded the flap and buckled it, yanked the tails as tight as they allowed.

Some of the staff applauded her. While we all stood in silence, and Mother still sitting on the rocks and looking at her lap as if this had nothing to do with her telling, with our story. Papers packed up in a satchel that'd fly back to the States where she knew they belonged. Nothing to do with our Troy and why he'd chosen the ocean.

Then Claudia turned to me. "Murna," she said. Surety in her voice, no look in her eyes asking, *Am I getting your name right or are you someone else?* "I'll let management know you've been hired back on as a temporary renovation worker. We still need a painter."

I flinched a little at that, but she said nothing else. Not waiting for a response, she walked toward the snack bar, thumbs active on her phone, and a few minutes later got in a car driven by a man. I guessed her husband. A small face with her same faded sandy hair peered out at all of us from the back window.

Lionel started muttering. "White people always think they can fix everything with money."

Miss Patrice was right behind him. "Well, you got something better? Not fixing, but, you know, a job does help. Right place for the money, anyway," she muttered back.

The small circle near me close enough to have heard the muttering started debating:

"I think she thinks it'll fix everything, like a domino effect or something."

"Maybe she didn't know what other step to take and did what she could."

"Don't even know if the one who pulled her in is fired, let alone anything else."

"But Lord knows Myrna needs the work."

"If I were her, I wouldn't take it."

"If she doesn't, know some folks standing right here who will."

"Well, hopefully all of this'll help some, then. All we can do is hope for something."

"Something had to happen to a Missus U.S.A. to make it all come down, you know. Not too hopeful looking to me."

"Missus wasn't white, remember?"

"Still."

A flash: many, many years ago. Moping when my parents argued at the dinner table. Mother turning to me, saying, *Myr-na, my ma always said that to sit and argue with people at a table is a good thing. Remember that.*

I let all their voices drift away from me, no matter who I agreed with or not. Not even Mutiny Day could always change the next day. Let myself just look at Mother, sitting on the bench by the gate. Not trying to sell to tourists. Not working. Not waiting to work. Bench I made for her to sit on.

He report back, Stones   Ask him, Stones?

She stayed on stones, not talking   Look Son in eye

Rubbed out lines where stones been with my own foot

These words from the book they took from me: still lodged in my brain like nettles.

Chapter Nine

T he security staff stepped aside as we passed through the gate. We made the long trek to the hotel entrance and passed through the lobby to the pool deck, Mother's arm looped in mine.

The deck was dappled in light and shadow. Debris an abstract panorama. Anyone who hadn't experienced the banquet would've sworn an awful storm had bullied its way through while we all slept, trampling our island while we dreamed of marauding bogeyman, escaped cows, people we'd let loose.

"Damn, look like a cow went through here," Mother said. "Bunch of them even."

There was only one lounger that hadn't been split to pieces. As I reclined the back just a little more, I could see the crispy folds of Mother's clothes slipping through each rubbery slat of the chair. A posture I'd never seen her in. I made sure she was facing the ocean, since I knew she'd never sat down like this, relaxed, and just looked out at the water because it was nice looking. I made sure she could also see the pool, just a little bit, so that when I lowered myself in she'd know that I'd taken the paint supplies from Troy's room.

I moved a cup of water closer to where her hand rested on the arm of the chair. Her hand so relaxed, fingers splayed all around, looked like a creature unsure of which way to go. Un-purposeful.

Opposite of my hurried hand puttying and painting the graffitied *Cruffey* out of the resort sign before we passed under it.

But she must've—sometime, someplace—she must've sat and looked out at the water just to look. Just sat there because she had nowhere to be and because the sun wasn't so strong as to nudge you inside and because the water was turquoise glass.

"See you," I said.

She smiled.

"Tell me again, Mother," I said.

"Each night just look out there, and I'd start counting all the stars. And each night I'd count the same number. And when they did not come to be counted, I'd count the holes they'd left behind."

My eyes closed, my breath adjusting to the rhythm of her words.

"See, that's poetry, girl, by a poet who plucked his own name from the sky. Not mine. Something I read."

"You read poetry?"

"Didn't you ever look under the table?" And then my mother laughed like I'd never heard a woman on this island laugh. A man's laugh. A squawk. An I-don't-give-a-fuck-who-hears-me laugh and a let-them-think-I've-got-nothing-better-to-do-than-open-my-big-mouth-and-laugh laugh.

"Some of those lines stay in my head like they've been sewn in there with my ma's hand, you know what I mean?"

My feet felt numb, like when I sat on the ruined walls for too, too long and worried I'd be missed. "Yes'm, I do," I said.

She closed her eyes, and I backed toward the pool until all I could see was the way the rim of her sunglasses met the plump of her cheek and her hand going on sitting there like it could saunter anywhere on the island whenever it damn well wanted. The shushing of the waves came and went. Quiet, then roaring, then quiet again. There was no music from the speakers today. Mother and I could feel the desertion of the resort all around us.

Typically on a group of tourists' last day, the Independence Departure ritual happened on the beach next to the pool deck. Columbus and his backup players would trade in their hats for clothing plastered with the asterisk of the British flag and march the tourists down to the boats. A few of us would stand on either side of their parade handing out suckers and palm-sized shells. Without our sheets at least. The steel drum band would play on the beach as the boats sailed to the key, re-caped Columbus promising new adventure on other islands, distributing brochures for the management company's other properties.

The animals who'd surrendered their shells were long disintegrated under our feet. Usually that sand was full, too, of sucker wrappers and tiny white sticks. But none had been left behind: there must've been no time for any Independence Departure. Management getting those tourists off the island at top speed. Far as I'd heard, Lionel hadn't even gotten a secondhand good-bye from Katelynn before she flew back to snowy lawns and semester textbooks. (Or was she taking care of Nathan Manion full-time, since the incident?)

No signs of the departure ritual, but I kept spotting hurriedly left behind things. A beer bottle on the gravel path, a sarong snagged on a broken chair, a pink flip-flop half buried in the sand. Blood. And a cloth sack shunted under a broken lounger. Inside the sack: a raft of paintbrushes in much better shape than the ones I had to work with. Art brushes. Not like the collection Troy had of any brush that might hold paint.

Looked around me and memorized the image of my mother reclined almost all the way, so I could find it in my mind again and again. Just a few notches up from flat out on her softened back. Sunglasses over eyes I was sure were closed or almost closed. Her lips sliding up in a smile. I'd never seen them from this angle. Her fingers raised every so often, tinkling at me: a contented fringe, a don't-bother-me flick. Every once in a while asking me how it was going.

Dinner the night before she'd looked so much stiffer as frail Uncle Q slowly slung the sack he always carried on the back of Dad's chair, then lowered himself down. When he thought I wasn't listening I heard him tell Mother, with a nod in my direction:

"That is why our fore-parents ceased talking about all of that. No matter how many times you may travel inland, with however many reasons you may have for doing so, you will end up thrashed, yes, but without a single new answer."

"Yes, Uncle Q," I'd said, sitting back at the table so they'd remember I was part of the question. He was right: my scars from the thrashing haulback weren't answers. But at least they were visible. "Guess I'm still kinda glad, though, that I read about them up there. Can picture them now, up there."

Uncle Q nodded.

How it makes me feel to find out where the pain is coming from, Dad had told me about his dentistry work. *To know exactly how to dig out the source of the pain,* he'd said. Not one of us had said whether we were glad we'd heard Andre's story of Troy's death. Much as I hadn't wanted to know it all, Mother was better off knowing. The knowing had at least opened her throat. Let her lie back now on the recliner to laugh, voice spilling sunlight.

Standing on the deck, looking out at the ocean with the pool dropping in front of my feet, something like the livestock and their people standing at the watering hole on the estate. Lifting their eyes to take in the view: the innuendo of a mast at their horizon. Imagining an end to the day's work. The horizon an illusion that this oval, this warped circle, had a straight line in its future.

Painting the bottom of the pool: last work I'd do for the resort. No matter how many brushes it took to prime the electric blue of the pool's interior that resisted covering, I didn't feel like I was working for them anymore. Painting away without an ache. Full of my own mother's voice like wind in a sail, like I was drunk on the airiness of it. Hearing each note felt like the last few sucks on a thiflae flower, when you could sense the sweetness ebbing away. You had to draw your lips in extra tight just then.

Management, their adjusters, and their lawyers were sure busy around the resort "investigating" what had happened to the

American woman. That's what most of us kept calling her, though we all knew her name. (*B3* stayed in my muscles, too, my nails tracing the letter and number into my palm. The pregnant curve of the *B*; its repetition in the *3* hugging close as our knees in the truck.) All knew the woman with the family we couldn't help but notice from their first steps on the beach—her foreign bag laden with our own history.

At night on barstools at Thiflae, it seemed like the whole island debated whether any of it would make a difference, to her or to us or to anyone.

Some folks said keep on keeping on hoping that something would change.

Some folks said you'd have to have crazy in your head to think anything would change for the better at that place. Just hoping for better like believing you could empty the ocean with a bucket.

Some folks said organizing was the only way.

Some folks said good luck to that without the government's eyes on any of the resorts.

Some folks said all you could do was keep your own eyes open, and we will see.

Some folks said maybe I should negotiate with management about giving tours of the estate.

Some folks said last thing we needed were tourists slithering up paved paths, taking snapshots, not knowing what on this earth they were looking at.

Most folks said at least there still was work to be had at the resort. At least there was work.

All folks said there was no good solution for the tangled puzzle of the inland. Knowing how to untangle it like thinking you could catch all the invisible cows on this oval.

I said the knowing just how to fix things was only for ghosts.

Listening to it all at Thiflae, I turned into a migrant: sat on a barstool a spell, stood out back on the pier of the porch a spell, came back inside to linger by the stereo system that tremored my insides.

Always a mix of people on the porch, adrift from the day. Later it got, more the mix was just folks my age or thereabouts: crowd that could include Lionel, Christine, Lem, Hebbie, Andre. Like plants that grew up together into a tangle of different-tasting tea leaves; me still the prickly haulback. All of them were willing to have me there, it seemed, even with my hanging on just to the edges of their conversations. Until some point when the porch would shudder beneath me like sand pulled under by the tide, and I'd step back into the bar. Out of the sloshing water, onto firmer ground.

Andre was still visiting and trying to convince Hebbie to move to the capital with him, now that their ma was getting sick enough to need the hospital there anyhow. Andre always with a new idea for contacts, settling, living. Hebbie's humming back to lining my ears. Let their voices, let the smell of his cologne, settle onto me till Andre started describing how they'd live: Hebbie bunking in Troy's old bed. Took my step backward from the wooden slats of the porch to the bar's linoleum floor. Felt a soft wall behind my back and turned to see I'd backed right into Lem.

"Sorry," I mumbled.

Surprised like I always was at how slight he looked out of his resort jumpsuit. Only about a week past the yellow paper sticking out of his pocket that I'd well enough put there. He looked over my shoulder at the others. Just wanted to get by. His T-shirt looked like one of Andre's, shiny navy with a black arrow traveling around his back and coming front again. I could see the creases where it'd been folded. Must've come in on the mail boat that'd docked just that morning. When his eyes came back to me, I saw the bitterness softened away. But also gone: the owing-ness, the willingness. He nodded and stepped off onto the pier.

"Here's our other bredda that will be coming with us, too!" Andre shouted. Clink of bottles behind me. Neither of us going back to the resort, then.

Realized I'd thought of Lem like Junkful, like Thiflae, like Troy's beach sculpture: always waiting where I'd left them.

"Really, Lem?" Christine's voice sounded full of the same thick surprise that clogged my own throat.

"Not going back to a job they don't trust me to do no more," he answered. Another clink of bottles at my back. My yellow paper of overtime, his of demotion.

Mr. Ken gestured for me to sit at the bar with him. I stayed past closing and helped him pick up empties. Walking home, I watched Queen Isa's low shadow swimming in and out of the brush alongside me. After I stepped off the road at our house, she went on toward the road to the landfill; she'd find her sleeping spot in Lionel's three-sided shed, mostly out of the wind.

In school we'd learned to smile at anyone who visited our country, to conceal its pains like an old dog passed off as a puppy. I was not a hostess. No matter what, I was glad never again to stand on that western beach as the boats of tourists came in.

Yet I could stand for hours these days on Junkful Beach, stare down the east. Wait for whatever the ocean saw fit to bring in to me. Some of it skipping up onto the sand and staying there, some of it washing in only to be immediately pulled back out. The ocean deciding whether to bring me some luck. That's what all of it seemed like: choosing or un-choosing my luck. But it was just the ocean.

Even when a drizzle rose up and the water was roughed by a cold, cold wind, I was willing to stand there. Stand there and stand there while frigates with their steeled wings thrummed overhead. Kept imagining, no matter how hard I tried not to, one more arrival: the book washing up at my feet.

No one marching around the resort with their clipboards and their corporate pens could tell me what had happened to the book Claudia had confiscated the night I'd been fired. Had they sent it off the island with Jasmine Manion's husband or with the nanny? Had they shipped it, with all of the Manions' stuff, on a flight trailing the helicopter that came for her? No one knew. Blamed the confusion on Claudia's departure.

Except Lionel and me, not a single person on this island even knew the book had ever existed. And no amount of online searching turned up a trace of another copy. Like a ghost, that book came out of the darkness and then disappeared just when you were looking for it.

Lionel agreed with a futile shrug to keep an eye out for it in all the resort's mountains of garbage. Agreed not to bury it in a day's work if he could help it.

He grumbled: "Why do you want that thing anyway? Just master's voice in there, master's picture of the world only." Which was all true, yet I still wanted it.

According to Mother, the book wasn't really what I was looking for. They were just words that pointed to the words that weren't there.

"But that's just it," I said.

"Anything and everything gets lost eventually, Myr-*na*," Mother said, "and so often lost to the sea."

But no matter how wrecked by water it might be, even if all the pages had by now washed away to white, I kept dreaming of the book coming back to me as flotsam. Washing up from everywhere and nowhere.

A book to help support the pedestal of the table where I took meals with Mother. A book that could sit atop and below the poetry books that I now knew—though I'd never witnessed her doing it—Mother bent down for, pulled to her bosom, read so deeply she let her three fingers stop marking out ailment and the measured tails of her sweater stop spelling messages for me. The cracked pedestal unmoved by her indulgence. A book I could pull out after we'd eaten dinner and remind myself of Tildy in the kitchen and, while I sat in my chair, Tildy on the bench. A book that could let my eyes go partly unfocused only scanning for *Divvy*, finding each corner of the estate he been found in or taken to. A book that could let me imagine some the pointed rock in his little hand as he found hiding places to press his ships into those stones.

Each time Lionel joined us for dinner, he dragged behind him the non-news that the book hadn't shown up at the landfill. Still, something about him choosing any chair he wished—no extra settings for Troy or Dad—made the air lighter. I asked whether he was bitter about his college girl flying home without him, and he shot me the slit of an eye. The same slit I gave him when he used to tease-tease me about Lem.

"Wasn't just like that. We were working on a business deal."

"You and who? An American?" Mother asked, laughter in her voice.

"Katelynn was helping me work out the details with the American woman. That day I gave the American woman the tour, we had a whole plan going. When she saw Junkful Beach. You heard she had a junk shop, Myr."

The scheme: he'd export items from the landfill and from Junkful Beach for the American woman to sell from the nook in her consignment shop. She'd pay the shipping, plus he'd get consignment. It sounded silly to us, Mother and me, at first, but I knew Jasmine Manion was probably a sharp businesswoman if that nook alone paid for her family's whole vacation at the resort. And Lionel assured us she seemed agreeable, too, and business savvy, when he told her they should consult Miss Patrice about the ins and outs of shipping merchandise between Cruffey and the States with the capital in between.

"Not a living, but a piece of one," Mother said, considering.

"Mutually beneficial," he kept saying the American woman had kept saying.

Katelynn had promised him that Jasmine Manion's customers would get excited about a boxful of our most common chipped or halved shells. True enough: we were all experts in marketing what Americans wanted from this island.

It would be so good, he pointed out, to have some *real* island things arrive in and depart from that Out-of-the-Mind Nook. Way he talked so chest-puffed about it, as though he'd already stewarded that nook. Already packed up the slick brochures' impossible beaches into cardboard boxes and wound them tight with tape that screeched like birds.

"And by getting some garbage off the island, she'd be doing part of my job for me—and paying the shipping fees," he joked. Or half joked.

Mother laughed like it was a whole joke. "And? So? You gonna try to find out what happened to her after the accident, if she's still running her shop and into this deal, then?"

I couldn't tell if Mother was convinced or skeptical. Most likely somewhere in between, as was her way.

But we all looked down, thinking of the possible places she might be—the different *hows* she might be. Maybe she'd come home from the hospital and rehab with half her hair turned gray, the way Miss Philene's had turned and stayed when Jimmy died. Maybe she'd come home walking with a cane. Maybe she'd be fine with the two-toned hair: it would show people she was artistic. Maybe she'd chosen a purple cane, the color of the storybook birds of Quickly Island, so her little boy wouldn't be as afraid of it. Reading her childhood book at night, the two of them, so the images of the pool deck could be replaced by the pictures of mysterious birds making it over the ocean. (Or maybe I was convincing myself of too much. Me, so often on the skeptical side of Mother's in-between.)

Lionel didn't answer either way; went back to leaning over his dinner plate, eyes hidden by his braids. The three of us dined on in semi-silence. Books at our knees. Dad's machete rested outside in the shed, awaiting gardening.

And then the cardboard box arrived on the mail boat, so we knew she was out there. Full of pinecones. Addressed to *L.—or Any— Cruffey on Cruffey Island* in thick black marker, shaky letters. Crumpled corners from its travels but taped expertly. No return address but stamped *Wisconsin, USA.*

Couldn't hardly wait until the mail boat staff had moved it off the platform, kids were already tearing at the tape. Wrenching the mouth of the box open and then untangling the knotted neck of the garbage bag inside to reveal the mound of pinecones. Pulling one out and the next and the next and the next and the next and the next. Passing them around the group. Every one of those kids, the wetness of their eyes and mouths quickening with sunshine.

Like I was floating in the sky watching myself the way I conjured my own arrival happening. First the sea spitting out a book at my feet, waterlogged and unrecognizable. Then my face exploding into a smile when I saw this was *it*, *the* book, my eyes busting big as potholes. Same as the kids gnashing at the box that came all the way from Wisconsin.

"Just look to me like short haulback branches fattened up," Miss Philene had said about that hoard of pinecones. She'd shaken her head at the grabby kids, perplexed by their joy.

That's how I'd be, too. Joyful. Perplexing.

In the meantime, I waited on Junkful Beach, trying to shore up a little luck.

Lionel found me there one day, nudging crude ships into the wet sand around Troy's sculpture with my toe. I didn't sit on the sand; I stood like the sculpture that never keeled no matter how hateful the storm. Like Troy himself standing, still and bent, waiting to be airborne—the last time I saw him after Dad's funeral. Like Troy the way Andre had seen him freeze, last time he was standing at all. Standing and seeing what made him need to run to the end. Stood and stared at that sculpture like maybe I'd understand *the sensibility of its maker.*

That day I was tracing with my foot the kind of boats my brother'd taught me to make when I was little: a triangle sail, a smile running beneath, both connected with a line straight as can be. I drew them all facing out, departing.

Saw Lionel before I heard him, waving something in the air. *The book?*

Then he got closer, and I saw it was just a letter—a letter from the capital fulfilling his requested grant to implement the landfill's next ten-year plan. He'd spend a year and a half in the capital, with Lem, being trained in the latest engineering and both of them learning to build the new cells. Less headroom needed for the liner of each new cell, he explained, giving us the space we needed to contain it all.

"*If* the resort stays at its current dump rate," he said, his face more hopeful than the sarcastic way his lips pressed out *if*. A year-plus of training, then they'd come back and start the expansion.

Lionel renamed the Landfill Engineer. Me: the new Site Manager. I'd get my paycheck from the guy on the mail boat, who would bring it from the public works office in the capital.

Lionel and I both looked down—marveled—at an unshattered lightbulb washed up with its filament intact.

First Andre and Lem floated to the key and then boarded the plane to the capital. Few weeks later, Hebbie and her mother. Already gone for the boat when I, misjudging their flight time, showed up at their house to say good-bye. Looked through the window at their bare table, kitchen cupboards all closed, a single sponge in the sink.

Few weeks more, I waited with Lionel for the boat to the airstrip. Different swarm of bags at his feet. Our good-bye went the way leaving-for-the-capital good-byes always seemed to go: saying a jumble of things like we were parting for a short time and a long time both. Whichever it took. Tugged on Lionel's braids in exchange for the weeks he'd driven me to crazy hill while he trained me. His cloudy eyes looked almost childlike-scared.

I knew he wouldn't go looking up his father. For all I knew, if Lionel was finally so willing to go there, his father wasn't in the capital anymore. He pocketed the note I handed him from Mother, asking him to go looking up where Dad and Troy were buried without markings. *Under a tree like they told me?*

Tide highest of the day as the boat pulled in. Would drain away soon enough, I knew, like always. Lionel had driven the two of us in his truck, and I drove it back alone.

And then Queen Isa and I reigned over the landfill.

Lionel and Lem in the capital learning how best to seal away toxins and make room for more. While I spent my days saving as much as I could from having to be sealed, from taking up room. Every phase of the resort's renovation marching on, every arrival of the mail boat, every littered wave crashing onto Junkful, even every lingering item on a shelf in Miss Patrice's store, had me wondering what would alchemize soon enough to garbage and lengthen my days at work.

Days there were often as long as working overtime at the resort. Some evenings the bridge of my nose rippled with tiny sun blisters, and most mornings some different muscle-of-the-day let its complaints be known. Some days like my body was still their *Maid.* But my mind: free of ID tags, papers. Just Hyphen Hands deciding which detritus should be buried under our feet and which reinserted into our homes. Standing up there on the landfill cells, had to remind myself I wasn't just walking around on a natural hump of the earth. It was a sediment hilltop we'd grown ourselves. *Anything and everything gets lost eventually.* Disintegrated into sand we walked on. Unremembered but carried in the soles of our shoes.

Came home each night to gossip Mother had heard floating around. She reported, through Miss Minnie, that Amerie had offered Lem a janitor's job at the vet clinic where she worked, and so he'd decided to stay out there. I'd known that he probably would.

Lionel went on learning the engineering, planning on arriving back. Plenty of folks would be looking to take Lem's place building the new cells for everything on this oval we—and the resort—had cast off. But Lionel was living with Dr. Amerie and his e-mails sounded all-through airy about it. Some nights my body buzzed above the mattress like a ship on the waves as I dreamed he never came home, never expanded the landfill. Only up to me to keep the oval from being swallowed up by everything we'd collected. Mother didn't object when I scraped out the pots and pans for Queen Isa after dinner. Left Mother to her poetry books while I sat on the steps watching Isa scarf and swallow. Waited for her to be done so she'd climb up next to me and nudge her snout onto my knee. She started sleeping on that broken step each night. Inside, Mother in her room, and Troy's room now mine. Moonlight peeped in and out of the dish towel curtains, like always. Each morning I found Isa waiting on that doorstep for me like a tourist beguiled by broken glass. Off to work we went.

Days I worked the hardest, Isa pouted around by the office shed. But sometimes kids came round to run with her along the landfill's swooping corridors. Watching them from afar, looked like marbles dropped into a big, shallow bowl. Isa's second person after me was Angelina, Lem's kid sister. Manny and Gussie and some others would come say hello and good-bye after their playing, take swigs of water from me, or see if I'd salvaged anything interesting from the resort's bags. But Angelina didn't edge too near the Site Manager who'd gotten her brother a yellow paper write-up and, with it, a one-way plane ticket off the island. Only half waved from afar. If Angelina'd come close enough, could've told her what I knew of a scrunched heart when a brother had gone off to the capital. What I knew of a heart not un-scrunched enough to bring one home. In the expanse between us, growing piles of water bottles that moved in the light and moved the light around them. I hadn't figured out yet how to pallet them and send them back in through the truck entrance without Lem.

I started putting the box together without really thinking what I was doing. Just tossing into an old box in the shed:

One, the small yellow mitten she'd found on Junkful, with its winds bringing flotsam and its myths bringing luck, and had left in the erasable art studio at the resort. Two, the plastic shampoo bottle with Portuguese labeling. They'd both come back to me, dumped by the resort. Three, a whole mess of sand dollars. Most of their shoulders crumbled like sugar, but two were pristine. I taped a label saying *For Nathan* to one, *For Katelynn* to the other. And, four, her cloth bag. I'd kept her brushes wrapped, clean and dry, inside. She was going to want them, I thought, no matter what her life had become.

I didn't put in a note asking if she had the book, missing pages and all. Had no way to ask for it, after everything.

Miss Patrice let me use the store's computer—fastest Internet on the island outside the resort—to look up "Manion Cottage Consignment, Wisconsin." Once I had the address, I toggled to the satellite image of her house. Lionel had told me the shop was inside her house, a converted garage. Her garage door was the same blank white staring at the street as every other house on their block, hiding what was behind: the shop, the nook, whatever had happened to Jasmine Manion, who seemed well enough, at least, to send us her northern version of shells. I waited until a month when the shipping cost wouldn't press on us so much. Then off it went, northwest past Quickly, past any landscape I'd seen with my own eyes.

Maybe her scissors stalled against the tape as she considered whether she ever wanted to see anything from this island ever again. Maybe once the box was opened, she'd taken her bag of brushes into her lap the way I'd seen her son hold tight to his blanket.

No matter how busy or dead-on sunny the day, I slowed down for every rustle in a pile that could be paper. Every book I found, which was never *the* book, came home with me. Cleaned off. Put under the table. Never called them *our books*. Just *the books*. Folks started coming by to borrow and return them more often than they came for Mother to check their mouths for pain. Sometimes came for both.

One day same as any other: Isa waiting for me on the step; two of us walking the dusty road with a wave and a wag to whoever passed going the other way; resort truck beeping its way in for the first of three visits that day and letting down its avalanche of sacks; sun in the sky as ever. Day same as any other, except: there it was. Those words that pointed to the words that weren't there.

Binding glue dried and broken, two of the five stitches loose. Cut map pages still cut. Gone. I sliced my fingertip on their remaining edges, but I didn't bleed. Sat and didn't work the rest of the day, without even looking inside. Just set it on my knees. Not as heavy as it had once seemed but a weight on my legs all the same. My fingers tensed into clamps—almost as if it were mine.

A few days later I scratched up the words to tell Mother the book had turned up. Really *turned up*: poking out of a pile of what had been thrown away. And should I send another box to Manion Cottage Consignment, though we'd never received word about the first?

"It wasn't really hers," Mother said.

We ate dinner that night with *The Cruffey Plantation Journal* against my mother's bare left foot, where we knew it was there.

Bench Story No. 17: Myrna Daphanie Cruffey Burre

Crouched at the bottom of the pool, I leaned back on my heels like a child and hugged my upper arms, etched as they were with fine white lines written on me by the haulback. I could no longer see up onto the empty pool deck. In this cave of the pool the sun didn't even descend to cast its shadows. If a cow had come thundering through like the worst storm I wouldn't have known: nightmare vanishing before a memory of it nestled in.

Troy had said that to be a watercolorist, you had to know what not to paint. Where to make yourself absent, leaving slices of paper blank and bright as light. Mother had been such a good watercolorist of the past, strategically tiptoeing around the blank spots, guiding around their treacherous edges. I was not a watercolorist.

Where Jasmine Manion's blood ran brownish: I had covered it in some places but left it visible in others. Red gone brown, like a thiflae flower that had leaked out its sweetness.

Mine was not the brush of an artist. It was a brush for painting the outsides of houses or for painting fences, quickly and coarsely. The handle was thick in my hand like rope. The brush was wiry. I had to muddle the bright paint colors I'd been given to find the grays, browns, and dark greens that I needed. I mixed gray and white with blue for the swaths of sky: the true blue of the sky, not their fake blue that had been so difficult to cover. My knees got in the wet paint some-

*times. I was not such a painter. But I could still see it all emerging.
As if I were erasing a false bottom to reveal what was beneath it, not
like I was composing it at all. I slid back and back to keep the mulchy
paint from getting all over me, until I was against the side of the pool.*

In front of me: the ruins.

*The chains of stones that cut the brush meeting the lasting corners
of buildings, like ghosts reassembling themselves to claim the shoes
they'd left behind. With their crumbled corners, their cracks, and
their diamond-shaped scars left for all to see. With the whipping post
drawn as what it would always be. A whole bird's-eye view map that
had been only in the book, only in my mind.*

*And on the map, as best as I could locate it by the watering hole, I
made a tiny painting of a pile of stones humped into a bench. And I
stippled in shadows beneath the roughly rendered stones, the way my
brother had taught me to tuck them under.*

*I imagined the lumpy forms of tourists, like manatees etched with
bone, buoyant in the pool. Hovering between water and sky. How
they couldn't help but reach out to touch this scratchy floor of ruins
and post and dreamed ships and stones. How if they just put out their
hands, they'd find our different island.*

A Note from the Author

The narrator of this book is a Caribbean woman. You may have noticed that the writer of this book is not. I've heard many propose that imagining another's experience is all part of a writer's job. I don't disagree about the skills necessary for the job, but there's more to the story. Focusing only on the writer's imagination glosses over a history not just of absence but also of damaging misrepresentations of "others." As a scholar of nineteenth-century U.S. literature, I think first of fictional idyllic plantations that persist today, for example. This book does not depict life on a plantation but rather a character haunted by *not* knowing what such a life was like for her ancestors. In following my imagination (when I first encountered a beach littered with international garbage and piles of stones U.S. researchers machete'd to but islanders did not preserve), I've been tasked both with creating a work full of empathy and realistic characters and with doing the research required to be truthful about a culture that's not my own. Though the island of the book is fictional, I'm still a tourist there; the writing must exceed my own personal perspective. But just as empathy is not the only requirement, research isn't either. As Kaitlyn Greenidge wrote, writers shouldn't go about their jobs "with an implicit insistence that writing and publishing magically exist outside the structures of power that dominate every other aspect of our daily lives" ("Who Gets to Write What?" *New York Times*, September 24, 2016). A novel such as this requires an awareness of those structures, too. Derek Walcott, in "Isla Incognita," invites his readers to proceed backward from knowing, from all the stories they've been told about islands—what he calls "the wrong or casual naming of things." Proceed with "the opposite method to the explorer's," he instructs, and find your way only "by a great deal of principled doubt." I believe doubt and trepidation in the writing process can be productive. And I hope that the book will lead to productive conversations with and among all kinds of readers.

Acknowledgments

of people, dogs, schools, funds, and texts

Thank you to my family for their support in all forms: Esther and Leonard Entel; Gabrielle, Eben, Ethan, Jonah, and Dalia Hattingh; Mark, Brie, and Adlai Entel.

Thanks to my agent, Allison Devereux, for being such an enthusiastic champion of my work at every stage and to my editor, Olivia Taylor Smith, for her remarkable commitment to this book.

Special thanks to Karen Rile and Lorrie Moore.

Friends, relatives, colleagues, acquaintances—writers and not, too many to name—buoyed me up during rough patches with questions about the book. Special thanks for advice from Jennifer Ambrose, Tori Barnes-Brus, Clara Burke, Glenn Freeman, Patrick Naick, Michelle Sizemore, and Rachel Swearingen.

The staff of the Gerace Research Centre, past and present, gave me a space for research (and taught me to use a machete). Various residents of San Salvador answered questions, provided directions, and even offered me rides to historical sites. Colleagues I traveled with provided collaborative thinking and snorkeling partnership.

My colleagues in the Department of English and Creative Writing at Cornell College helped me take a full-year sabbatical, without which the first draft would never have been completed.

Brooke Bergantzel offered expert technological advice. Students in my Bahamian literature courses shared my interest in the big questions of this book.

Much of this book was written at the Writers WorkSpace in Chicago. Thank you to director Amy Davis for making me feel at home there.

My aunt Patty Jempty and my grandmother Frances Feigen passed away while I was writing this book; I already miss their reactions as readers.

My late sweet dog, Charlie Brown, took me on incredibly long walks during which I often untangled knots in the plot.

I appreciate the creative writing opportunities I had in the public schools in University Heights and Shaker Heights, Ohio; from first grade on, my schools made space for reading, writing, and writers. Thank you, too, to all the writing teachers who both encouraged and challenged me at the University of Pennsylvania and the University of Wisconsin.

The McConnell sabbatical fund gave me the gift of time to work on this book and the opportunity for a much-needed research trip. Through a Mellon Foundation grant for environmental studies, I first traveled to the Gerace Research Centre to plan a Caribbean literature course and afterward began a short story about a debris-covered beach that eventually became this book.

A few lines of Amiri Baraka's "Preface to a Twenty Volume Suicide Note" were adapted for Daphanie's story. The book's epigraphs come from Derek Walcott's *Midsummer, IX*; Emily Dickinson's "Pain—has an Element of Blank—"; and Toni Morrison's "A Bench by the Road" speech. Among the many texts important to my research and writing were: the only surviving Bahamian plantation journal, republished as *A Relic of Slavery: Farquharson's Journal for 1831–32*; John Cummins's translation of Columbus's journal, *The Voyage of Christopher Columbus*; Ian G. Strachan's *Paradise and Plantation: Tourism and Culture in the Anglophone*

Caribbean; Virginia White's *The Outermost Island: An Oral History of San Salvador, the Bahamas*; and Eva Jane Baxter's work on ship graffiti.

About the Author

Rebecca Entel began this novel while teaching on San Salvador Island in the Bahamas. She is Associate Professor of English and Creative Writing at Cornell College, where she teaches multicultural American literature, Caribbean literature, creative writing, and the literature of social justice. She holds a B.A. from the University of Pennsylvania and a Ph.D. from the University of Wisconsin. Her short stories have been published in *Guernica, Joyland Magazine, The Madison Review*, and elsewhere, and several have been shortlisted for awards from *Glimmer Train, Southwest Review*, and the Manchester Fiction Prize. *Fingerprints of Previous Owners* is her first novel.

@unnamedpress

facebook.com/theunnamedpress

unnamedpress.tumblr.com

www.unnamedpress.com

@unnamedpress